MadCap

By: Charity Ayres

Published by Three Ravens Publishing
threeravenspublishing@gmail.com
P.O. Box 851 Chickamauga, Ga 30707
https://www.threeravenspublishing.com

Credits:
MadCap was written by Charity Ayres/ Three Ravens Publishing – 1st edition, 2020
Cover art by Ravven www.ravven.com
Trade Paperback ISBN: 978-1-951768-10-2

Chapter 1

A growl echoed through the tiny room and shuddered up my spine, causing me to drop the nub of lead I held in my hand. The sound was guttural and vicious enough to make the fine hairs on my neck lift and quiver. I closed my eyes for a moment and took a breath in before turning my head.

"Dammit Jim, knock it off! You know you spill rot on the floor when you get worked up. Calm down." I tapped the writing utensil against my chin and looked over my list again. "Hmm, bearings, bioelectric graphene, nanite nodes...wait. That's not right."

A moan answered me, and I took a breath, eyes closed for a moment before turning to the horror that was chained by my door.

"I won't forget to save a pound or two of flesh for you."

I was rewarded with a dopey, pink and yellow grin that wafted the scent of trash and decay across my quarters. I fought the urge to cringe, playing it off as a heavy sigh to show how I felt about Jim's lack of appreciation for my efforts. The smile drooped a little, and his body wiggled like an ashamed puppy from where I had him chained by the door.

"I *am* the one and only Captain Magerious Low, and you know my word is treasure enough to cover my first mate...alive or undead, Jim." I gave him a saucy wink which he tried to emulate, albeit in a much slower and disturbing way.

With an unladylike grunt, I looked back at my list and scribbled out the entries. I was rewriting the most important items on my pilfering grocery list when the sound of shouting from outside of my cabin interrupted me. Damned if I could ever get my list sorted in time with the constant interruptions. If my crew was fighting again, I'd feed the troublemaker who'd started it to Jim.

"We'll get fresh nanites to fire up that brain of yours and get you back to work," I arched one side of my mouth up, "or play, Jim."

Jim rewarded me with his dopey grin accompanied by a long strand of spittle that hung in a rope down to the floor.

A knock at the door to my quarters made Jim let out a snarl, and I barked out, "What?"

"Captain Maggy, we've spotted the *Interrogator* on the horizon!"

"Excellent! Get the crew prepped to capture and board," I crowed. "And tell that bastard Smitters that if he even thinks about firing one of the cannons toward the hull that I'm going to stuff him inside it first."

I stood, pushed my curls back and stuffed my tricorn on my head. I had a moment of vanity where I thought to check myself in the mirror but sneered. I knew what I'd see: a lush, feminine face with curling black lashes over pacific-blue eyes; a gift from my whore mother. That look had drawn my nefarious father into her charms. It'd brought enough offers of pleasure when men saw my full lips and ample bosom. Seafaring life had even kept my waist trim without the help of a corset, though the leather one I wore did double duty as armor against sword or knife. I thought about battle and curled my lips into a wider smile. It was an unpleasant look that was more likely to have a man wetting his britches than wanting to drop them; especially when the bloodlust tattoos made my lips go flush red. It wasn't cosmetics that enhanced the color, but magical necessity for my job.

I'd paid several years of my life in an oft-avoided area of the Caribbean. The witch there gave me the tattoos that detailed my lips, fingers, and the calves of my legs. Pirates didn't end up living long lives as it was, so it seemed like a good trade. It had remained a good purchase in the five years since I'd used the enhancements to wreak mayhem on the high seas.

I was the terror that strode up and took what I wanted no matter the cost or risks. I was Captain 'Maggy' Magerious Low: commander of the *MadCap* and her mismatched crew; unclaimed heir to the toughest and most feared pirate lord; and I was hell-bent to reinstate my first mate, James Naderblast.

Jim had been my First Mate since I cut my teeth on my first hostile takeover of an alliance vessel. I would never replace him: dead or alive.

Or *undead*, you could say.

A few months back, while in port on a temporary leave, Jim had a run-in with a group of fire-sirens. Jim managed to bungle into their territory during a dispute between them and their water-siren sisters. The fire-bitches blasted the shit out of poor Jim, and the water-wenches damn-near melted his brain. The combined magics put him on the verge of death, but strangely did not kill him. When I found him, I immediately knew he was different, but all I could see was that he was bleeding and dying in my arms.

I checked my blaster and pictured firing it between the eyes of the next siren I met before sliding it into the holster. I tightened the belt and reached for my cutlass with the black blade that marked it for the deviousness it was normally used for.

Thank-Odah for the nanites we'd recently stolen from a group of smugglers who'd docked at New Sky, a waystation between sea and steam-air travel. What a bunch of idiots they were, betting and bragging at the card tables. It had been a simple score to follow them as they broke port and relieve them of their booty. They're lucky we took their cargo and left them their lives – other pirates wouldn't have done them such a solid.

A little-known fact about nanites: they can heal what ails human cells, but when you add them to dead or near-dead cells, they get eaten by the cells they're trying to repair. Apparently, something in Jim's slow-rotting carcass went cannibal on the blasted buggies. We realized it as Jim started gnawing on the cook who had been asking about his lack of appetite. After that, it was just a slow dip in the waves before Jim began to rot.

Don't get me wrong: he's still in there. His appetite, however, has shifted from wenching and booze to the aforementioned pound of flesh and pint of blood or entrails. Lucky for him, we often had both. Pirating was a messy business, and no one ever seemed inclined to give over without the loss of life.

Each score since then has been focused. Salable goods aside, the nanites were what I was after. The more I could gather, the more likely we could keep Jim from turning to goo on my freshly swabbed decks. I wasn't a fan of his gooeyness and liked him upright and calling my orders instead of crawling and slathering at everyone's heels.

And oh boy was I ready to rip into the *Interrogator*. Rumors surfaced that they were carrying a new form of nanite – one that was damned-near indestructible. Hope can be a tricky and untrustworthy bitch; I usually didn't waste my time on her. On the scarce occasion that I tipped my hat in courtship of the feeling, it rarely meant anything good for anyone involved.

"Stay here, Jim," I patted his head before reaching above him to pull down my monoscope and nail blades. He swiped at my leg, trying to grab a bite, but I didn't fault him for it – I just swung out of the way. "My boots didn't taste great the last time, you'll recall, ya drooling bastard. Clean up a bit while I'm getting you a meal and some much-needed healing."

Jim groaned and scrubbed his sleeve at the pool of drool on the floor. I shook my head once at him before pulling at the rings on the fingers of my left hand. Each ring was topped with a wicked blade that I slid forward to cap my nails, creating claws of the finest steel. Why settle for one blade when I could carry five?

On my ring finger was a special bit of tech lined with steel and quartz. Something in it caused more than a physical spilling of a body's guts when I needed answers. A quick jab to the temple and my opponent wouldn't hesitate to tell me anything I wanted to know. It was the only way I could get a quick bit of information before the wretches slit their throats or took a damn suicide nanite in their gullets. I rarely got to use it; truth be told.

I patted the holsters at my hips before swinging open the door to my quarters to step into the passageway. I made a face as a memory tugged when I was in the doorway, so I leaned back and poked my head back in.

"Stay in the chains this time, would you, love? I don't mind a bit of sparring to stay on my toes, but you almost bit a finger off last time," I gave Jim a wink, and he curled his mouth into that goofy grin.

I stepped out from the p-way and into the dapper glow of afternoon light. I grinned and sucked in the air like it was the first good breath I'd have. Of course, being closed into my cabin with the stench of Jim meant it probably was.

I launched from the top step and onto the deck, my heels hitting the metal-glazed planks with the sound like a mallet hitting a gong. It was starting to thin in spots where we'd taken a cannonball from a less-than capitulating quarry. I'd have to see about making for port to shore up my defenses sometime soon. My heels clanged out my entrance, but my crew continued working at the rigging, turning necks, eyes, or eye stalks to look at me.

"If even one of you bastards takes your share before I've gone through it all, I'll carve your heart out with a shrimp fork before tossing you into the cabin with Jim," I snarled before pulling the monoscope from the pouch at my belt and fastening it across my eye. The crew cheered and called out, to which I flipped them off and focused on the ship we were approaching. I could see the movement as the crew of the vessel tried to prepare to face us through the magnified lens. Our speed meant they didn't have long to do whatever it was they thought they could. I grinned around the lens where it pushed into my cheek; it wouldn't be enough.

The *Interrogator* crested the waves and shimmed down the side as though she, too, were trying to escape at the behest of her captain and crew. The Alliance thought they could keep the vessel under wraps by using a water-cloaking technology to make them invisible. Too bad we cracked that shit like a rotten oyster, and they were without the tech to swap engines and lift off. This was even before one considered that there were a good ten ships taking skies with an eye out for the nanite tech *Interrogator* held within her hulls. If they'd spotted us, and there was a good chance of it, they likely weighed their odds as better against little 'ole us rather than ten super-cruisers outfitted with steam engines and cannons.

I preferred to keep my keel wet and my blade sharp.

Well, a yo-ho-ho, and thar she blows. Adrenaline pumped through my body, fueling the bloodlust that was always there and honing the edge of my urge to battle. I felt my lips curl into a sharper, poison-tipped version of the grin Jim gave me. A squidropod to my right inked on the deck at the look on my face, and I was tempted to nail blade his tentacles away.

"Clean that up, you salty bastard," I curled my lip at him, feeling the red bloodlust flush my lips to swirl the colors of old blood and fresh injury. He, or she – I could never tell, gurgled a response and scuttled away, the humanoid legs were at odds with the anxious rustling of his tentacular arms.

"Cap'n, we should overtake her in a few ticks. Who's lead for the boarding team?" Smitters was powering up the lines and looked at me from his hunched position. At least someone had given the fat walrus-humanoid something useful to do. Those lines would be imperative for disabling the ship through charged bursts. Then the grappling lines could be sent with skimmers attached for boarding.

"Are you volunteering?" I curled my lip at him, and Smitters shrunk his one ton-plus frame down. He was slim for a walrusoid, but I knew his ass would never cross and would likely snap a skimmer in two if he tried. His center of gravity meant he was good on the main deck but not anywhere else.

"If you rat shits can keep my boat safe without pissing yourselves, I'll go myself. Scrags, Trag, Swifty, and Hacks: gear up."

There was a quick scurry of movement as my orders were followed without hesitation. Three of the four I called were usual additions to the boarding parties except for Trag. She was a shred-wing Aerieoid who'd had her wings stripped by some sick bastard before joining my crew. Despite her handicap, I'd seen her shimmy up and down gear lines like a hungry bilge rat. The raven-girl had earned her place at my side.

Scrags was a crab-hybrid creature with a blue-green exoskeleton and pincers for hands. He could carry most of the content of the hull from the ship without any help and do it while scuttling across a fraying line. Swifty was a Bastetite with dark golden markings on her pointed ears and curled whiskers in her feline face. Her teeth overlapped her lips, and her nails were more wicked than the blades over my fingers. I'd also never seen her miss a shot with blaster or blade.

Hacks was the only other human on my crew now that Jim had gone to the zombie dark side. He was a tall, wiry guy with strange lines of tattoos scrolled across his body in wild colors. I had a feeling he and I had a couple of those markings in common. I knew for certain that I had seen the rusty color of blood pool in the curvature under his pectoral muscles and crisscrossing his biceps in much the same way as my own markings.

Perhaps once Jim was better, I could investigate the hidden markings on Hacks a bit further. He ruffled the shock of reddish-brown hair on his head and gave me a wild grin that made me think he had read my thoughts. I curled my lips at him, feeling my teeth and senses sharpen to a knife's edge.

Yelling drew my attention back to the *Interrogator*. Another few heartbeats and we would practically be on top of her. They fired a slew of interlocked mini balls at us from their starboard cannons. One came at me, and I swatted it away with my blades, careful not to let skin touch the spiked acid-coated metal. The Squidropod from earlier wasn't so lucky and the mini ball sunk several inches into his/her skull before the metallic mesh shot out. In an instant, a net wrapped around the Squidropod crewmember, turning it to goo as the mesh closed, crushing and binding like squeezing out a wet sponge.

"Electro those damn balls, ya fat bastard," I yelled at Smitters who hustled his swaying mass across the deck to click on the Dragger. The barrage of mini balls stopped their assault on my crew. Instead, the munitions were pulled to the electromagnetic Dragger like a shark to chum. Once it was covered with them, it would surge and shoot the mini balls back to the steam cannons they came from, destroying them from within. It was a beautiful sight, like fireworks.

"Tag the ship and send the lines," I yelled. Deck crew scurried forward to flip switches on the different line-launchers like the one Smitters had been prepping. "Take them alive, so we have some new playthings when we're through."

I would need information in case the nanites didn't pan out, but you could never tell a group of pirates to play nice without offering them a boon. I would have preferred capture and release, but that never seemed to be the way with Alliance vessels: be they privately owned or run by the government.

Several crewmates tossed out insults and catcalls at the crew of the *Interrogator*. I jerked my chin at my boarding party before rolling on the balls of my feet. I crouched and felt the blood fury roll through the tattoos as the muscles in my legs bunched and I launched.

The hefty price I'd paid to get the witch woman to give me these particular bloodlust battle tattoos was about to show how good a trade it was. I jumped about thirty feet up in the air before coming down to land on the opposite deck amid *Interrogator* crew and soldiers. The blast of my landing caused a shockwave across the deck, and those nearest were thrown to the port side. By the time I'd cleared the center part of the deck with blades and cutlass, it seemed as though crewmen were coming from all angles. My boarding crew was nowhere to be seen.

"This isn't a gods-damned tea party; we don't have time for you to lag, you sorry dogs! Get your asses over here," I called as I continued to wade through sailors and Alliance soldiers. My teeth lengthened and my gums hummed as I felt the venom that the magic in the tattoos created coat the enamel and fill my mouth. I turned my head and spit the excess. I was immune to it, but it still tasted nasty: like a mouthful of burnt metal.

The *Interrogator* crew closed in from all sides. My desire to keep some of the enemy crew alive went out the window when I saw they had no similar inclination. Blood sprayed across the deck of the MadCap as a crewman took a direct shot to the face from an Alliance crewman. I moved to return the favor when I leaned back and booted the closest sailor to the chin with a jaw-crunching kick. My boots were weighted to help keep traction during rough weather. It was just a nice bonus that they could break bone when paired with the power in my legs from the tattoos.

I crouched down as I spun my nail blades and cutlass in a whirlwind of dismemberment. I wanted to holler for my crew again but couldn't spare the breath or time. Distraction would have me overtaken in a heartbeat.

Onboard screaming shifted attention away from me and drew a few of the *Interrogator's* crew. I smiled and reconsidered the possible hamstringing of my crew. A woman with cat ears, a feline mouth, and piercings running along both lips dove at me and found that my cutlass wasn't just for show. The gash across her cheek streamed quickly to her mouth. She spat blood and landed several feet away where she assessed me while I grinned. Her quick moves had helped her keep her head for the moment. Claws sprung from her fingers, she crouched into a position I was very familiar with. I recognized her as a bastet humanoid and knew she'd be quick.

"Here kitty, kitty," I crowed, gutting a male to my left and dismembered another at my right. The feline woman made a hissing noise and sprang at me, claws out. Before she got within reach, an arm came out like a clothesline and caught her square in the sternum. I heard something crack as she was launched away where she crumpled. It was probably her breastbone. She didn't get back up.

"Hullo Cap'n. Mind if I cut in?"

"Yes, I do, you smarmy bastard. She was my kill," I snarled, and the bastard gave me a wink before bowling through several enemy crew and breaking their main mast with his arms. I had even come up with the perfect taunt for putting her down.

"I was going to tell her it was time for a catnap or that she was a cat-astrophe at fighting," I muttered.

Hacks danced back by me, chasing one of the smallest sailor's I'd ever seen on an Alliance crew. The sound of my voice stopped him, and he gave me a grin and a shrug. Cocky bastard.

I didn't see Swifty, Scrags, or Trag and the enemy crew was milling around something near the starboard side. I swung my cutlass and swiped with my nail blades, cutting through the enemy crew like grain until I saw what was in the center of their maelstrom.

It was a someone: Jim.

Chapter 2

"Dammit Jim, what's in your head for coming over here? I told you to stay put," I snarled and drew the attention of the *Interrogator* deck crew back to me. Jim dove for and grabbed the nearest one, biting a chunk out of the Walrusoid's shoulder.

"Fine, we're to biting over fighting now, are we? Well, that's just dandy," I grabbed a giant of a man and yanked his head back by the hair before letting my tattoo-sharpened teeth rip out the central veins in his throat. His skin was the color of sunset and quickly shifted to tallow as he crumpled to the deck in a pool of blood. I spit out the bits in my teeth and snarled at my first mate.

"Jimmy boy, I suggest you head back over." I shifted to slice through the throat of a raggedy old sailor who thought to charge me whilst I was talking to Jim. Rude. "Take your meal to go, would you?"

Jim had latched onto the body of a scraggly old pirate whose face, neck, and upper body were covered in white hair, though there was none on his head. I guess it just goes to show that some men's hair migrates south with age.

Jim made happy noises and I couldn't help but chuckle. He acted like an oversized zombie puppy when the nanites died in his system: non terrifying growls and cute vicious noises. I shook my head and stepped away to let him eat in peace. At least it would keep him stationary for a while.

Most of the crew was dead or tied to the broken mast in the center of the ship. Hacks and Scrags were guarding the *Interrogator* crew while Swifty crouched in a fighting stance with a nasty cut bleeding a river down her face. Trag came up from below deck with an odd, ball-shaped canister in her hands.

"This seems to be it, Cap'n," she called out to me, lobbing the ball at me which I caught with one hand. "I'll need Scrags to break through the harnesses for the rest of the booty."

"You heard her, Shellback," I called and stepped over to the hostages with Swifty. "Anything important here, Swifty?"

"Looks like a load of riffraff hired just for transport and delivery, Cap'n," she told me and leaned in to sniff the nearest one to her. She winced and gave me a look. "You'd think Alliance hires would be a bit better-smelling."

I narrowed my eyes at the comment and looked over the rag-tag bunch of captives. All of them looked like they had been scraped off the bottom of the ship: patched uniforms, starved appearance, and little in the way of hygiene. It didn't match the normal Alliance crew type with their neat beards or clean shave and regular meals. I felt an itch pull at the back of my neck.

"Swifty, send a few more across the line and start transporting our new guests to the *MadCap*," I heard her assent and turned to walk over to Jim who was still making happy noises and gnawing on the carcass of the old man. I wrinkled my nose but shrugged. A boy's gotta eat. Hell, fifty years ago, we would have been dining on the ilk of Swifty or Trag. Some of their distant evolutionary relatives were still on most menus.

"Jim, we need to do some hunting, friend." I drew my cutlass and curved my lips into the grin that generally made an opponent lose the ability to swallow. The still-pointy teeth probably would have helped with that reaction. "Methinks some of the crew is playing hide and seek, and I need my best hunter to sniff them out."

Swifty made a sound behind me, and I gave her a slow neck roll until I met her eyes.

"You don't smell food, lass and ye best remember that. The first mate will find them by their heat and not be confused by the nasty reek left behind by those sacks of meat," I jerked my head at the crew who I started mentally calling *the decoys*.

"There's better treasure aboard, methinks," I laughed, and Jim echoed an odd parody of it before dropping his snack and scuttling over to crouch beside me. His laughter and quick willingness to take orders reminded me that there was still some of Jim inside the drooling, flesh-eating creature he'd become. "Go find the warm bodies, Jim."

He took off at breakneck speed: a handy benefit of what he'd become. As a human, Jim was good at following my directions but slowly and with less enthusiasm. He half ran, half lumbered across the deck, heading for the interior. The dog analogy in my head went wild at his loud sniffing and panting. How he climbed down the ladder into the belly of the ship, I could never explain without puppets and a ship's model.

The overgrown toenails on his bare feet scraped and scrabbled across the planks. He shifted around and tried to follow the enhanced senses that I was now counting on to find me the missing link in this venture. I was tempted to go back for the nanites but wasn't sure if he could mindlessly continue pursuit without my presence for redirection. The further gone he was, the more it seemed that I was the only one he recognized.

Jim paused, his body quivering like a rogue gale on the horizon. I felt my teeth prick my lower lip with a vicious grin. Jim took off like a merman in heat, cutting down the passage and began pawing at a part of the hull that looked like any other part until I got closer. I could see that the decking mesh here was different. The wood tones and metallic gleam seemed just slightly newer than those around them. I couldn't see a latch or trigger along the frame at any point and leaned back to holler.

"Somebody get Scrags down here!"

Swifty relayed the order, and I heard a new sound of scrabbling down the ladder. It made me arch an eyebrow at how quickly the order was obeyed with how slow the previous ones had seemed.

"Your orders, Cap'n?"

I met the beady gaze of my crewman and nudged my head in the direction of the hull where Jim was still sniffing and scraping like the good hunter he was.

"Release the damsels hiding in the petticoats of the ship, would you? I'd like an eye on my treasure," I quipped. Scrags twitched whiskers that looked too much like antennae and nodded.

Scrags clicked his pincers and scuttled forward, mandibles rising from his back to brace him as he wedged into the ship's hull, popping the boards out like cracking open a clamshell. Jim made a lascivious noise at the exposed contents, and I let out a wild laugh, disbelieving my own eyes but thrilled at my luck.

"What's this I see but my favorite Alliance Marshal and one of their scientists? Oh, this *is* my lucky day," I crowed. I stepped forward to push Jim back before he decided to take a taste of one or both. "And here I was just hoping for information on the nanites, but I never expected the bonus of having my own source! The sea gods are truly smiling on me today."

The marshal in question was none other than Marshal Thaddeus Spinner, the foppish, self-absorbed ass who had attempted to arrest me on more than one occasion. It might have to do with my own pirating ventures, or it might be that he had some major beef with my father, the traitor-pirate, Captain Ned Low.

His appearance screamed everything that was wrong with Alliance sailors: there was never a mud-brown strand of hair out of place, he was always clean-shaven and polished without a speck of dirt under his nails. I wasn't sure he'd ever touched anything with grime on it.

My men, on the other hand, were often coated with random ship sludge, had rough hands to match their manners, and were calloused on every patch of skin that could be utilized in the line of work. Yes, some of them smelled like week-old sewage at times, but they were less concerned with their appearances than they were getting their work done.

Spinner, in his pressed uniform and trimmed facial hair, was always looking for a way to make himself look good at the expense of others. Our first encounter had been embarrassing for him and today wasn't going to make him any happier. I was thrilled at both his displeasure and my own good fortune.

"No one would smile on you, Low," Marshal Spinner stepped out of the enclosure. "You've just made the bounty on your head go to head-hunter levels with our capture."

"Well..." I gave him a saucy wink. "I do have a head, so it really just makes sense if you think about it." Scrags snapped his pincers at Spinner, who jumped, and I laughed. I jerked my chin at the shellback. "Take them to the *MadCap* with the others."

Jim started to spin around as though chasing his tail the moment Scrags had the two human men above deck and I knew that these walls held more than one living being in them. It didn't matter though; he would have homed in on the humans first with his hunger and the rest...well...

"Swifty, are the other hostages on my ship yet?" I called up, and the Bastetite girl looked down into the hull with me.

"They are, Cap'n. What're your orders?"

A smile spread across my lips again, and Swifty's ears went flat on her head.

"Tell Smitters that today is his lucky day. Arm the cannons and prepare to blast this ship to the depths," I whistled at Jim who quickly scurried above deck ahead of me and maneuvered like a monkey back to the *MadCap*.

I crouched, feeling the energy building in my calves before pushing into a high leap back to my ship. The moment the lines were set, I spotted Smitters grinning wildly at me. The thought of destruction always put the Walrusoid in a good mood.

"At your leisure, Smitters," I grinned back, and he nodded.

"Aye, Cap'n," one of his tusks got caught in his toothy grin, but he didn't let it slow him. "Blasth 'er, ye batherds!"

The cannons let out a gust of steam and belched flaming balls at the *Interrogator*. They were wrapped in a micro-lattice that released tiny spores of acid on impact. Multiple shots later, they were cutting through the other ship like a dorsal fin to water.

Screams erupted; guttural sounds that mimicked the cry of gulls overhead when pulling into portside for the day, but I shrugged it off. The men they'd left on deck had been given a death sentence so that the Alliance could hide below; it was a fitting punishment for self-serving cowardice. Though the sound pulled at the fine hairs on my neck, my brain recalled other screams and my spine turned to steel. Screams of Alliance were like whispers of pleasure to me at this point.

I headed to my quarters, knowing from the bloody trail that Jim had taken his meal to the only room where I could keep the crew safe from him. Inside, I found him chewing on something grisly that I decided not to look at too closely. It was one thing to hear the screams and know that justice had been served in its own, cruel way. It was something altogether different to watch my first mate make a meal of the enemy.

It just wasn't natural.

"Okay Jimmy boy, set it aside so I can give you the newest dose." I pulled off my nail blades, setting them in a cylinder that would eat away the biological matter left on them. Next, I hung my belt up next with cutlass and blaster still attached. Gore clung to them, and I knew they would need a good cleaning later, too.

Jim continued to make growly-chomping noises on whatever it was he held. I put my hands on my hips and watched him chew for a few moments before my disgust and impatience took the fore.

"Hand it over, Jim," I reached forward, and he made a low growl. "Cut that shit off, you scurvy dog. You know I'm not above taking a rolled newspaper to you. Do we need to do retraining?"

Jim whined low in his throat and slowly let the fleshy lump drop out of his mouth with a wet plop onto the floor.

Yuck. I really needed to find the cure for Jim, stained decking aside. His flesh-eating side was getting more and more aggressive as the days went by. I just hoped the nanites would make a better repair that lasted longer this time around.

When I twisted the ball, a gust of white air puffed around the seam with a hiss. In the center was a tiny, round, glass container. It was different from the others in that those had come without a sort of vial and syringe to inject the nanites. I wasn't sure what to do with this. I twisted free the lid and found a creamy substance inside, like the fancy lotions women of fortune used on their soft, pale, useless hides. If that's what this was, I certainly didn't want anything to do with it. My sun-browned skin would never look or smell like money; I would be salt, ocean, and sun until my last breath. I noticed a flicker in the cream as though it were moving within the confines of the tiny container.

"I'm not sure about this, Jim." I watched the cream's tiny movements for a moment and showed it to Jim. He sniffed a few times, made a face, and resumed chewing on his treat as though unconcerned or uninterested. I looped the metal cuff around his arm, pushing long enough for it to click into place before I opened my door.

Hacks was walking past, carrying a crate of something to the hold. He gave me a wink and a grin. He paused in the doorway, looking at me with something akin to expectation. Apparently, I wasn't the only one wanting to get a closer look at tattoos.

"Later. Get me the Marshal and that scientist," I slammed the door without waiting to see if he'd comply. I knew he'd do as I ordered as much as I knew the look he gave me was an offer. I paced the cabin with the round canister in my hand.

There was a knock on the door a few minutes later, and both men were led in. Hacks had them cuffed, collared, and leashed. Jim growled from his corner but kept chewing at his treat. Spinner looked put together despite his likely manhandling from my crew, and his eyes darted around the room but held no useful intelligence that I could exploit. With him was a messy-haired older gentleman with white-streaked hair that stuck out at odd angles. His eyes, though dun-colored, were sharp as he looked in every aspect of his surroundings immediately.

"What do I do with this?" I held up the half ball with the glass tub nestled in the middle.

"You give that back! That's not for you." The ballsy or foolish scientist started to stagger forward but Hacks jerked his leash, and Jim growled.

"For me or not, it's mine now, so tell me how to use it. Normally nanites are injected, so what do I do with this?"

Neither man answered me, exchanging looks.

"One way or another, I'm going to figure it out and use it on Jim over there," I sighed. "You can tell me how to do it now, or have the information tortured out of you later. If you die in the process, I'll try to use it anyways."

"You'd use it on that...thing," the scientist snorted in disgust at my first mate. Jim lifted his head to the man and clacked his teeth together to make a snapping. The scientist jumped, and Jim let out a low rumble and smiled. Bits of his snack poked out between his red-stained teeth.

"He's much more pleasant after a dose of nanites," I shrugged. "But if you don't help me, you might end up as his next meal, instead. He prefers the taste of humans for some reason."

"What do you mean he's better after nanites," Marshal Spinner enunciated every word as though I'd spoken in a foreign tongue.

"Oh Spinner, it isn't as though you haven't met Jim before. James Naderblast is the only first mate I've ever had and the one who took a chunk out of your side with his cutlass three years ago. How soon we forget!"

"That's Naderblast? What the hell happened to him?"

"Siren civil war almost killed him. Saved him with nanites…" I paused to watch him chewing on whatever limb he'd torn off, "...mostly. He didn't come out right from the first dose, though."

"Fascinating," the man leaned down as though he'd poke at Jim or was figuring the best angle of dissection. Jim ignored the Mad Scientist as he continued to munch and slurp, causing everyone to cringe at one particularly loud wet, sucking noise.

"I cannot believe that nanites turned him into...this?" Mad Scientist was shaking his head, but the slight quirk of his lips showed interest rather than disgust.

"And sirens but enough with the chit-chat," I scowled. "How do I give it to him? Does he eat it like caviar? Wash with it? What?"

"Just apply it," the scientist whispered, inching closer to Jim, who was watching a new meal get almost within grabbing range.

"Professor Talimuck!" Spinner grabbed and spun to the scientist as his face went an interesting shade I would call eggplant. His best shade, really. Talimuck, aka the mad scientist, pushed back and reached one hand a little too close to Jim for my own comfort. I might need him to answer some questions if the nanites didn't work or possibly see about keeping him on payroll if what I was guessing from this conversation was true. I made a low growling noise to warn Talimuck away, but Jim stayed still. Interesting, he usually bit first and snarled later.

"I don't think you understand what we have here, Marshal," Talimuck's eyes had gone wide, and he was practically salivating. "This is a breakthrough, and my nanites might do amazing things with this subject."

"Damn Professor, what happened to 'keep your mouth shut' and 'don't let them in on the nanite secrets' in the hold?" Spinner was frothing at the mouth in his rage. It made me grin, a lot. I thought I was the only one that pissed him off that much.

"This is a unique opportunity, Marshal," Talimuck said with a shake of his head. "I cannot imagine a better way to test out the nanites."

"Wait, test? Did you say test?" I narrowed my eyes. "Have you used the nanites before this?"

Fuck if I suddenly wasn't hesitant to try this on Jim. Who knew what the nanites would do to him? I didn't need him any worse than he already was.

"What are these particular nanites meant to do?" I scowled and fought the urge to start punching people. "Are they built to heal, too?"

Every nanite in existence, that I knew of, was built specifically to speed healing in the living thing they were put to. I had never heard of them having any other use.

"Yes, yes of course," Talimuck said with a vague wave of his hand. "But they're disease fighters and powerful nanotechnology. The Admiral wanted to try them on his soldiers as the first trial."

From the look on Spinner's face, I knew the Professor had run-of-mouth disease and was now incapable of shutting up about secret information. Looks like I wouldn't need Hacks to torture out information. He'd be so disappointed. I couldn't have that.

"Take Spinner back, Hacks," I jutted my chin at the crewman. "Release the professor. I'll watch him."

Hacks did as he was told, cuffing Spinner hard enough to make it noisy when the marshal tried to argue. Just before the door closed behind them, I gave Hacks a wink and spoke again.

"Have fun, but don't break our new toy just yet," I smiled, and the pirate's lips lifted in an evil grin that I liked a whole lot. Yeah, that boy was proving to be fun.

"So, Professor...Talimuck, was it? Tell me what to do next," I took out the tub and opened the lid again.

He looked from the tub to me to Jimbo, and something passed through his eyes for a moment before he clenched his jaw and nodded to himself.

"Just put it on like moisturizer," he moved his fingers in a circular motion as if I'd never put on moisturizer. I hadn't, but that wasn't the point. "I recommend you put it on his head first so that it seeks out his brain."

He took a step back away from Jim to let me move closer. He still watched my first mate gnawing at his treat, and I couldn't help the smile. The professor's skin had gone pale.

"You sure you don't wanna do it?" I chuckled. The other man swallowed hard and shook his head. I then noticed that the end of the chew toy had bony fingers and I shook my head, feeling my own gorge rise for a moment.

"Drop it, Jim," I snapped my fingers at him, and Jim lifted baleful eyes to me. He huffed once and let his treat drop again. This time, there was a lot less wet to the thump as it hit.

I scooted forward and unscrewed the cap. Dipping my fingers in, I pulled a liberal amount out and began rubbing it around Jim's temple, jaw, ears, and eventually into his spotty hair growth. He'd always been a touch balding, but it had gotten worse after he'd gone zombie-dog on me. I got a bit more and rubbed it into his skull and neck while he made happy noises that made me chuckle. Vicious dog, he was not.

After I rubbed it in as best I could, I stood up and backed away, looking at the professor who watched Jim as though he was waiting for horns to sprout.

"I wonder if horns will sprout," the professor said softly, and I choked. He looked at me and gave me a small smile. "Joking. That's never happened before."

"How many times have you tried it?"

"Once or twice...on mice," he said, his eyes locking back on Jim.

Great. We went from mice to the equivalent of a zombie doggie. I was beginning to doubt the usefulness of this venture when Jim seemed to give himself a shake and stood.

His curled, claw-like hands straightened, and he reached over to unlatch the cuff that held him chained to my wall. I gasped, lifting my hands to cover my mouth. Previous nanite transfusions had taken the better part of a day before Jim started looking even slightly human-like.

"Ready for your orders," Jim said, his voice raspy from misuse as he gave me a wink. I lowered my hands and gave him a grin, throwing a punch at his shoulder which he caught before sweeping my legs out from under me and knocking my ass to the floor. I cackled and jumped back to my feet.

"You ugly bastard. It's nice to hear your voice," I grinned for a moment when tingles started to run up my arms and across my face. I looked down and saw the tattoos on my fingers crawling away from my nails and turning into sun-golden skin. My razor teeth retracted, and I reached up to pat at my mouth to make sure my teeth were still there. My stomach dropped into my feet and I had the horrible feeling my tattoos were fading from around my lips as well.

I rushed to the small porthole-sized mirror over my water basin and saw that my face had lost all tattooing. Even the piercing at my nose fell out, and the scarring along my jawline from many a near beheading faded to nothing but clear skin.

"Fuck me, what'd you do?" I turned to the professor who looked a little smug. "What's happening to my tattoos?"

"Too right, whatever have you done to the fine Captain?" Jim's voice grew strong and had an almost polished sound to it. "Never mind. I can see the answer: you've taken her power markings from her. Clever plan, that."

"Indeed," Professor Talimuck stood tall. He cut his eyes to the now-upright Jim and then slid them to me. "All of your ill-gotten magical gifts are gone, Captain Low. You'll no longer have the battle power you once did and will be forced to live like the mortal you truly are."

"I will not," I hissed, grabbing a dagger from my nightstand and diving at the man.

Jim stepped in my way and disarmed me in a heartbeat. I gaped at him as he twisted me around and caught both of my wrists in his one before he cuffed me in the spot where he had always been chained.

"Oh, and James here now works for me," Professor Talimuck said as an afterthought. "Those nanites are linked to me. I just needed you to touch them to yourself and your first mate here to take over."

"Fu—"

"Now now, Captain...or should I say former Captain? No more language like that, I think," Talimuck wagged his finger at her. "We'll leave you cuffed for now, but James and I will now take your ship. You did give him the lion's share of nanites after all and the ones in you will be busy eating the magic in your blood for a bit longer. They'll probably be spent doing so, unfortunately."

Jim stepped away from me and stood by the professor who cocked his head at me with a vague grin.

"I can't believe how well this worked out. Now, you'll just keep your mouth shut Magerious, like a good girl. If you behave, maybe we'll bring you a little treat when we reach the Alliance."

James, I couldn't call him Jim in my head anymore with the starched posture and strange confidence in his glowing face, held the door for the professor and they stepped out. I slumped down, trying not to feel the chafing of the cuff at my wrists and stared at the bone left behind on the deck. Who was the good doggy now?

Chapter 3

"**O**h, my parents taught me well to shun the gates of hell, as I sailed, as I sailed…"

"Shut yer trap, sea whore!"

I snorted. Everyone was a critic when it came to sea shanties.

"I'd rather hear my singing than your whimpering in the middle of the night," I called back, fighting a cough. The jug on the floor beside me was as dry as my throat was becoming. "And if you have a problem with it, sidle on up, gent. I haven't killed anyone in weeks!"

Chains jangled as I reached to scrape broken nails at my head, pausing mid-scratch as I wondered if the lice had finally found my oily, unkempt skull. It was vanity that struck for a moment before it turned into a laugh that caught in my throat and pushed out a previously quelled cough.

I could go on about how I didn't deserve the treatment I was getting or how they had the wrong girl, but that would just be a waste of time. I'd fought like the dickens to keep my ship and break free every chance I'd had after they'd taken *MadCap*, but arguing against the mayhem and murder I'd done? I'm nothing if not prudent.

I'm also damn good at pissing people off. I'd proved it at the trial they'd had when they brought me ashore. As though the Alliance could do a fair trial? It was more a list of some of my many misdeeds up to that point. They'd missed quite a few. I'd mostly laughed my way through it.

They'd told me to apologize if I wanted a lighter sentence and I'd flipped them off. I wouldn't bow or scrape for what I knew I'd done. It kind of comes with the territory when you act like you don't give a fuck if you live or die. The hatred I spawned had brought a sort of fanaticism from those around me in their efforts to express it.

Now I was in an Alliance prison on some Odah forsaken rock somewhere. I'd guess somewhere off of the Gold Coast as that seemed to be the nearest and dearest hunting grounds for the Alliance. I know I'd only been tied and hooded for a couple of days without food or water. Smart of them to just stow me and forget about me until they threw me in my new cage, really.

Marshal Spinner, of course, was the head of my devotees in the Alliance and had the expansive good fortune to be one of my jailers. I'm certain our extensive history of near-death, pissing contests, and screams gave him quick entry to his happy place in having me as a prisoner. One of these days, I'd have to make sure he truly remembered our first meeting, but that would have to wait until I had blade or blaster in hand without shackles holding me in place.

Since I'd been in prison, the Alliance, via Spinner, had gone through the whole gracious question and answer period, but it always ended the same. That morning had been no different than the many others.

"Are you sure you don't want to tell me where you've hidden the tech you stole," Marshal Spinner asked, a dark eyebrow arched at me as he waited for my very polite response.

"Fuck off," I hissed.

Spinner jerked his pointed chin, and I knew what was coming next. I fought to relax my body as the lick of leather stroked my back like a burning brand. Agony shrieked in screams that I wouldn't let pass my lips. When it became too unbearable, I sunk my teeth into the soft skin on the inside of my cheeks and lips. The coppery tang of my blood made me think of other things: fighting with fists, the blows of blade against blade, and Jim.

I thought of Jim, pre-zombie and post-lackey, a lot

When the ripping blows of the whip stopped, I swallowed. I pursed my lips and lifted my chin to look at Spinner. I let myself focus on his greased appearance instead of the pain that radiated across my back. His hair, facial or otherwise, was much too slick and black to be natural. I wondered if he greased it or if the color came from being such a kiss-ass.

The thought had me curling my lips and I gave him a wink as I was hauled out under my armpits by forces unacknowledged yet ever-present. Spinner watched; he looked more natural with a tinge of purple flushing his skin, and his gray eyes practically black.

The experience was just one more lashing to match the at least twenty or so more on my back. I had stopped counting them even though they gave me a sense of time through regularity. Spinner only bothered to visit with me once every few days to ask a general question, whip me, and then send me back to my gilded cage. There, my only company was rats, the screams of other prisoners, and the bones of some forgotten soul that had occupied my cell before me.

"Hullo Steve, how's today's fare?" I looked at the skull and nodded. Steve wasn't much of a talker, but that was just fine with me.

"I have to tell you, friend, the dark, cavernous lifestyle is wearing on me. As captain of the *MadCap*, I once ruled the blue seas and open skies. The gentle caress of a Northwind was better than the memories of my whore mother.

"Not that it was all glory and pleasure cruising! Her comfort was generally a kick or punch if she was lucid or a bland, vacant smile if her opium had come in. The balm of Southwest wind was better than the touch of a lover, even when a storm whispered warnings on the breeze."

I paused with a smile.

"What can I say? I like dangerous lovers." Steve didn't respond to my wink or smile, so I continued.

"My love of the ocean changed me. It was small when compared to who I'd become with a capable if psychotic crew to take the place of family. We faced all comers, Alliance scum included, with sharp blades and jaunty smiles. We stole with reckless abandon; it didn't matter what the other land or sea vessel had; we took it just the same. It had been a glorious life filled with new excitement and danger each and every day. Pirating was an art form meant to encourage the sampling of everything the world had created. It was freedom without consequence so long as we could continue without getting too greedy or getting caught. At least, until one of our own became infected with something that changed the tide and found us under rough weather.

I knew, outside my cell, there were often guards wandering back and forth. I found that if I was quiet, they tended to try to visit me. I think they thought quiet meant vulnerable. I guess no one'd ever told them that a pirate is never more dangerous than when they're half asleep. I kept up the talk because I'd gotten sick of being beaten or starved for fighting back when they tried to take advantage.

"Now, here I am, chained at the ankles and wrists by a short leash," I jangled the chains. My arms were caught above my head while I sat with my legs getting the lion's share of freedom. I couldn't stand up; my wrists were cuffed to the wall at waist-length for a normal person. I couldn't lay back because that would press my ruined flesh into the wall. I also couldn't tuck my legs underneath me because the chains were short enough to keep them to the sides a bit, even if I could straighten them or bend the knees a little.

"Pick a lock and free yourself one time and they lose all trust in you," Steve didn't respond, but I knew he commiserated with me just the same. I started whistling and tapping out a different sea shanty with my cuff against the wall.

"The worst part though, Steve, is that my nose itches," I twitched my nose, but it wasn't helped by the clump of black hair that hung lank in my face. I half-wished that the bastard who'd chopped my mane away had shorn it close to my skull just so I didn't have to deal with the sweaty, dangling locks.

I snarled and rubbed my forehead into my arm in an attempt to see. It didn't matter. In every direction, I would only find a damp, malodorous prison that had become my castaway home. I waited, imprisoned, for the Alliance to decide what to do with me. At current, that meant figuring out who to send into my cell with my daily rations. I smelled the poor slob coming before I connected the sound of his scuffle to who it was entering my corner of bliss.

"Dunno why they can't just stand ye up and chain ye to the wall like e'ry body else," he grumbled at me. He said the same thing every time he came. It was becoming an annoying attempt at being conversational like wishing someone a good morning.

"They could just let me go and then neither of us would be in this conundrum, friend," I shifted. The feel of the cold from the wall kissed my back before the irregular stone bit in with needle-like teeth. I bit into my lip and cursed internally at myself. I couldn't seem to move away from the pain this time around, not that it ever went away, but I had always been good at ignoring what I didn't care to think about. I also kept hearing Spinner's asinine question in my head.

I rarely bothered with whatever modus operandi was on Spinner's agenda for when I was returned to my cell. Today, his words were like a song that hummed inside my brain, scraping at me almost as much as the wall.

The waiter of the day tossed a dried bit of bread at my head as he walked past. His lips were drawn into a thin line; I'm not sure he appreciated my humor.

"Yer water, my lady," he gave a low bow before setting a small pitcher near the wall and well out of reach. Maybe he did get me.

"I didn't want it right now, anyways," I yelled at his back as he shut the door and walked to another cell.

I sighed and shifted my arms to try to push the hair out of my face, yet again. I had a hard time deciding on the why of the issue of my hair: why hadn't they just shaved it all off? Were Spinner and his alliance cohorts hoping that I'd get lice, or did they want to keep me looking just a little less like the other prisoners, so I'd never blend in any sort of way. The barber had taken a barely sharpened blade and sliced away the lengths around my ears, nicking my neck and leaving me with a new scar to remember him by. The hair would grow in its uneven length, but I would have that itchy, semi-infected scrape to remember my time in prison.

I looked down at my ankles. The chains were a simple single-lock cuff system, but I didn't exactly have anything to slip in and shift the pin. The last cuff had been set with a biological reading that was strangely sensitive to heat and cold. I think it worked more to identify when I prisoner had died than it did anything else. It had been easier to break. I'd only needed to add body fluids, and I had an unconventional key. Sadly, my rag-clothing had suffered for that freedom.

I slumped against the wall and hissed. My back felt wet as though I'd been toiling in the heat instead of letting my insides seep out into the ragged scrap of cloth that passed for a shirt. The fresh pain did not clear my thoughts. I knew that I needed something small, preferably slightly flexible, and sharp if possible, to dig into that cuff.

"Couldn't you have settled a bit closer, Steve? I'm sure one of your finger bones would have been perfect for the job of lock pick." I frowned at his thoughtlessness and scratched at my head, a fleeting thought of lice distracting me. Vermin on the brain, I caught the sound of scuffling in the room.

I stretched my foot and caught the edge of the dried, rancid bread that had bounced off of me to land on the floor. Snagging the edge with a ragged nail, I dragged it toward me. I moved less than half an inch over the course of a dozen or more heartbeats. I heard the sand-on-stone sound again with a slight whispering squeak. I shuffled the bread again, letting it wiggle a little like a massive, chubby finger beckoning my tiny guest.

Through a crack in the stone, a tiny face peeked forward, whiskers twitching. Mottled brown fur covered the lean body and stopped at the whip-like tail. The rat was surprisingly fat considering the accommodations in my hellhole, but there was probably a good share of meat that the critter included in its diet. Some prisoners were only taken from their cells when the smell of decay became overwhelming.

Whiskers twitched and the rat looked from side to side. I kept my breathing slow and soft as though just a sleeping prisoner and nothing for the little furry fiend to worry about. I stopped wagging the bread and kept my foot near the hard crust. The rat stood still for longer than I would have expected before rushing forward to grab for the bread. My strike was just a tiny bit faster.

When I took to sailing, all I had was the clothing I wore, and it hadn't included shoes. I'd run barefoot for most of my young life and didn't see a reason to change once I was on a ship. Thankfully, sailing and bare feet work well together more often than not, and the hard soles of my feet were tough like quality leather boots. Or in this case, as hard as a spine-breaking metal trap for one overly-ambitions rat.

I looked at the limp, lifeless creature and dragged it toward me with one foot. I caught the tail between two toes and tossed it up toward my hands. It hit the wall a few times and fell before I managed to grab it. I slid my feet underneath me enough to push me up; my back screamed at the drag of flesh on stone while my mind screamed at what I was about to do. I looked at the furry lump in my hand and shook my head at it before raising it to my mouth. I bit down hard before turning away to spit out blood, rat fur, and heaven knows what else. I dropped back down to sit with the ravaged body still in my hands. I hacked and fought the bile in my throat. My hands went to work ripping through the tear I'd made in flesh and fur. I worked at the flesh by feel alone, tossing scraps as I went until I was able to snap off a leg. I'd gotten the portion I needed and dropped the rest of the body as I stripped the limb.

Part of me realized I should have made a meal of the critter, but I was simply not hungry enough to eat raw rat. I'm not sure pure starvation would ever make me *that* hungry, no matter the circumstances.

The largest bone in a rat's body is the same in that of a humanoid: the leg, specifically the femur, or thigh. It is also the densest bone and the only one that I thought might hold up as a lockpick. It was a little on the lumpy side and I was going to have to sharpen one end if I wanted it to fit properly in the keyhole of the padlock.

I rolled my head back to look up at the bone in my hands. It was covered with gore and smaller than my pinky; it wasn't much, but it would have to do. I dragged the smallest point against the rock wall to give it a slight edge.

I missed my tattoos. I kept thinking about how I could have gotten free with a good burst of energy in my legs or sharpened my choppers and bit through some of the smaller bits of metal. I couldn't break chains with a bite, but I certainly could have worked against some weaknesses. The nanites that took my first mate also took my witch-given ability to convert bloodlust into powers. I'd felt the powers drain away when I'd been locked away in transport after my capture. I'm pretty sure I screamed and cursed the ship's crew. I hope Odah had been listening and would look kindly on one of his rebel children. I shook my head as I thought about the loss. It was a sad world when a pirate would have to rule by skill and fear but not with ill-gotten witch magic.

By feel, I found the lock and then the tiny keyhole in the padlock that kept my cuff closed. I wedged the bone pick in, feeling the knocking around from the surface of the metal. I closed my eyes, letting the blind movement of the pick draw out the interior through clicks and clacks of bone against metal. Eventually, I was able to *see* the pins in my mind's eye. I wiggled the bone until I could shift against the tension enough to pop it loose. It took several tries and a lot of swearing. I think it may have been that couple of really good, colorful curses that did the deed.

When the lock released, I almost fell backward into the wall. It wasn't pressure from the lock, but the strain of focus. I shifted to work at the other wrist until it, too, popped loose. The second one came easier since I'd learned where to push.

I rubbed my wrists for a moment before checking the bone. It was a little cracked but would probably hold up a bit longer. The body of the rat was within reach, so I had a spare pick if I needed it; I knew there was a good chance I would.

The wrists, though awkward, had been the easy part. My ankles were chained with very little available movement in a somewhat straddle position. Put it this way -- if Spinner had decided I needed to be on a low pony, they could have backed one in without unchaining either foot. I would have no choice but to either drop my butt to the ground and try to reach one foot while the other was helplessly pulled in the opposite direction or twist into a stretch and hold my feet while working at the cuff from an upright position. Both had pitfalls: stretching meant straining my back, more so from a seated position. Bending over meant less stretching but having the blood rush to my head from the extended time it would take. The latch was under the cuff attached to my ankles and facing away from me.

I'd heard women in the brothel my mother worked at talking about how some women could stretch their legs out flat to either side. I remembered thinking that there was only ever one time that could be useful and was glad it wasn't a skill I wanted. Now though...

I stood and decided to try the face-down approach to relieve some back strain. My left leg protested as I bent over my right. I used one hand to brace myself while I worked the pin under a little more than an inch of space between cuff and floor. I couldn't lift my foot for long and work at the cuff, so I realized that upright was not going to work.

From a sitting position, pins of agony rippled through my back as I curled my body toward my feet. I felt the moment the skin tore open. The wetness on my back became a fresh red stream. On the bright side, parts of the cloth that had been stuck to me when the blood dried were coming loose due to the fresh deluge. At one point, the bone pick snapped, and I had to stop and dig through the stiff carcass for the other femur.

I was panting as I grasped my ankle. My vision blackened as the pressure on my body seemed to only intensify and never release. Sweat beaded on my upper lip as I maintained the strung-up position like a chicken on a spit. My free arm wound around my leg, locking me into a folded pose as I wedged the new tool into the tiny hole at the base of the cuff. I wiggled, feeling the metal bits inside pushing back or shifting around. My focus was not strong as it was divided between listening to the screams of my body and visualizing the interior of the lock. Suddenly, I felt the bone against tension in the lock and heard the angelic sound of it popping loose. I think I would have cried if I could have.

Before I could talk myself out of it, I released the grip on my leg and my back muscles pulled me from the hunched over position I'd locked myself in. The shift upright dragged the fabric across my back, ripping at skin where new patches had dried and made a sickening sound similar to the one I made ripping the fur from the rat's body.

"Odah's balls," I hissed. Blood ran freely to make slick pools on the floor, and fresh pain followed a moment later. Too bad I didn't need any more rats; my blood on the floor was going to attract a lot of them.

My energy renewed with the pain as though I'd just been slapped awake and I half-crawled, half-dragged myself to the remaining ankle. What seemed like a sweaty week later, the pin tumbled loose, and the cuff rolled on the stone floor like it sought to escape as much as I did.

I crawled forward and unrolled my spine, one vertebra at a time until I came to lay face-down. The fetid, cold stone felt good on my legs and side as I lay there, just trying to breathe. After my breath slowed, I rolled to my hands and knees and crawled to the pitcher of water my server du jour left for me. It was tepid and tasted like stagnant pond water, but I gulped it down for a moment like it was wine from an Alliance vineyard.

Halfway through the pitcher, a memory snagged my attention as my insides twisted. I cocked my head to the useless pile of bones near the wall.

"Right-o Steve! Drink slowly so I don't throw it all up like last time," I whispered before taking a small sip and then another. The first time they'd brought me water had been around two days into my captivity. I'd inhaled it and ended up spewing it all over the floor and the hay that filled in as bedding. It had been another day before I had a chance at a drink of water again.

Once I felt steadier, I crawled forward and half curled up in a ball with my face against the floor. I was dirty enough that I doubted I'd get much dirtier. Plus, the cool floor felt good on my flushed skin and the pain in my back made me fight the urge to whimper. I came to a decision; I reached back and grabbed the bottom edge of my shirt, hissing as the fabric tore away from my skin and ripped open the wounds yet again. I brought the hem up over my head, keeping the front of the shirt in place to cover what was left of my limited dignity.

"What I wouldn't give for a few of the older-tech healing nanites I used to feed Jim," I mumbled.

Jim.

I pictured the slobbering cannibalistic fiend he'd become. Jim had been inches from death when I'd found him after his unintentional siren civil war guest appearance. The volcanic islands we'd made port at had been rumored to be paradise and it had seemed like a good stopping point. When I'd found his mangled body, blood bubbling out of his mouth with each breath, I hadn't thought of anything other than trying to save him.

Training a new first mate wasn't on my to-do list. Unfortunately, I had no idea that magic could become so muddied like what I saw as a result of his healing. I'd often wondered what Jim had done to turn the wrath of the sirens on him like it had. My first guess would be something along the lines of, "Ladies, there is plenty of ole Jim to go around."

I snorted and a puff of dirt or something less savory lifted from the stone floor near my face. Ladies' man, he was not. Jim had definitely done more to deserve what'd happened to him than just bungling into the wrong place at the wrong time, but he'd never been coherent long enough to give me the full tale. I did know that he'd been caught up in a siren's kiss. Sirens were kin to the succubi. and there was magic laced in their kisses that many men, and women, have paid dearly to experience. Some traded treasure while others traded years of their lives to rest in the arms of a siren. I don't know what Jim offered in trade, but the medicine man we visited later on the island said that Jim had managed to be kissed and hit with some other type of magic.

The life magic opened Jim up to faster decay of organs, brain, and body. It also made him ripe for some sort of magical ancient parasite to slide in and start feeding on him. Almost everything that had been done to him was beyond what I'd even known to exist prior to having to deal with the fallout. Jim's malady made the physical diseases one could get with a traditional harlot seem like a calm sea rather than whatever the sirens were singing into your blood.

The only thing that prevented Jim from becoming part of the sea foam was the nanites that we'd stolen. I'd been en route to meet a potential buyer, when one of the deck lads came barreling down the road, looking for help. I'd almost started calling out prayers to Odah and planning where we'd send Jim's body to the depths, but the fact I actually had the nanites seemed like a sign of salvation instead of profit.

Honestly, I couldn't have turned away from him if I'd wanted to. The education about magics we should avoid came later. After dosing him and getting Jim to town, I learned a lot about sirens from the island witch doctor. I'd say Jim and I both got the education of our lives that day. What I didn't have to learn was that my first mate was worth more alive for future hauls than the payout for the nanites would have likely gotten.

"Zombie," I whispered to my empty cell.

That's what the island man had called Jim. I hadn't thought they were real. They were a myth created by the Alliance to keep bad little boys and girls in check and away from their science labs.

I remember my mother saying, "If you don't behave, you little shit, I'm going to send you to an Alliance lab, so they can turn you into a slobbering zombie!" Scare tactics were preferable to what my mother usually did to keep me in line. My mother's brand of discipline was usually accompanied by a cuff to the ear or a swift kick in the ass. Words usually only came when she was too drunk to move quickly enough to grab me.

"I should have stuck to straight pirating, Steve. In pirating, it isn't about feeling, it's about profit. If I'd accepted that Jimbo was a lost cause, I wouldn't be here."

Damn if I didn't need to get out of here. Talking to that damn skull had started to become more than a diversion tactic. I'd had enough diversions in my life as of late. If I'd not tried to help Jim, I'd probably be on the deck of my ship instead of in a prison.

While seeking nanites to heal the slowly decaying and carnivorous mind of my First Mate, James Naderblast, I had put myself directly in Alliance hands. I shook my head and huffed up another dust cloud. There was no choice. Seeing Jim on the verge of death kicked something inside me into gear and caused me to believe in luck for at least a moment.

Weeks went by after I'd given Jim the nanites without any hint of what had happened. It had seemed that we were in the clear until Jim jumped me in the corridor near my cabin. Despite the lack of overture in our relationship up to that point, I assumed it was due to the animal magnetism that was *moi* overtaking his good sense.

I had been trying to pat him and push him away; the thought of being intimate with Jim was as appealing as the idea of being with Smitters. But as I was trying to let him down gently by prying him off my person and avoiding kneeing him in the family jewels, Jim tried to take a bite out of my arm.

A few crewmen pulled him off before he could do any damage, but he'd gone feral. We had to chain him to keep him from trying to eat other crew members. I had our weaponsmith pull a slave ring from belowdecks and weld it into the bulkhead near the door. I attached a short length of chain, figuring despite the previous and isolated incident, that I was the least likely to get randomly eaten by my first mate. I also knew, as captain, it was my job to keep the crew in line, even zombie crew. Besides, Jim was also a great company deterrent for randy males that wanted to try their luck with the captain. It made fewer bodies I had to heave into the ocean.

The nanites we stole or occasionally bought if we found a semi-reputable buccaneer looking to make an honest living, had varying effects. After the third try, we had a portion of nanites that seemed to be made of sterner stuff and it held Jim over for a few months. The only side effect seemed to be occasional drooling, but several of my crew did that anyway so it wasn't too noticeable.

When his condition started to degenerate, I went on the hunt again. General nanites carried in most ship's medical supplies were easily attained, and not all made equal; Jim's body was the testing ground for quality. He had become almost a connoisseur of what good nanites were made of and I learned what types or makes to look for. The ones that only lasted a day or two were not worth the effort, but those few batches of month-long buggers were a fine wine to the discerning palate.

In Tortuga, we heard about an experimental nanite that could create a sort of super-soldier for the Alliance. I knew that I had to get some. Not just for Jim, but to stick it to the Alliance by stealing their new, best toy. I knew that if it was something they were making for their people that it had to be something good.

It did not work out the way I wanted. Jim was healed, that's for sure. I still see how quickly he became a puppet for the Alliance. The nanites shifted him into something, someone else. It wasn't just Jim that was affected, though.

Aside from the tattoos, I'd been incapacitated for a bit. I don't know if it was my body trying to deal with the magic being eaten away or something similar to what took Jim's will. Whatever it was didn't permanently take, thank Odah. My brain remained my own and I didn't go lapdog like Jim had.

If I could have just tested the nanites, maybe I wouldn't have lost Jim. Maybe I would still have my tattoos, too. I shook away the memories as though trying to fight off the prison lice infestation. I pushed myself to my feet with slow deliberation, sipped at my water, and considered my prison-scenario circumstances.

Ship gone. Crew gone. The first mate gone. Trapped in a dungeon with my only responsive conversations limited to an Alliance marshal that wanted me dead. Overall, I was in a shitstorm without so much as a hanky.

I heard movement in the hall outside of my cell while I sipped. I could charge at whomever my next visitor was, but my back felt like it was on fire and I could barely control the wobbling in my legs. I shifted backwards and upright so that I could use the wall to stand if I became brave enough to press against it. I lifted the pitcher and placed it in my lap so I could grip both sides like an oversized tankard of ale and waited.

My brain cataloged the multiple clicks and eventual clack of the locks being released. I heard the drag of rusty hinges and old metal of the door sliding open. My lock-picking skills would get a work-out once I had the energy to plan my escape, that was for certain.

A lantern entered before my favorite marshal came into the cell. I grinned as he looked from the chains overhead, around the cell, and then finally to me. He was clearly expecting I would still be doing my best whipped dog impression at his behest.

"Hey Spinner, is this a social call or are we going for two lines of questioning today?" I lifted my pitcher in salute and took another drink. I was proud that I'd managed to keep my arm from shaking. I kept my eyes locked on him as he slowly neared so I could shift if I saw that damn whip coming out again. Back scarring was one thing, but I didn't need him messing with my pretty face. It took a well-paid whore and a swashbuckling pirate captain with a devil's face to create this look and I was disinclined to lose it.

"Actually, I brought you a visitor," he motioned behind him and up stepped the man of my musings.

"Jim," my voice came out level and without inflection. I bit down hard on my lip to keep any hint of hope for the return of my first mate. I knew better than to think he had been returned to his true self. Spinner brought Jim to see me as a sucker punch to my morale. He thought to break me with the sight of the shell of my former first mate. A shell, that's what I had started seeing him as; he was no longer my Jim, but a Jim-resembling Alliance man.

"Captain...er, Maggy," he nodded after looking to Spinner for confirmation. The casual voice hinted at humanity, but I refused to fall for it again. I had let myself hope for at least a minute each time Spinner brought the fake Jim in to see me; I wouldn't do it again.

"You'll be happy to know that Jim will be taking command of your vessel and crew on the *MadCap*," Spinner's teeth reflected the light from the lantern-like tiny white blades. "They'll be running Alliance missions for us now under his leadership."

My teeth drew blood from my lower lip, and it helped me keep my damn mouth shut. When I lifted the pitcher to drink again, it was a slow, thoughtful movement that had both men watching me warily. They should be cautious; I had good aim when I threw serving ware.

I lowered the pitcher and said nothing. Hate and rage simmered in my eyes. The Atlantic depths of my peepers would likely look like the frozen arctic from the ball-shriveling violence in them. It was a good thing the two men were closer to the door than they were to me. I didn't credit myself with much restraint. Rage was giving a renewal to my empty energy well.

"Is that all?" I asked. I knew there had to be more; they were baiting me.

"No," Spinner stepped forward just one step, his jacket nearly brushing the stone wall. He thought better of approaching the barely caged beast. His arm stretched forward; long fingers stroked the chains that ran from the base of the wall. They made a soft, musical sound as the movement ran like water along the links. The chains rippled up to the ceiling and back down to the cuffs I had been clasped by minutes earlier. Spinner's thin lips curled into a smile. His grey eyes settled on me as he ran a finger down the length of chain like a caress.

"You'll be happy to know that your time in this cell is coming to an end," Spinner finally said. I arched an eyebrow and waited for the ax to fall.

"Don't look like that *Magerious*," Spinner loved to enunciate the syllables in my name as though he were speaking to me intimately. "We aren't going to kill you."

I shrugged and took another drink from the pitcher, letting my gaze drift to Jim and back to Spinner. "Your funeral, then."

"False promises do not become you, Magerious dear," Spinner dropped his hand and hazarded another step toward me. It was as though he wanted me to kick his ass and the stick jammed up it. "I would think you'd be happy to know that you're moving on. Without death, no less. Don't you want to know where you'll be going?"

"Why do people insist on asking questions that they plan to answer? Is it a call for attention? Are you truly expecting me to say: oh, please tell me, Spinner you god-like marshal?" I rolled my eyes. Spinner's smile slipped, and I barely restrained the grin that twitched at my lips.

"Yes, well...we're sending you to the Continent Alliance holding. The capital, at the request of the chancellor himself," Spinner's smile brightened again. Had we been in natural light, I would have likely been blinded at his new fervor. Instead, I sipped water.

"Didn't you already tell me that?" I asked. Spinner's smile froze.

"No."

"Are you sure? I'm pretty sure during one of our talks--"

"I never told you that--"

"--you said, 'Tell me where you stashed what you--'"

"--I would never have told you that."

"'-- took or I'll send you to the Continent Alliance holding,'" I finished. He opened his mouth to protest and I raised my hand to stop him while I finished the water in the pitcher. I set it down and let out a loud belch of contentment before motioning him on with my hand.

Spinner's face was caught halfway between the smile he fought to maintain and a look of embarrassed confusion. I guess I remembered more of our conversations than he did.

"No matter. That's where you're going," Spinner moved his hand in a chopping motion. "And do you know--"

"Oh balls, not this again," I sighed.

"--what's going to happen?" He took another step toward me and I'd had enough of his brand of stupid and decided to explore some of my own.

Rage can energize even those weakened by whipping, hunger, and... well escaping metal cuffs when locked in a prison. I chucked the pitcher at Jim and dove at Spinner with a snarl, knocking him to the ground. I crawled up to straddle him and started pummeling his cocky face for everything I was worth. Even without the magically enhanced tattoos, I knew how to throw a punch.

Jim grabbed me by the scruff of my neck and pulled me off of Spinner. He spun me around and pinned my arms at my sides, holding me about a foot from the ground. The buttons from his jacket dug into my ravaged back and I hissed. Spinner sat up and pulled a handkerchief from his pocket to dab at his lip in a dainty, ladylike way. He completely missed the blood dripping from his nose and seemed not to realize how much his eyes were already swelling. I spat at him and he shuddered before wiping at the saliva on his cheek almost frantically.

"Carry her to the guards, James," Spinner stood slowly, and I cracked a grin despite the pain. His face, once handsome and lean, now resembled a meatball. He glared; Jim tightened his embrace. I could barely breathe around his arms.

"Been working out, Jimbo?" I gasped out. "Good for you. Near death can bring clarity, but it would be good if you eased up a little before I black out and become dead weight."

"I'd still end up carrying you, so it makes no difference, Magerious," Jim paused at my name as though he needed to remember it. I had a renewed need to punch someone. I settled for several well-placed kicks with my heel that failed to garner any reaction other than a few grunts from Jim.

Jim carried me up the stairs as though I were a sack of flour. The buttons on his coat dug grooves in my back with each step up. I passed out at some point either from pain or lack of oxygen. When I came to, I was in a room with dusty rays of sunlight coming in through bars on the upper portion of the walls. After the dark I'd been in, it was glaringly bright. I had been re-cuffed and chained to a bench beside a skinny-looking wench.

"Cozy," I muttered and the girl beside me shot me a death glare that made me smile. At least it looked like they were going to provide me entertainment on my journey if her reaction was anything to go by.

"Magerious, I wouldn't get too close to that one: she bites," Spinner wagged his finger in the air at the girl as though chastising a naughty child. The girl snapped her teeth in response.

"Considering who's giving the warning, I think she's my new favorite person," I drawled, tugging quietly at the cuffs behind my back. I only had jagged nails and no bone pick. Logic told me that escape right then, with no clue of where I was in the prison or where the way out was, would just lead back to my cell.

I settled in, feeling the cool air caress my bare back. A breeze puffed up and I couldn't help but fill my lungs with the briny smell of the ocean that drifted in. It was like home was calling me to release my burdens and return to its embrace. Heaven probably smelled like the ocean, I decided. Of course, wherever I was going was likely to lead to my death which meant live or die, I could at least enjoy the smell of home.

I closed my eyes and tasted the wind. There was no mist to the air, so we weren't close enough for me to dive into the depths of that blue heaven, but the smell was strong and salty on my tongue. It was a balm to my frayed spirit and a shot of liquid courage to my rage.

The jangling of chains drew me from my reverie, and I opened my eyes. A bearded, haggard-looking man slumped in chains to the other side of the angry wench. He looked as though life had kicked him in the balls repeatedly, a kindred spirit.

"That's the final load," Spinner called out and a few very large male humanoid creatures came forward. One looked to be of the same ilk as one of my former crew members: a Walrusoid with flat arm-width tusks sticking out of his mouth and mounds of fat rolls to make a Buddha statue jealous. The other was something I had never seen before. It resembled a mound of rocks piled on top of each other until they somehow became a humanoid shape.

Or possibly a giant pile of shit. I looked the creature up and down and realized that the more I thought about it, the more I felt like a pile of crap was carrying myself and two other prisoners away. I could see no eyes, mouth, or nose on the thing, but it had gaping holes on either side of its boulder-head that I assumed were ear holes.

The two stepped forward, each carrying a long staff. They slid the staff under the bench, pushing through until each ran the length of our chain-accessorized seating. I hadn't noticed rings under the bench, but I saw curved metal when I leaned forward to see what they were doing. The sudden shift of the bench made me sit back up quickly. With a grunt from the Walrusoid and no sound from the boulder-sized-poop-man, they lifted the bench and occupants before carrying us out of the prison.

Chapter 4

Pure, stabbing sunlight slashed at my eyes like claws and I curled my head away from it. With my hands chained, I couldn't temper the onslaught, so I alternated opening eyes and blinked a lot. I could feel the unnatural bump beneath me that told me the two massive pack-carrier males trudged along.

I wondered if this was what it would have been like to ride a camel. The bumps and shifts caused no end to the discomfort for us. Had I been less chained in place, I would have fallen to the ground and likely been dragged. The girl in the middle dug her fingers and nails into the bench next to her legs to keep from falling. Maybe if they'd done more than just loop a few ropes around her in a way that would hang her if she fell, then the poor thing wouldn't look like she was holding on for dear life. The man on the end was curled in upon himself and bobbed limply with the movement. For a moment, I wondered if he had already died. I certainly couldn't tell by his smell; what I wouldn't have given to be upwind of him.

My eyes started to adjust to the light. Just the same, it didn't decrease the pain or clear the blurred white spots on my vision. With my vision hampered, my hearing and sense of smell seemed to take up the slack. I closed my eyes again, letting the sun heat the skin of my eyelids and dance across the dirty bits of exposed skin.

I could hear the roll and slap of the ocean on the docks. There was either a storm coming in or one had recently passed from the violence of the waves. The smell of the salt, when untainted by the odor of my companions, was warm. It was as though it had been boiled before wafting across the air to reach my nose. The heat of the sun and the damp humidity in the air tickled immediately at my scalp and the rough press of cloth on my body. I wasn't sure if I could sweat with the limited water I'd taken in, but my skin felt like it was being gnawed by horseflies where the cloth bunched up.

Through the heat, a spray of moisture danced at the bottom of my feet and I opened my eyes. My lips curled at the soft pleasure of sea spray hitting my skin. I could almost have ignored the scenario around me: chained to a bench, boarding a ship that I had never seen before, positioned between a strange woman making odd noises and a walking pile of shit.

Almost.

Boulder-sized-poopman and the Walrusoid plunked the bench down on the deck. They withdrew the staves they had used to carry us and stood beside the bench. They practically made the three of us invisible in the shadows of their mountainous forms.

"Thanks for the lift," I winked where I figured the crapman's eyes would be. The head of the massive creature shifted down at the same time the Walrusoid turned to glare at me.

"I'm unappreciated," I sighed.

A clatter of noise drew all of our attention. I shifted to rub my eyes into my shoulder because I was pretty sure I was seeing things. When I opened my eyes again, the image remained.

The figure that came toward us was like something that had stepped off of a propaganda page about pirates. From boots to neck, the man was everything one would expect of a pirate: missing both a leg and hand, a cutlass at his waist, and a blaster in the holster. He had a metal leg to replace his left and some kind of claw form on his right hand with a metallic run of limb up to the elbow. I'd seen both prosthetic forms on various sailors or soldiers in my life but these were truly quality from the brushed look. I had a feeling they were titanium or an alloy.

Despite that, he cut an impressive figure. He had a lean sailor's body under a jacket of Alliance blue and gold. His arms were crossed at his chest over a narrow waist with legs like tree trunks. His hands were unmoving, but I could see that they were more calloused than my own. Apparently, the Alliance had found themselves a working captain instead of just a rich prat with powerful connections. He was a healthy, impressive figure from the shoulders down; enough to make a normal girl want a peek under the blues for a bit of fun. That, however, was where the normalcy of the figure ended.

From neck to hairline he wore a metallic faceplate --
likely also titanium but shinier than his leg or claw-hand.
I was pretty sure no one had figured out how to make a
prosthetic head and general healing was done via nanite,
so I was understandably confused at the metal-mawed
captain.

"Take them below with the others," the captain pointed
a crewman in our direction as he jerked his chin at the
Walrusoid and his trailing shit pile. His voice was
smooth and even; another thing I didn't expect. I think I
was waiting for something tinny or echoing like he was
speaking through a tube. In my mind, it would have
shown that he was severely damaged under that metal
plate. Instead, he had a young voice with a deep timbre
and confident quality to it.

The crew member stepped forward. He was tall and
lanky with sand-colored hair and freckled skin. He was
young and looked like he would be more at home on a
farm than a ship. He unlatched the male from our bench
first, handing him off to another crew who'd followed
him down the gangplank. The second man manhandled
the prisoner away to the p-way that I knew would lead to
the lower hold. When the man was out of sight, the
sandy-haired crewman turned back and did the same
with the scowling biter before moving to me. I felt his
hands settle on the cuffs around my wrists and I
narrowed my eyes for a moment as I waited. I watched
the shadows around me through lowered lashes and felt

the touch of pressuring on my cuffs, knowing I would only get a moment to react once the cuffs were opened but liked my odds against the captain and his young crewman.

"Hold," the captain lifted his hand. The movement behind me stilled with the cuffs still latched.

"Richter, do you know who she is?" the captain's voice was warm as though he was about to welcome me, but I heard the steel snaking through.

"No Captain," Richter said from behind me.

"That's Maggy Low."

I fought the smirk that pulled at my lips as several unseen crewmen drew in their breaths. I kept my eyes down. Making eye contact right then could easily have signed my death warrant. The crew was not impressed so much as they were angry. I could feel it swell around me like a new storm waiting to whip the seas into a frenzy.

"Your orders, Captain Sloan?" Richter's voice came out like he was trying to grind wheat in his teeth. I didn't so much as twitch. I kept my breathing slow and calm despite the chaos that swelled in me directing me to fight, kill, and run.

"Get her the collar," he said softly, almost lovingly and I knew I was in a lot of trouble. A moment later, Richter was back putting a leather cuff around my neck. It had a chain attached that linked first to the wrist cuffs and then to my ankles. The chain running between them would restrict all movement and keep my hands locked almost to my chest with less than six inches of movement in any direction. There was an additional lead going to the back of the collar, but I didn't think this captain would be the sort to use it.

"Cuffs to the front, Richter. We need to keep our eyes on the *former* captain's hands," Captain Sloan sounded like he was talking about a bright day after unseasonably cold weather. I raised my chin. The emphasis on my lost title made me want to hiss and claw, but I kept it in as I took in my newest adversary.

Eyes moved behind the metallic face. They were a surprisingly pale shade of blue and were narrowed on me. I could see maturity in his gaze; not too young then. A seasoned sailor, for certain and quick to sense danger even when it draws into its shell. I could feel him taking in my bedraggled and beaten form and found my spine stiffening just a tiny bit. I fought it because I would have preferred to be underestimated but I knew he saw me as to what I could be instead of what was standing in front of him and let my posture lift. The predator in me sized him up in return.

"There she is," Sloan said slowly as I met his gaze. "I knew the demon within you would show itself sooner or later. Look close, mates: that is the look of evil that you never want to be on the other side of. She may hide it with a smile or a joke, but it's always there just below the surface waiting to come out and strike at any show of weakness."

"Either my reputation precedes me, or we've met," I said with a curl of my lips. "So, which is it?"

"Wouldn't you remember me if we'd met, Low?"

I narrowed my eyes at the non-answer and cocked my head to the side for a moment as though I was trying to place his face. My fingers tapped at the wrist cuff as though I was puzzling it out.

"You're right. I would remember a man with a titanium ass attached to his neck," I gave him a sweet smile. "I'm glad I won't have to kill an acquaintance then. I have so few of those left alive."

"You have no power here on the HMS *Draconis*, Low," his voice held laughter. "From what I hear, you have no power anywhere anymore. Nanites are tricky little buggers, aren't they?"

I let the smile drop to a sneer as I stared down the metalhead. I imagined a dozen scenarios of his death and let each play through my eyes. A lesser look had males pissing their britches, but Captain Sloan calmly stared back, waiting for me to look away. When I didn't, he cuffed me with his claw-hand. My teeth pierced my lip and blood dripped down from the edge of my mouth.

"I hope you enjoyed that. You won't get another," I snarled and stood as the crewman, Richter, finished with my ankle cuffs. I walked for the p-way before anyone could shove me forward. Quick steps behind me turned out to be Richter.

"I prefer a cabin with a view," I told him as he nudged me into the hold with his shoe on my ass. I only barely managed not to fall down the ladder.

"I prefer a captive that shuts her damn mouth," Richter grumbled. I arched my eyebrows.

"Do I sense a bit of steel under that boyish facade? Lovely. When I get loose, I'll leave you your tongue, so you can tell me how wonderful I am," I grinned. He didn't speak as he slid the door shut with a loud chop. Darkness was only sparsely interrupted by rough edges and cracks in the decking above.

"Good comeback," I muttered. I closed my eyes as I waited to adjust to the lack of light. You'd think it would have been fast and easy after how long I'd spent underground in a prison cell, but nope. After several deep breaths, I opened my eyes and turned to look over my fellow captives.

All twenty of them.

The crazy chit that had been on the bench beside me was nowhere to be seen, while the bearded gent was looking a lot less on the verge of death and standing right at the front of the group. Several looked me over with my chains running from feet to wrists to neck and stepped away. Not the odd bearded guy, though. He didn't take his gaze off me.

When the *Draconis* raised anchor and the hold we were all in shifted, the group was like a mass of reeds hit by wind. I spotted my bench-mate curled up in a ball on the floor behind the group. At the movement of the ship, she made an odd keening sound that did not immediately make me desire to renew our friendship.

I shifted away from the wavering group that didn't seem to be able to keep their feet under them until I found one of the walls in the dim exterior. I lifted my shoulder and leaned against it. I probably looked like I intended to nap upright, but it couldn't be helped with my hands in their useless state near my chest.

I focused on my new restraint. It was intelligently designed in that it limited my movement. It did not, however, keep my hands from touching and that would mean an escape was in my future. You would think with the extra precautions of chaining me this way, they would have gone the extra fathom.

Hours of seasick companions later, there was a scuffle at the hatch opening to the hold. It slid open and I had to cringe away even though I had my eyes closed in preparation for light. A few buckets were dropped down with some water skins. I had heard the clank and wet flop enough to be able to identify that mealtime had come.

I squinted my eyes and stepped forward to pull a hank of bread out of the bucket. It was likely that the bucket would do double-duty in holding our food before consumption and after. It wasn't unlike what I'd done on my ship with prisoners. I had insisted that, for passengers I wanted to be kept alive, food be lowered in burlap and buckets emptied regularly. It was the stink I hated. I also never saw a reason to lower hired help beyond what they'd already endured through service to the Alliance. Officers rarely made it to my holds.

I looked up through the hatch at the grinning face that stared down. I couldn't help but wonder if he wasn't seeing the chains on me and that made him brave and caused the leering look on his face. Then again, the fact that I was trussed like a pig for the spit might have been what caused the look.

"My compliments to the chef," I said, taking a bite of the bread. "Much less mold on this than what they served in the prison."

The leerer let out a wild laugh and slammed shut the hatch. I heard the latch slide into place and turned back to my fellow passengers. They started forward once the hatch was closed. I helped by shoving the bucket of bread to them with my foot. I grabbed a water pouch out of the other bucket before shoving that, too.

I sipped at the water and gnawed the rough bread. It was likely to be the same bread from the beginning of the voyage until the end. Of course, it would either be gone or be a different color by the time we reached where we were headed.

The others descended on the rations as though wild beasts unleashed which made the hair on my neck curl and my skin crawl. My bench-mate was still curled up in a ball at the back on the floor.

"She dead?" I asked around a bit of bread, jutting my chin at the ball of girl.

No one spoke but a few looked from her to me. The eyes of the other prisoners had taken a somewhat feral gleam that did not bode well for this journey. I knew what happened when humans lost touch with reality: they would rip each other apart like beasts. It made me realize that the girl and I were probably the only prisoners that hadn't spent as much time in prison before being shuttled off. The bodies I was looking at seemed as though they'd been squeezed from the cracks of the prison or pulled from the very mortar.

I stepped forward and one of the prisoners in the crowd made a low sound in their throat. I hadn't a clue if it was male or female, but it was a definite warning, like stepping toward a starved dog. I curled my lip and shifted my weight. I took slow, stalking steps circling the group. I was intent on shifting around them to keep the hatch at my left. Hungry eyes watched me move and I knew that if I rushed them, they would move as one beast to tear me apart. It wasn't much better to have them so intent on me, but it would at least give me the advantage of forewarning if they decided to rush me.

Between steps, I slide my hands slowly forward as I shifted my posture to a slight hunch. The movement was done as slow as I could. I counted heartbeats between curling one vertebrae at a time. I hoped if I did it slow enough that it wouldn't seem as though I were moving at all. My fingers danced down the chain, taking one length at a time into my palms, careful not to let the links clink together.

Small sounds came out of the crowd of people. I was sure there was a mix of sexes and species in that group, but just then they looked identical. Twin sets of glowing, feral eyes built the image of a pack of ravenous wolves to my senses.

I spread out my hands to hold the length of chain between them, thankful for the lack of light and therefore the tell-tale reflection on the metal. One tiny step and I felt eyes shift back to me. It wasn't the whole group, but just a few of the nearest outliers that watched each breath and shift of my body.

I sidestepped to move toward that back wall where I had seen the curled-up girl. I found myself hoping that she was still alive, or it was going to be a waste of my time trying to get to her around the pack of crazy.

Ever noticed that when you're trying to be careful and sneaky something seems to get right in your way at *exactly* the worst time?

I was looking forward and not down, which meant that the massive, rotted knothole in the flooring was an extremely unfortunate surprise. It was so unexpected, in fact, that I fell toward the pack of wild predatory humanoids in the center of the room and lost my grip on the length of chain I had intended to use as a weapon. The chains hit the floor just ahead of me, making a lot of jangling, crashing noises. The raucous noise was followed by the loud banging of my body weight crashing down and my instinctual, but agile curses aimed at the sea god.

On a good day, my curse phrases were almost poetic.

I felt the turning of the pack instead of hearing it. It was as though someone had sucked all the air out of the room in one massive gulp.

"Oh shit."

No poetry there, just plain as fuck fear.

I hissed and rolled away from the knothole of doom as toenails dragged and feet scrabbled as the mob charged me. I took the first attacker with a good kick from both legs that launched him or her -- they all looked like hairy burlap sacks by then -- back at the rest of the deranged mass. The flying attacker took down two others in his or her short flight. Two grabbed at my left arm and hauled me sideways while others grabbed for my legs or arms. I don't know what the intent was other than ripping, tearing, and/or destroying, but I wasn't planning to find out.

I swung toward my captors and caught them with the mass of chain. I clipped grabby hands with my swinging feet and shifted with the direction of the swing to land behind one of my attackers. I caught the man -- I hoped. A full beard is not an absolute marker of gender -- in a headlock and threw my weight back. I was thankfully close enough to the wall that I used it to surge both my body and the captor forward into the slowly shrinking crowd.

If I heard the hatch open behind me, it was blocked by the rush of bloodlust and survival instincts that were ringing in my ears. I struck with feet, chain, elbows, and grabbed random body parts to knee as I waded through the fray. I knew I was winning even though the number standing still outnumbered me by more than five. Then, it was over, and I was on the deck with a boot to my neck and the sound of a whip sending my fellow passengers into far corners of the hold to quiver.

"Take 'er up to the Captain," the male whose boot I had become intimately acquainted with said to someone behind us.

"The girl," I grunted. There was no way I was letting my efforts go to waste.

"What the fuck's she talking about?" a voice that I recognized as Richter called from near the hatch door.

"What girl?" Booty leaned down to ask.

"In the back…" air was being cut off from the weight on my neck and the press of chain to my sternum.

"You should worry about yerself," Booty snarled just before blackness took me.

Chapter 5

I jolted as cold, salty water hit me square in the face. Aside from being cold, it forced oxygen in my lungs at a gasp. Light glared down at me and made me wrench my head to the side. I spit out ocean, bile, and probably blood before my lungs remembered to work. I curled my body up so I could spit out everything but air.

"You aren't even aboard the *Draconis* for a day and you're trying to destroy some of my cargo, Maggy," Sloan didn't sound as annoyed as his words led me to believe. He sounded amused. I sadistically wondered what he would sound like when I pissed him off.

"The girl," I gasped out again. "Did you bring her up?"

"I don't know why you care, but yes."

A shadow blocked the sun from glaring at me so that Sloan could glare down from his metal face. I could see the contemplation in his eyes even if it wasn't evident in his voice.

"She alive?"

"Yes. Again, why do you care? What is she to you? Former crew?"

"Didn't want a dead body stinking up the hold," I rolled to flop my head to the side and shut my eyes. "Brings the rats in faster."

"Right." Another bucket of salt water washed over me, making me gasp in surprise and pull a bit too much into my already aching lungs. "Were the bruises and broken wrist a gift from you?"

I rolled to my side and coughed up more sea water but didn't bother to respond even when my airways were clear. It was a stupid question, and he knew it. He was trying to tell me how she fared, so he could gauge my reaction. He wouldn't get one.

I flopped back and hissed at the pain of the deck touching my back before I could think to cover it up. When my vision cleared of red pain, I looked up, squinting at the glare from his metal face. Sloan said nothing for several heartbeats, and I knew he was waiting for something from me. Questions? Snarky comments? My body was still trying for a reasonable amount of air, so I couldn't help him on any front.

"She's being tended to," Sloan stood up and scratched his forehead by running a fingernail around the hairline, wiggling it as though trying to peel the metal away from his hair. He caught me watching and stopped.

"The question is, though, what to do with *you*? If I put you back in there, I could lose profit," Sloan watched me, but I stayed where I was at. I could feel the rough boards digging into the exposed skin on my back. I wasn't sure I wanted to sit up and risk peeling away more broken skin. "I can't let you loose, or you'll kill some of my crew. I can't shift you to work with the cook like the girl

-- there's no more room and a dead cook can't feed us. What am I to do with you, Maggy?"

"I hope you don't think I'm going to make your plans for you, metal face," I lifted my hands to wipe the remaining water away from my face. "Why don't I take in some sun and nap while you figure it out."

The kick was hard enough that it knocked some of the wind from my sails and made me fight the urge to gag. I rolled and tried not to scream as I left skin behind on the deck. I'm sure I made a noise like a hot air balloon being popped, though.

"Looks like you're damaged goods anyways," Sloan tsked. "Richter get over here. Clean and wrap our guest. We don't need her dying of infection before we reach our payday."

"Yes, Sir."

"After that, attach her chain to the anchor line and set a guard," Sloan waved them away as though shooing a bug.

"Yes, Sir."

Richter yanked me to my feet and hauled me by the arm to the officer's mess. He pushed me inside and motioned toward a stool. Richter closed the door before he walked to a hutch to pull out a mass of cloth and tubes. He kept his eyes on me with every movement. I shot Richter a grin when he pulled out a glass bottle that I recognized.

"I'll take a double if you're pouring," I wagged an eyebrow at him, and Richter narrowed his eyes. I was truly not winning the boy over. "Okay, a single shot will do for now."

He grabbed cloth from the pile on the table and poured rotgut from the bottle.

"A glass works better," I twisted my mouth and held my breath. He pressed the soaked fabric into my back as I waited for the urge to scream to pass. It took a long time for the sting on the alcohol to dim enough that I didn't want to run my voice hoarse in yelling or stomp my foot like an angry mare. Richter patted down my entire back with the rotgut alcohol which intensified the pain. It also didn't help that his patting was more like a steady slap against the tender, ravaged flesh of my back. A gentle touch this gent was not. I managed not to say a word or let the slightest sound escape my clenched jaw while he cleaned the lashes on my back.

"At least now I know how to shut you up," he muttered, and I lifted one finger to show him what I thought of his ministrations. He laughed quietly despite himself.

"One of these is deep and jagged," he mumbled.

I knew from the feel of the whippings I had gotten what he was talking about. Spinner had remarked on the guard's ability to strike the same spot more than once as though it was a true accomplishment. Maybe it was. Maybe it was just fucked up.

"I could cauterize it, but that might do more damage at this point," Richter was obviously not speaking to me and I didn't see a need to interrupt his thoughts just then. He made noises and mumbled to himself before applying a salve that had an immediate cooling feel on my battered skin.

In the wave of cooling bliss, I realized that he had been silent too long. I shifted slightly so I could turn my body without twisting my waist to look at him. His face was flushed, and he was holding a wrap in his lap and chewing on the edge of his lip.

"I'm not sure if I should have the captain decide about that deep one," he said.

"You know, you could just use nanites to heal it," I suggested and the flush to his skin got darker.

"Slaves don't get nanites," he sneered at me. The hesitant look left his face while he glared but he didn't pick up the wrap in his lap to finish. I realized that the blush hadn't left him either. I didn't try to stop the chuckle that fluttered across my lips.

"I forgot: no female crew members on Alliance vessels," I smirked. "Do you want me to take off my shirt, *Richter*?"

I made the question come out as a taunting purr. The flush spread to his neck and I thought steam came out of his ears for a moment. Freckles take on an interesting, spotted look when a body is flushed with deep discomfort. It was kind of like looking at a leopard and trying to decide which part was spots and which was skin tone.

Richter flung the wrap at me and took a step away.

"Wrap yourself then," he growled. I laughed harder. There was no modesty in my own crew. I'd seen more body parts from various species than I wanted to think about. There had even been this odd insectuous creature that apparently had an appendage on his chin that was for mating. He left it dangling out for months before any of us knew that's what it was. The sound he made when he stroked it should have clued someone in.

I shifted to pull my shirt away but realized there was no way I could do it. The way my hands were chained to hang at my chest meant there was no way I could reach the fabric at my waist. I shook my head and arched an eyebrow.

"We have a couple of choices here, Richter," I drawled and managed to contain the humor I still saw in the situation. "Either you unchain me--"

"Like hell."

"-- or you wrap me," he was silent at that possible option. "Or, I go barebacked and risk undoing everything you just did."

A sharp sound like someone knocking with the hilt of a blade came from the door. Richter jumped up and opened the door. His arm popped up in a salute and Sloan stepped inside.

"I thought maybe Maggy had talked you into an afternoon diversion, First Mate," the captain looked from my exposed back to Richter's clenched hands and bowed posture. "No? Good. I'd hate to have to feed your corpse to the creatures of the deep."

Richter's gaze zipped to me again before he fought to straighten his posture.

"What *is* taking so long, then?" Sloan leaned to look at my back but didn't step any closer. Richter swallowed once but didn't speak.

"He was tending to a gash that was deeper than the others," I shrugged and was surprised it didn't hurt as much. "I tried to talk him into nanites. I won't repeat the words. They aren't becoming of a lady such as myself or permitted in such sensitive company."

I eyed Sloan up and down in case there was any question as to who I was calling sensitive. He made a noise that could have been a grunt, but it was hard to tell with the low echo from his faceplate.

"Cut away her shirt and get on with the wrapping then," Sloan waved his hand forward as though inviting Richter to dance. The first mate nodded and pulled a knife from his boot. It was a good, sharp weapon and cut the cloth like a thought.

I lifted my arms and hardened my blue gaze to meet Sloan's across the room. Richter didn't hesitate this time around, but I didn't bother to look and check his embarrassment level. He pressed the bandage to my chest and quickly wrapped it around my body several times before he tucked it off near my side and stepped away for a moment.

Sloan's eyes never wavered from mine despite my partial nakedness. There was no change in his gaze, either. Forever a challenge with this one, it seemed.

As Richter returned, he sliced a length of cloth and used it to tie the wrap. While he was occupied, I leaned into him and gave him a kiss on the cheek, making him jump. When he looked at me, I gave him a wink.

"Thanks, darling. That was great," I curled my lips into a smug smile that had color rushing up the sailor's face in a way that tickled me to no end. I decided to tally how many times I could make the first mate blush in the course of the journey.

"Get a length of chain to the anchor line. I'll bring Maggy out in a moment," Sloan's voice held a hint of the humor that I was feeling. "Dismissed."

The first mate saluted and tore from the room as though his ass was on fire.

"I knew you wanted me all to yourself," I settled on the stool and gave him a wide smile that was more shark than flirt.

"I wanted to get that sailor out of here before he started swinging," Sloan lifted a finger to rub at a spot just above his ear. He seemed to remember something and dropped it. I watched his chest rise and fall in a sigh that I didn't hear.

"Any chance you want to tell me where you hid some of the spoils of your previous venture?" Sloan asked, and I quirked an eyebrow.

"I'm thinking there's more to this question than I previously thought," I told him. "Spinner was obsessed with asking me that every single day and now you're asking. Do you want to tell me what in my stash you're looking for?"

"Bringing back the stolen items in your 'stash' would be very beneficial to me. Not only would I get a pay raise, but I'd also likely get a medal or a commendation," Sloan lifted one shoulder.

"All logical reasons and your metallic maw is hard to read, but I can see something else in your eyes," I shifted to cross my arms and settled for lacing my fingers together. The chains were seriously in the way of my posturing. "You should know you can't kid a kidder so why don't you just tell me what you want? The odds are against me escaping; why not just ask?"

"I would never lay odds against you doing or not doing anything, Maggy," Sloan said slowly. His voice sounded tired and unlike the content, upbeat persona he had postured with prior to that moment.

"I wouldn't either, but I don't play the odds. I always go for the underdog out of instinct," I told him honestly. Who didn't love an underdog?

"You think you qualify as the underdog, Maggy? Aren't underdogs usually heroes who just haven't found their moment yet?"

I found myself liking the way he thought and nodded slowly.

"Sometimes. Sometimes they're just the one that everyone else thinks will lose."

"I'm not sure I've known you to lose, Maggy," Sloan stepped around me and pulled a shirt out of the cabinet.

"See, there's that familiarity with me again," I tsked. "Care to clue me in as to how you think you know me, yet?"

"What would the fun be in that?"

He took a step toward me and I fought the urge to take a step back until he held up the shirt like a white flag. I nodded and lifted my arms. I felt only a slight tug of pain in my back now that it was medicated and wrapped.

Sloan grabbed the chain that held my arms and pooled the loose shirt at my feet for me to step into. He held one wrist at a time in his metal claw as he uncuffed but didn't release me. The angle he kept me at left no movement for my arms. I could have head-butted him, but I'd likely crack my own skull in the process, so I waited.

"Do you often take the time to dress your captives?"

We were in the galley from the looks of it and the general geography of the ship. The *Draconis* was a bit larger than *MadCap*, but the layout was very similar. Sloan had moved to latch the chain to the bottom of a long table welded to the deck. He paused and turned his metal maw back toward me at the question.

"I'd rather not put dangerous ideas in the minds of my crew," Sloan said softly.

"I suppose it would be a bit too tempting for them with the lack of females on ship," I shrugged. Sloan clapped the lock shut and straightened.

"It isn't about temptation in the same vein that you're referring to it, former-captain," Sloan drawled. "Do you have any idea what some of the crew would do to you if they had free reign?"

I turned to look at my surroundings and lifted one shoulder. "That's the crux of being a pirate, I suppose."

"That's the crux of being a mass-murderer," Sloan hissed. "How many have you killed, Maggy? Do you even know?"

I turned my blue glare on him, cold enough to freeze. He wouldn't know the screams I heard in the quiet hours of the night that called for vengeance.

"Do you?" I whispered. "Your hands are no more clean than my own."

Sloan grabbed my wrist and pulled it forward, looking down at the palm for a moment then lifting his face to look at me. His hand was callused, and I could smell the salt coming off of him from endless hours on the deck of a ship. He wrapped his metal claw around my wrist and undid the lock before pulling the sleeve of the shirt up and over before relatching the cuff.

It was a deft movement and he barely took his eyes from mine as he did it. When the metal of his claw released my wrist and grasped the other, I knew that his metal hand was possibly worse than a cuff as it was controlled by hate. Justified hate, to be sure, but righteous it was not.

Faster than I would have thought possible, he had me in a new shirt, re-cuffed, and was shoving me out into the passageway where two waiting crewmen to escorted me to my new imprisonment. I looked back once as I felt his gaze on me but couldn't decipher the look in his eyes even though I felt the weight of it.

My new home at the anchor was guarded by an arthropod humanoid who spent his time knitting. I watched him use the pincers that it had in place of hands and the first set of jointed appendages under its arms to hold the yarn. I figured with how fast it went that it would have a blanket done by the time his watch duty with me was over.

"You missed a spot," I settled against the bulkhead beside the anchor. The arthropod made a noise in response that turned into a shrill chattering as it found the spot I had been referring to. I wondered if he was cussing at me or himself.

"I wouldn't tick him off if I were you," a burly guy who was looping lines near where I was chained commented. "He's been known to like the taste of human flesh now and then when in a rage or if he's mating."

"When's his mating cycle?" I lifted my head and curled my lip at the scorpion-looking guard before gazing in the direction of the speaking crewman.

"In a couple of days. Tick him off and he'll go out of his way to find you if he gets hungry," he let out a belly laugh, and the arthropod guard made a squeaking noise while gesturing at the other crewman. I may not have understood what it was saying, but I could gather from the gestures that it wasn't about me.

I flopped my head back, thunking it against the wall a few times when I heard shouting. I popped upright as though I was on a spring and winced as pain shot through my back. Despite the discomfort, it was better than it had been.

"Incoming vessel, six o'clock," someone yelled. My guard dropped his knitting as he stood to his full height and ended up hunching when he reached the planks of the deck above us. The other crewman ran off while my guard looked back and forth as though questioning what he should do. I shrugged and threw my hands as wide as I could to make the chains rattle.

"It isn't like I can go anywhere," I sighed and flopped my head back again for a moment. I turned my head and watched the guard ripple and shift forward a little. It made a noise and the 'yarn' it had been knitting was sucked up into a hole that I hadn't noticed between its legs.

"Ew! That's disgusting!" I yelled as I realized what it had been knitting. "And to think I was going to ask you to make me a blanket."

The guard skittered and scuttled away from me, weaving back and forth as it dropped onto all appendages like a centipede. I waited until he was almost to the stairwell before shifting under the chains. I rolled my right shoulder for a moment and grasped my right bicep with my left hand. I curled my body and braced against the wall behind me. With a hard yank and shove, I dislocated my shoulder and rolled it forward, so I could move my hands closer together. Sloan had tightened the chain after he dressed me, raising my wrists and making it so I could reach my hands.

I checked to make sure the scorpion/centipede crewman was still distracted before I curved my collarbone forward and spit a pin with the first mate insignia on it into my right hand.

"Thanks again, Richter," I murmured with a grin. I'd caught his collar with my teeth for a moment when I leaned in to give him a kiss. I started working the lock on my barely reachable left wrist. My shoulder hurt like hell, but it wouldn't matter if I could get free. This wasn't the first time I had ever popped my shoulder out. It always hurt like a sonofabitch, but I'd never struggled with putting it back in afterward.

I tripped the pin and the cuff popped open with a click that made me flinch. I looked back at the guard who was now circling the ladder and making a lot of noise. Thankfully, his noises did an amazing job of covering the sounds I made.

I started to work at the left cuff, but the pin was bent from the angle I used to unlock the first cuff and I was struggling to get it into the pinhole.

"Pirates! Man, the cannons!"

The shout was like a southern breeze after days adrift. I grinned as the shuffling and called orders became frenzied on the deck above me. Maybe Odah was smiling on me this time.

"Prep the divers and load the cannons. Drop mines," Sloan's voice was easily recognizable both in timbre and command.

"Mines?" I gaped. No one had developed a safe mine for dropping or launching. Even the landmines weren't safe and tended to overheat from steam and chemicals before taking a target. Stupid Alliance taking risks as usual with their own damned lives and those of anyone around them.

The sounds of clunking came from all directions as crew members flew down the ladder to take items from pulleys that were drawing something up from below decks. I watched a crewman pick up a flat disk about the size of a pie and place it on the deck beside him. He pulled three more before the cranking stopped and no more were brought up.

Escape attempt forgotten, I watched as the crewman twisted something in the center of the disk to pop it open. He then pulled a flask from the belt at his hip, poured liquid in and twisted it closed. He did that with each disk before picking up the first again, pulling flint out of his pocket and waiting. The urge to yell questions at him was, thankfully, waylaid by the captain yelling a command that was echoed by other voices around the ship.

"Drop mines!"

"Drop mines, Aye!"

The crewman and several others struck flint along the top of the casing; some several times as they watched the center of it for something before throwing it in the ocean. The disks hit the water, splashed once and then flew up in the air, with a huffing whizz before continuing the trajectory with which they were thrown.

After the initial throw and hop, it was hard for me to see where the disk went, but they made a lot of noise. More when they hit the unseen target. A clattering clang sounded in the distance as though someone had slapped two pot lids together. It was followed by screams and popping noises.

"Fire cannons," came the call and the crewmen called back the order before they took aim and began firing. I could hear the cannonballs striking a ship in the distance. Why didn't the fools draw back and skirt up behind the *Draconis*? What kind of blasted pirates were they if they couldn't do a simple boarding maneuver?

In my head, I continued to rail at the poor excuses for pirates trying to take on the Alliance vessel before I remembered my own plight. I shook my head at my own wasteful actions and resumed picking at the cuff, trying to get the bent pin to connect and release the cuff.

You'd think I would have noticed when silence surrounded me instead of the sounds of battle, but I was so focused on mental berating the other crew and picking the lock open. The split focus caused me to descend into my own silence and leave my surroundings behind.

The cuff dropped loose, and I squirmed to roll out from under the loose wrap of chains that had secured me to the anchor line. I rolled my shoulder and arm back as hard as I could and felt it, painfully, pop back in. Something bit down hard on my shoulder.

"Sonofa--"

"And here I thought we were coming to an understanding, Maggy."

Right then I decided that I hated the sound of that smug bastard's voice. I hated the calm, mocking roll of it that under other circumstances in a different universe I would have found almost sexy.

Chapter 6

I struggled to break free, but Captain Sloan's metal fist was clamped around my shoulder, possibly hooked under my collarbone and prevented me from doing much more than twisting in midair. I'd be lying if I said it didn't hurt like hell.

"If the pirates hadn't been so easy to disperse, I would assume that you had somehow managed to plan that diversion for your escape," his voice, though still light and friendly, had an undertone that made the hair on my neck rise.

I kicked out but all I managed to do was windmill my legs since they were still cuffed together. I looked like a child's toy for a moment without the full body movement and Sloan made a low sound in his throat that I took to be amusement.

"It's too bad we aren't on the same side of things, Maggy. You are pure entertainment," Sloan reached up and touched something on his arm before the clamp dropped me to the deck. In less time than it took me to regain my senses, the claw-like metal hand was hauling me by my chains like a mother cat carrying a kitten. I was just as helpless. He touched something on his arm again and took a step back without releasing the clamp.

Even if I threw my body weight at him, there was no way I would be able to make contact over that distance other than to brush him with the still-hanging chains. He hauled me around like a puppet on a stick. I decided that hanging limp was my best play for the moment.

If I still had my leg tattoos, not only could I break free of the damned chains that bound my ankles, I could give Sloan a boot to the head that would dent that metal face of his. Too bad that my quest for nanites had taken my best weapons. In my time in captivity, I'd replayed the moment over and over, thinking about how stupid I'd been. It wasn't just that I'd blindly dosed Jim, but I hadn't even thought to put on gloves. It had never occurred to me to try to protect myself from the nanites. The worst that had ever happened from direct contact with nanites had been baby-soft skin and the random scar heal.

The super-bots had been programmed for a different endgame. Granted, I wasn't focused on anyone else's needs than my own for a working, non-cannibalistic first mate, but I still should have dug a little deeper before accepting the wind change. I let that bastard, Talimuck play me like a bad bluff in a poker game. Normally, I wasn't so unequivocally stupid.

Jimbo was headed somewhere to take over my ship if Spinner was to be believed. The loss of Jim and the tattoos that I'd paid dearly for with part of my life that was now forfeit had set me to now dangle from an

Alliance captain's grasp like a puppet on a string. It pissed me off to no end that I'd paid a price I couldn't undo. Hope was a bitch.

It might have been the limited oxygen to my brain as the captain carted me around like a toy, but I daydreamed about the glory days. The bloodlust tattoos made my legs practically steel-skinned without the unattractive look that Sloan had. I'd leapt the lengths of ships almost to the point of temporary flight and I'd only had the abilities just over a year. One year of being the terror of the seas was not worth the ten paid for the advantage. The marks had faded to ridiculously smooth skin. But I could deal without my hard-earned scars easier than I could the loss of strength. The feel of the tattoos bleeding away was second only to the other-ness I'd felt. It was as though the blood was drained from my body and replaced with ice water.

Finally, we reached our destination and Sloan tossed me to the mizzen mast. He gestured a few of his men forward; they brought chains, several cuffs, and a leather belt hooked with more chains. They secured me to the mizzen quickly.

"Apparently a collar restraint isn't enough, though I would like to know how you managed to get loose," Sloan cocked his head at me. The sun reflected off of the surface of his face and I couldn't keep eye contact. "No? Trade secret? Pity."

I grunted and looked past Sloan to see a mass of men wrapping chain around the main mast. In the links, I saw men cuffed and tied as Sloan's crew continued to secure the new captives. My eyes caught on a flicker of a tusk and realized at least one of the pirate crew was familiar. I dropped my gaze to keep Sloan from noticing the shift, though I'm sure it showed in my posture.

"Do we have a friend on the crew there, former-captain?" Sloan turned slowly as his crewmen continued to secure me. "Interesting. We'll have to see about getting you a reunion."

"With those scallywags? Do you honestly think I would ever take riffraff like that in as part of my crew?" I spit at the deck to show him what I thought of it. "They were so quick to lose to you that I would have killed them myself if I had been given the chance."

"Would that have been before or after they had taken you off of the *Draconis*, Maggy?"

I shrugged.

"I wouldn't look a gift horse in the mouth if that's what you're asking. However, I would have sacrificed most of them to Odah as we sailed away."

Sloan looked back at me and nodded slowly. I was pretty sure it wasn't in agreement so much as his recognizing that it was the sort of measure I would take. I began to wonder how someone with the ability to think like a pirate had managed a position in the prissy-assed Alliance. I couldn't see him playing their game easily with how quickly he took a more direct approach to failure. He'd have done better as a pirate. I would have definitely taken him into my crew after only speaking to him for a short while. His intellect was obvious.

After all, he immediately recognized me as a dangerous, skilled adversary.

"Possible, but I'm not convinced enough to let you anywhere near them," Sloan shifted to stand behind me. "I'm also no longer certain having the crew guarding you is in my best interest."

"I prefer the view from here, anyways," I told him. It was the truth. I was near the helm under the bright light reflecting off blue waters and able to smell the salty brine of the tumultuous world around me. Other than being chained in place and not on my own vessel, there was nowhere I'd rather be.

"I might need to put you elsewhere then," Sloan drawled. "We can't have you enjoying your journey."

I shrugged. I wasn't sure he would be happy with the situation after long. I bored easily, especially when I couldn't move around. Other than the fact that I would do anything I could, including kill, to escape, Sloan would have been better off putting me to work. I was, after everything else, a sailor.

"Are we there yet?" I huffed. I had been chained to the mizzen mast for hours.

"You've only been chained up for five minutes and I already want to kill you, Maggy," Sloan said. I shrugged as much as I could with the chains clamped down.

"Five minutes, five years… Are we there--"

"No," he huffed and walked over to one of the captured crew and punched him square in the face. He seriously needed to work on his people skills.

Sloan gestured and gave orders to his crew about the prisoners. I was guessing he planned to put them in with the feral slaves in the hold. It would at least thin out the numbers of one group or the other so long as he didn't need anyone for information.

I watched the pirate prisoners taken away one by one until Sloan came to a very familiar, Walrusoid figure with a broken tusk and a bloodred rag tied around his head. I knew underneath the rag would be a shining bald head and a series of piercings that ran from the tip of his head down to the top of his spine. Smitters always hid the piercings when he fought another crew to keep them from getting ripped out of his blubbery hide. I'd seen it happen once and it was not a pleasant sight. His species apparently had fat that existed underneath the upper layers of his skin.

Smitters gave Sloan a bow and simpered at the captain in a look I knew very well. He was trying to convince Sloan of his worth as a sailor. I wished I was closer. I wondered if Smitters was reciting the same bull he gave me when he hired on to be part of my crew. I remembered thinking how rehearsed it was and considered turning him down, but we needed the muscle. Walrusoids were good at going without food due to their fat stores and were extremely violent when provoked, perfect for pirating.

Sloan gave a sharp motion to Richter who gut-kicked Smitters and tugged at his cuffed hands before leashing him and leading him away. I barked out a laugh, not bothering to bite it back when I saw the captain's reaction. Apparently, Sloan saw the same amount of charm in Smitters as I had without any of my desperation.

A few more captives were taken away after Smitters, but none had familiar faces. I wondered if I could find a way to speak to my former crewman but doubted the captain would let me near a single member of the group they'd taken below. After the last few had been walked away, I found that I couldn't hold my tongue.

"You're going to lose a few more in doing that, Sloan," I drawled when he returned to the helm. "The new additions won't start the fight, but they won't end it, either."

"Are you trying to tell me that a bunch of cowed, broken prisoners will attack a crew of pirates?" Sloan laughed. It was a rich, cultivated sound that made me wonder if he practiced it in his cabin.

"They aren't broken in the way you're thinking, or they wouldn't have attacked the girl and charged me when they deemed me a threat," I sucked at my teeth. "That group's gone feral. They'll look for weakness to control or strength to destroy. The pirates are going to look like something that needs to be destroyed."

"I don't know whether to listen to you or knock you out just to shut you up," Sloan looked at the horizon, made a small adjustment in the wheel and pretended our discussion was over. I considered it, but my tongue had other ideas.

"Your first mate would prefer the latter," I squinted around at him, my head tilted to the side. The mate in question looked up from the deck and gave a quick couple of nods in assent. I blew him a kiss. "I think he likes me and that pisses him off, personally."

Richter's eyes went dead, and he shook his head and curled his lip.

"Yep. He totally has a thing for me," I grinned, and the first mate walked away with a snort. "Better watch that one. He's going to try to free me at some point due to his strong feelings."

"To kill you maybe," Sloan's voice held disappointment but was light with humor that he couldn't quite hold back. He shifted into a comfortable stance that told me he was ready to man the wheel for a good while.

"Was that walrusoid yours?"

"Nope," I said without pause. "Too fat for my crew. My mates were a svelte group of fighting and sailing machines."

When he dropped my gaze, I looked at him for a moment longer to attempt to further my persona of ignorance. He was a smart man, though.

"Right," Sloan said. He called out to a couple of older crewmen, one of which I recognized from my time at the anchor. "Maggy needs a nap. Help her find one."

The crewman gave me a broad grin and I noted that several teeth were missing around the same time as Sloan's commands sunk in. A moment later, a massive boot came at my face and I saw no more.

MadCap

Chapter 7

I struggled to wake, bathed in sunlight and the sounds of crew and sea around me. I smiled as I pushed at my reluctant eyelids, wanting to call out commands to the crew of the *MadCap* and get on to...wherever it was we were going. I frowned and reality began to creep in until I realized that I *was* awake. I was also not on my beloved ship despite the warm sea smells and caressing spray.

Night had fallen, and I was seeing stars. Not the metaphorical, knocked-on-your-head stars, but actual stars. The moon had yet to rise and it was full dark. The only light was from pinpoints in the sky that did nothing to cast aside the darkness that fell like a cloak over the *Draconis*.

The imagined warmth of the sun lingered on my skin as I pushed to break away from the last bit of happy dreaming into reality. I shifted and felt the rub of my chains like cold metal fingers digging into my flesh just to remind me that they could. The exposed skin of my arms and face felt like they were coated in grit from sweat and spray. There was a limited amount of my skin exposed and I was going to have an oddly disjointed tan if I spent too many days chained up.

A cup rose to my mouth and bumped against my lips. I took a slow draught before lifting my eyes. Even though he was just a shadowy figure, I recognized the captain from the carved way the light spread around him. Skin would look faded at the edges in the dim light, not sharp as though the darkness was being split with a blade. His entire profile was outlined in the sparse light in sharp relief.

"Richter set your nose after Druber stomped down a little too hard one too many times." There was no apology in his voice, not that one was expected. "You killed his brother on the *Intrepid* a few years ago."

I was surprised that he shared the information with me. It was almost as though he wanted me to understand that the hate was justified. Hate is what it is, justified or not. Granted, I'm sure I deserved the ire of a great many people due to lives lost under my command or in the process of knocking down the Alliance whenever possible. It didn't matter if I felt the loss or hate; I was a pirate, and we wash our decks in the blood of our enemies.

I took another drink from the cup still at my lips before lifting my chin to meet his unseen eyes. I remembered the ship he was referring to with bitterness.

"Possible. I killed a lot of people on that ship. Their captain was an imbecile that wouldn't back down, so I had to *put* him down. It was only after most of his crew was dead that I succeeded in doing so," I frowned. It had been a waste of time on my part since they'd only been carrying basic supplies and no munitions. It hadn't hurt the Alliance or lined our coffers any.

"Do I hear reasoning in your response, Maggy?"

"No. I would have likely killed them all just the same for being Alliance," I chewed at my lip, considering. "If not as an outlet after finding that they carried a lack of useful supplies in their stores. They were worthless to me."

Sloan's head moved in the shadows and I realized he was nodding. Even as my eyes adjusted to the sparse light in the night world, I could only just make out the movement.

"Why do I feel like every interaction with you is mindfully done on your part? Are you still hoping I'll let slip where my stash is?"

"Slip? No. Outright tell me? Yes."

I laughed. The sound came out hoarse and choked. I was so dehydrated that I wanted to gulp down the water and my voice showed it. Sloan lifted the cup to my lips again and I sipped.

"Even after I'm dead, my treasure will remain hidden," I grinned. I was feeling slightly better, but my stomach rumbled, and I remembered that the only food I had consumed in days had been the bread heel in the hold. "Do you want me to make a cliched comment like 'Dead men tell no tales'?"

"Would it make you feel better to do so?"

"Nah. My preference is just to say fuck off," I watched his shrug and took one last sip from the cup before he stepped away.

"Richter will bring you some gruel when he takes the watch," Sloan stepped back to, I assume, the helm. By the light level and glow of the moon on the horizon, the captain had been at the helm, and I'd been unconscious, about four hours. There was no sound but the waves lapping against the sides of the ship and the creaking shift of the massive vessel. The crew was either silently attending their watch stations or below decks getting some shut eye. It was longer than most captains stayed at the wheel, to be truthful. I know I would have likely tied up and headed to my cabin by now or taken a few hours off and come back. I shrugged at the stupidity of Alliance training and leaned my head against the mast.

The wind rolled across the waves, warm and clean. I breathed it all in and felt the crust of dried blood around my nose when I tried to take a full lungful. It itched and made my nose feel a little full, but I didn't let that stop me from enjoying the balm of the seas. Of course, with every moment of peace, it must be shattered by something simple, yet vile to the senses.

"There's a high starting bid on your head when we reach land," Sloan said before I could annoy him with questions. "There's even a rumor that Ned Low will be in attendance for the sale, possibly as a bidder."

Fury welled up inside me and I didn't respond. *Of course*, my father would bid to buy his pirate daughter from the Alliance. I would rather spend a lifetime hanging from my ankles in their prison, though. I wanted nothing to do with that bastard and I would bet Sloan knew that or he wouldn't have brought it up.

"I wonder if he'll actually make you a slave or just kill you for betraying him," Sloan mused, and I couldn't hold my tongue.

"Betraying *him*? He's the one who joined up with the Alliance and killed off the Kinship," I hissed. "And for what? A pardon for his crimes and a big payday? Oh, and let's not forget making admiral of the fleet."

"I sense bitterness, Maggy."

I snorted with such vigor that a jab of pain sliced through my recently set nose. I frowned, knowing it should hurt a lot more than it did but shrugged it off. I'd always been a fast healer.

"Which is what you expected, or you wouldn't have brought it up," I rolled my eyes and winced. My nose may have been set, but the pain in my head and eyes pointed toward further trauma and probably a black eye as a reward for my 'nap.' Maybe it was less about healing and more about competing for which part of me hurt more.

"True. I have to say though, that I have great admiration for your father; he did what no other pirate has been able to."

"You mean he was the only one with his balls so shriveled that he didn't mind doing it, the yellow bastard," I snapped. "What kind of person hunts down his own ilk for a ravenous, power-hungry military power?"

"He didn't hunt *you*," Sloan pushed again at my buttons, but I shut down after throwing a suggestion for what he could do with his questions. Silence pressed down on us and I had no desire to press back. For a few heartbeats, at least.

"He didn't catch me, you mean," I growled, my voice low and barely above a whisper.

"If that's what you choose to believe," Sloan's easy tone was salt on my wounds, but it gave me a moment's pause before I dismissed the idea. My father would torture me once he had me under his control, I had no doubt of that. But, I knew Low'd had the opportunity to pull me in with the rest of the Kinship when he sold them out to the Alliance, and it rubbed like an old wound.

Light began to break on the horizon like a bright idea in the world of neglected dark. The moon drifted across the sky as a bare thread that was like a slash in the dark tapestry with a view to the universe beyond. It was so beautiful that I swallowed the bitterness in my throat as I tried to enjoy it.

Richter came up to the helm and saluted Sloan.

"Feed our guest, then take your post," Sloan said. Richter gave him a strange look and came forward with the bowl. The smell of the food hit me before he got close. I'd expected gruel, but it was some kind of fish soup. When he brought it over, I could tell it was cold having probably sat neglected while the rest of the crew supped. It was wet and edible if sour in taste.

I took spoonful after spoonful without a word. Light outlined Richter's boyish face and he watched me. With every spoonful, his eyes darkened with mistrust.

"I'll insult you after I eat, mate," I assured him and took another spoonful. "I would prefer to do so on a full belly, but don't you worry I'll mouth off, so you can feel at ease for the moment."

Richter's eyebrow lifted into his hairline and Sloan grunted from the helm, likely to stifle the laugh. When the bowl was empty, Richter took the bowl and went to where Sloan waited.

"Captain, I just had helm duty while you were checking the prisoners-- "

"That'll be all, Richter," Sloan stopped him short and I turned to look away from their disagreement. Apparently, I'd been wrong about Sloan staying at the helm all day, but why would he shut Richter down. Who cares if I knew he shirked on his duties?

They spoke in low tones for a moment before Sloan stepped away and Richter took the wheel with a glare in my direction. The captain walked over and crouched down beside me holding my empty bowl.

"Be a good lass, Maggy, and I'll have someone bring you *fresh* food when I return."

I rolled my eyes and turned my face away. I was too sore and tired despite my forced nap to bother with a response. The food churned a little in my belly and I hoped Richter hadn't decided to add anything unusual to it before feeding me. It would have been something one of my crew would have done to a prisoner they didn't particularly like...if I'd let the poor soul live that was.

I listened to the captain's clomping walk down the steps; one heavy stride and one light as he alternated between metal leg and flesh. It wasn't unlike the creaking of the *Draconis* as it shifted, but it wasn't a comfortable sound either. It told me that the metal leg was not something the captain had fully adjusted to. I made a mental note of that interesting bit of information.

"Alone, at last, Richter? How long have you been planning it out?" I yawned and fought to adjust under the chains. Parts of me were getting stiff from no movement and my butt was numb.

"Shut it, Low," the young first mate hissed from behind me. His temper was scorching, and I hadn't even started messing with him yet. This was going to be an interesting watch shift.

"Sure, sure," I rattled the chains a little. "Maybe I should have asked while the captain was still here, but when do I get a break to relieve myself?"

"You don't."

"I highly doubt you or the captain want to smell piss all day while you're minding the helm," I rolled my eyes. If they didn't care about prisoners going all willy-nilly on the decks, they wouldn't have lowered buckets into the hold.

Richter didn't deign to respond but also didn't make any move to help. At the start of the conversation, I hadn't had an actual need to relieve myself. In the course of discussing it, I was starting to feel an uncomfortable urge.

"Richter, I seriously need to relieve myself," I sighed. "Honestly, by the time you get me unchained, it may be too late, and I would rather not pee here since I'm sure I'll be locked down in this very spot for a good while."

He still didn't make a move or respond. The moonlight was starting to be overshadowed by the sun making an appearance on the horizon. The skyline brightened into colors that would entrance the eye, but I was too focused on my bladder to get beyond the thought that others would soon be coming up on deck and I was going to wet myself.

I could take a lot of humiliation, but wetting my pants was not something I'd be comfortable with. It's rather difficult to be menacing when someone's seen you in damp britches.

When the captain came out on the deck, I was truly squirming as I tried not to release. Richter either didn't notice or, more likely, decided not to as the sun rising highlighted my restless movement.

"What's wrong with the prisoner, First Mate?"

Sloan had spotted my movement or heard the rattling of the chains as he was climbing up to the mizzen mast.

"She says she has to take a piss, sir," Richter said, and the captain's eyes widened a little as he took in my now-pained expression and whatever look Richter was giving him. Sloan motioned for a couple of men to come up, but it was too late for me.

"Don't bother," my voice was toneless, and my nostrils flared with impotent rage. The smell was immediately picked up by the friendly breeze and swirled around so that anyone within a few yards could smell it. I narrowed my eyes as I thought about what I could do to repay Richter once I was free. Perhaps an eye for an eye? Tie him to a high mast and see how long it took *him* to wet himself?

The two men that came up the deck paused, looked at the captain behind me and froze. I heard a sound beside me punctuated by a thud. Richter came around with a bright welt on his cheek and a shocked expression in his eyes.

"Unchain her so Richter can mop the deck. Take her to my quarters and have Fletcher take the helm," Sloan's voice was deadly quiet; all the better to hear him by.

When the chains came off, I stood to the side and waited. I glared into the eyes of anyone who looked, daring them to say a word to me. Even though my hands were still cuffed to my hips and a chained leash ran the length of my body, I would tear anyone apart who so much as side-eyed me in my present state. The humiliation was bone-deep, and I was spoiling to fight my way back to the top of the food chain.

The two crewmen walked me to the captain's quarters and Sloan stepped in behind me. There was a metal ring in the center of the floor and Sloan hooked a length of chain to it. Meanwhile, the two crewmen unlocked my ankle cuffs and pulled the chain that ran the length of my body free. The captain loosened the leather belt that held my hands to my hips and scooted it up before retightening it at my waist, above my waistline.

"Go tend your duties," the captain hooked the chain to the back of the belt so that it ran to the floor like a dog leashed to a yard. The two crewmen saluted and stepped out of the cabin.

Sloan took a step toward the door but removed the lock from the chain links at the ring on the floor. I narrowed my eyes as he pulled the chain through the ring, drawing it tight like he was about to manually haul anchor. He opened a drawer to the left of the door and pulled out a pair of loose britches while keeping the chain taut. He tossed the britches to the floor at my feet.

"My water basin is just there," he motioned beside me. "I'll keep the length of chain tight and turn my back, so you can clean and change."

He pulled a steam hand-cannon from a holster on the table beside him and waved it at me.

"If I feel it go slack, I *will* turn and shoot you," he eyed me, and I nodded once. Even if this *was* my best chance at escape, I couldn't bring myself to do it in the humiliated state I was in. If I ever truly hated someone, I would choose my current predicament as inspiration for torture. Of course, that could just be the recipe for my own personal hell.

Sloan turned away, the chain clamped in his claw and the cannon in white knuckles. He lowered his hand to his side, but I didn't doubt for a moment that he could bring it up in a blink.

I didn't waste a moment in undressing and tending to myself, nor did I let the chain go loose. Sloan had pulled just the right length in to give me enough distance to reach the basin but little else in his quarters. I considered attempting to pour some of the water through my matted hair but didn't know how much patience he had in offering up this good deed. I would just continue to manage with the filthy rat's nest on my head. I finished and pulled on the clean pants before turning to look at his broad back and metallic head.

He hadn't budged during my quick clean-up and changing. I could see the tension in his hand where his finger held close to the trigger and the strain in his back and shoulders from holding the chain, but his head was firmly faced away. It was almost like foolish trust. Maybe it was understanding.

"Why?"

He heard me, I could tell it from the slight jump of muscles in his firing hand, but he didn't answer at first. The silence dragged on long enough, I thought he might not. Maybe it was the awkwardness or just the fact that he'd shown kindness where he didn't have to, but something pushed me to say something I never thought I would.

"Thank you," I mumbled softly. I couldn't bring myself to raise my voice, but he heard me just the same and turned back to face me. I had my face half-lowered and probably glared like a petulant child, but I was truly thankful for the small kindness. The blue eyes in the metal face filled with an odd expression that I couldn't quite read without the corresponding facial cues.

"I'm not a beast, Maggy. I know what you think of the Alliance and all of its soldiers, but most of us do try to treat prisoners humanely," his voice had lost the joking quality again, but it had a touch of steel in it. I snorted but didn't correct him with facts from my own dealings with Alliance sailors. Instead, I argued against his foolish act of kindness.

"Despite the good deed, your first mate wasn't wrong," I admitted. "I'm not the type of person anyone should let their guard down around. I will get free and I will kill to get that way if necessary...no matter how *humane* you are to me."

"Which is why I'm in here with a cannon and two of my crew are waiting outside the door armed to the teeth." His voice held humor and I wondered if he could smile under that metal plate or if there was even a face to react. My fingers twitched as I considered jumping him just to try to look under the mask.

"Good call," I curled the edge of my mouth. "I do think we need to come to some sort of arrangement, Captain."

"Oh? What about?"

"I want to know what it's going to take for you to free me."

Chapter 8

"Oh Maggy, amusing doesn't cover it. Outrageous? Pure entertainment? If I could laugh, I would," Captain Sloan pulled harder on the chain so that he could keep me controlled while he moved to the door.

"I'm not kidding," I watched him pause near the door. "I'm not going to tell you where I keep my treasure, but I can certainly make you a rich man. Rich enough to leave the Alliance and retire, I would say."

"You mean run for the rest of my life while the Alliance hunts me down for letting you escape," he huffed. It was an odd sound like someone blowing in a tube.

"I'm sure we could come up with a way for us both to look good in the leaving, Captain Sloan," I arched an eyebrow and gave him a slow smile. "I'm going to be hunted no matter what, but I could always give you a healable injury to make it plausible that I escaped."

"I doubt such a thing exists," he rapped on the door before popping it open. He hadn't been kidding me in his threat. The two crewmen sheathed their weapons and stepped into the room.

"I will, however, work out a deal with you in exchange for good behavior," Sloan said as the men took up the chain and reattached my ankle cuffs. "Keeping you under continuous guard like this is going to be exhausting, especially since it seems that I'm the only member of my crew who isn't going to slit your throat the moment they're alone with you or give you too much freedom."

He paused and looked me up and down for a moment before he continued, "And I know I can't put you down in the hold. Thank you for your advice, though." Sloan slowly cocked his head to the side at me.

The movement distracted me as my eyes snagged on an area above his collar where skin seemed to be peeking through just below his helm. It looked like a ridge just below his Adam's apple.

"The group from the prison did just what you said, and we lost lives on either side of our captive pool. I've had them tied together and moved into a smuggler's hold at the bow. We had to get creative with how our supplies are stowed, but it worked. Vicious lot, that group.

"Also, Bree is doing quite well with the cook, I'm happy to inform you."

"Who's Bree?" I blinked at him and wondered why I should care.

"The young woman you were adamant I get out of the hold...Wait. Do you mean to say you truly didn't know her?"

"I just met her as we took a fine transport to your ship atop mythical creatures. After hearing Spinners words of praise, though, I was already a great admirer of her work," I waved my hand and Sloan made an odd noise.

"Of course. She told Yeurin, the cook, that Spinner insulted her mum, so she took a bite out of him. I have to admit that I've never known a man so adept at ticking off women," Sloan nodded, and the crewmen finished with the restraints.

"Not just women. Spend some time with him and you'll likely want to bite him, too."

"Undoubtedly," Sloan watched the men fasten each buckle and close each lock on my very restrictive leash. "Tomorrow, we'll give you some cleaning to do. Likely my quarters since we know we can hook you to the slaver's ring in the middle of the floor.

"If you do well, we can see about giving you some small comforts or maybe a leashed walk around the deck as a reward," Sloan waved the men and me out of his quarters. His voice followed me out. "Back to the mizzen mast for the day though. Feel free to braid rope or repair nets for fishing while you're there."

The door slammed into my back as soon as I was through it. They didn't try to shove or touch me until I reached the mast. At the helm was the oldest sailor I had ever seen who grinned at me despite a complete lack of teeth. I arched an eyebrow and moved to the mast.

"Upright if you would, gents? I'm not much in the mood for sitting just now," I told them as I leaned back against the mast and waited. They made no moves toward me for a moment, then shrugged and started wrapping a length of rope around me instead of chains. They kept my hands out but wrapped the hemp strands around both wrists to keep me from moving them far.

"He's getting smarter, I see," I grinned as they finished. "Now, where is that netting I was promised?"

The two crewmates looked at each other, shrugged again, and took two steps away in tandem. I fought the urge to ask them if they were sharing a brain. One scooped up some netting and brought it back to me while the other waited.

"That'll be all boys," I was still smiling at their simple expressions or lack of reaction. I wasn't sure which. "Off you go. Back to work and all that."

They shrugged at me again and walked away. Sloan's crew was striking me as a bunch of rule-following, mind-their-own-business sorts. I'd yet to see any of them move in any way that seemed to be beyond their mission. Unless you count the times they took pleasure in dealing with me violently by captain's permission.

On the *MadCap*, my crew would have been yelling insults at each other or offering inappropriate suggestions on how to better do the work by now. The air would also have been filled with sea shanties and complaints at the lack of booze. The Alliance crew moved mindfully, efficiently, and with the intent of doing a good job.

I wasn't too keen on any of them.

Richter though, despite the humiliation I had suffered at his intent or neglect -- I still wasn't quite sure if it was an intentional slight or more the distrust that I bred -- I'd meant what I said when I told Sloane he had the right approach. Give someone like me even an inch, and we were likely to make you regret it, possibly at the cost of your life. Despite the internal acknowledgement, I was still going to see Richter suffer.

My fingers wove through the nets. I focused my movements on repair and re-knotting until my mind was able to re-energize the muscle-memory and I could let my thoughts drift.

A good deal of what I had seen on Sloan's ship didn't fit into what I knew of Alliance sailors and militia. Some were cut from the same cloth as Spinner: driven, arrogant, and stupid. They followed orders mindlessly without question, without hesitation, or asking intent. Sloan had a crew full of men who did as he said but still seemed to carry their minds in working order. They had a certain amount of tough bravado but didn't go out of their way to be cruel other than the typical approach to setting the scene for discipline. Even Sloan seemed to have interests beyond simple handling and transport of slaves or else he wouldn't have cared what happened to the girl, Bree. He wouldn't have cared how Richter treated me.

The conversation between him and his first mate kept tugging at my brain. I thought that the fact that Richter was being put to double helm watch was just a sign of arrogance, but Richter's complaint included that the captain had gone to check on the prisoners. I'd been out cold, put there after voicing my concern for the captives below deck, and that's when Sloan chose to act. Was he trying to hide his good intentions from me? I wouldn't fault him for that as I was loathe to let someone see the weaker, thoughtful side of my nature. From what I'd seen, as far as Alliance was generally concerned, prisoners were the lowest rung on the ladder of life and meant to tread on.

I tossed aside the mended netting and picked up another that had been tucked into the rope beside me at some point. I might have normally been alarmed that I had missed the addition of my workload, but I felt no fear that anyone on the *Draconis* would abuse me without the captain's say-so. It was another piece of the puzzle that didn't fit.

I looked down at the net. This one had some wire threaded through it, likely to use for skimming the surface to catch fish instead of dropping net or running lines. You could usually catch feeder fish or school-types with the line as the boat moved -- easy feeding for a ship's crew. The strands were too thin and ran the length of the netting. They'd never be any use to me and would be missed if I tried to unwind some for later escape. There was no point in making obvious attempts that would get me caught. It was better to bide my time and choose the right opportunity.

I plucked at the woven strands to try to remake some of the knots where it had frayed, missing my fingernails. I remembered that this had been one of the first jobs I had ever taken on as ship's crew.

The only vessels that would take me on as a lass were either fishing boats or, eventually, pirate ships. The commercial lots wouldn't take a woman as part of the crew because Alliance had forbidden women aboard sea-going vessels. There were women officers, mind you, and usually a prissy bunch of over-privileged daughters of Alliance brass, but they weren't put on the ships. They had cushy border-patrol jobs, desk jobs, or port call jobs where they could keep their hair, nails, and uniforms looking just so and their skin soft and uncalloused while they hunted for an officer husband. It wasn't a job I could apply for no matter my skill. My upbringing and parentage would prevent me from ever holding a job outside of what I'd found.

In my homeport, the first fisherman who hired me, Jed, did so because he'd lost a man during a particularly rough gale season. He's paid me less than half what he'd paid the lost crewman which was still more than double what I was getting from nicking wallets or purses. It wasn't that I couldn't thieve. It was that most folks were so poor on the island I grew up that there wasn't much to take. The only time there was any money to be made was when one of the big ships came in, but their money usually went right into a bottle or a handy whore like my mother. Neither left much for me to steal.

I knotted nets, learned to tend the sails, and found that being on a craft on the water felt more like home than anything else I'd known. I was always the first crew to arrive to prep for a day's fishing and the last to leave. It didn't hurt that I'd taken to sleeping at the docks since I'd lost rights to a cot in the bar when my mother died, and I refused to take up her place as a whore. The docks were friendlier when the inhabitants realized that I was quick with a knife to protect myself and had nothing salable worth stealing.

After Jed died, his son took over and I didn't like how he looked at me, so I moved on. Eventually, I happened upon the *HMS Honoria* and her captain, Zlytho. Zlytho was a sort of amphibious creature called an Amphodysis. I referred to Captain Zlytho as a 'she' because that was just how her personality struck me. You'd never tell just from looking at her reptilian and frog-like features. Her species was hermaphroditic, so it really didn't matter if you said, "Yes, Sir!", or "Yes, Ma'am!" so long as you did what she ordered.

I think her approach to women aboard her ship also made me label her as a friendly gender, which with my upbringing was rarely of the male persuasion. She didn't care who or what you were so long as you did the job you were hired for. In my mind, it was also a snub in the direction of the Alliance, despite the fact that she had us dress as men, so I liked her all the more for it.

A year onboard and I became her first mate in everything but title. The title belonged to an academy twit that the Alliance had stationed on her ship. Despite its inception as the *Honoria*, it later became the *MadCap* under my leadership. James Naderblast was the weapons chief under Zlytho. He was also my first and only friend.

Zlytho wasn't always on the right side of the Alliance line in her dealings beyond her crew choice. To be honest, I would say she pretended to be Alliance while actually being a pirate. It's probably why I didn't mind going full pirate when she died. As her death was at the hands of an Alliance vessel manned by a crew including Spinner, the approach seemed justified.

It should have been a normal supply replenishment between Alliance vessels. The *Majestic* gave me my first encounter with Spinner who was pretending to be a weapons chief while actually spying on any and all Alliance he came across. It was the only time that I would put Spinner's name in the same sentence as I used "intelligence."

HMS Majestic fired shots both at the supplier we were meeting up with and the ship I was on. They'd been given a tip, likely from Spinner's bungling fool sources, that rebel factions were using the UNREP to trade secrets and smuggle contraband. Complete poppycock, to be certain. The supplier was adamantly Alliance and Zlytho didn't care for secrets or questionable stores.

As far as I was concerned, Spinner had let his lack of good sense and follow-through cost the life of my captain and most of both crews. The shots sent the supplier and most of the crew to the depths. After interrogations came up empty, it also got Spinner busted down to Marshal for not waiting on a go-ahead from Alliance brass. Hence, the last time I would ever have to link his name with anything indicating mental acuity.

I guess his captain knew how to delegate blame to save his own hide, though I knew from later encounters that Spinner'd given him intelligence about a spy on the *Honoria*. He'd been trying to make a name for himself by busting some massive pirate ring inside the Alliance and his captain had likely seen a treasure trove in his future; and a fool to blame if it all went belly up.

I took as much of the supplier ship's crew as I could aboard before she sunk. We were ordered to the nearest port to await Alliance intervention. Jim and I had other plans.

I gave them a choice to stay and fight back or depart at the nearest port. Only a handful of the crew from either vessel elected to part ways. We went on our way once released, patched up the ship, and returned with vengeance on our minds and new colors flying. We blasted the shit out of the *Majestic* and left her crew to grab what flotsam they could from the debris. There was a string of islands near the site that would take them in or return them to Alliance on passing vessels if they wished it.

I didn't shy from killing if it was warranted but had no desire to blast or drown a bunch of military who'd just been following orders. It was one of my main regrets because part of the surviving crew contained Spinner. I knew him. I'd seen him on the island of my birth committing atrocities. I even stood on the deck of my new ship with a blaster aimed at his oily-haired head.

But, I didn't pull the trigger. Stupid, stupid softness in me. Had the whole thing happened even a month later and I wouldn't have hesitated. Becoming captain on the path we'd chosen thanks to circumstances, changed me quickly. I sailed away, leaving an insipid adversary to remember my face and wait for a chance to find me again.

I took over as captain thanks to skill and the support of my former crewmates. Only two from my new crew had to be dealt with when they challenged me for captaincy. I hadn't wanted to, but they forced my hand and I killed both to take the newly named *MadCap*. Jim stepped up as my first mate and we charged over the swells for a few years before being summoned in by the Kinship.

Kinship was the name for the coordinated efforts of the pirate vessels including my father, Captain Edward "Ned" Low. We met, agreed to help each other when absolutely necessary for an agreed upon fee, and went on our way. I didn't see my legendary father when I went in to swear my allegiance to the Kinship. I saw him not long after as my crew and I were on our way out, not knowing about a new meeting that had been scheduled. It was the first time I ever laid eyes on the sperm donor that made my existence possible. During my voyage back to the Caribbean, Low stepped up and the Kinship was struck down.

Captain Low didn't find me or mine, I'm not even sure how hard he looked. I wasn't in any mood to face him after hearing what he did to the other pirate captains that he had sworn an oath to. If I ever did see him, I wanted it to be only for the moment before I blasted his face from existence.

"Not bad." The voice snapped me from my musings and back to my present where blasting anyone's face off was not an option. A sailor stepped forward and took the netting out of my hands. I'd finished the wire-mesh but hadn't dropped it since I had no other work waiting for me. My fingers had been tracing the knots while I reminisced.

"You any good with braiding lines? We need to bind up some mast lines. It's getting close to squall season and we need extra bound and ready," he squinted at me before taking a few steps to spit off the side of the ship. His face was lined like old wood and his skin mimicked the color. His eyes were the faded blue of dungarees as he assessed me, flickering between the netting now in his hands and my bound position. His whiskers made me think him old, but he had a youthful vigor to him as he passed off the nets to another sailor. I could imagine him playing the bones and dancing a jig.

"I've some experience. I didn't start off as a captain. Does anyone?" I pressed my lips together and wondered if Alliance leadership did just that.

"Not if they're worth their salt," he chewed something and spit again before meeting my gaze for a long moment. Were we crewmates, I think we would have compared cutlasses. "Name's Malcolm."

"Cap... Maggy," I jutted my chin at him. "You'll either have to bring me the rope or talk the captain into tying me to a different mast, Malcolm."

"I'll do that," he walked off. While I waited to see if he'd return, a couple of sailors untied me and leashed me, so I could take a walk on the deck. I guessed Sloan had decided my quiet morning deserved a good return.

"Maggy," Malcolm returned on my third lap around the deck. It was a good thing as I was about to chew out some sailors for stupid mistakes in rigging and sloppy seamanship. I met his eyes and stood still.

"Captain Sloan says you need to clean a bit and he'll set up a station for you to work with the rigging," he motioned me forward and my two dog-walkers followed with my leash.

Inside the Captain's cabin, I was again chained to the ring on the floor and given rags and buckets to clean the space. Part of me wanted to tantrum for being set to servant work, but I knew it wouldn't do any good. Even with the wind in the sails, it would take almost a week to get to port. Besides, this was my chance to earn the captain's trust so I could make my move and escape when we got close to land. Though, part of me knew that earning trust from this captain would be a hard run to make.

Chapter 9

On my hands and knees, I cleaned and felt like a deck seaman again. It wasn't unpleasant work; at least the captain wasn't a squidropod who left ink behind or even an Amphodysis like Zlytho. She always left trails of scaly skin and pearlescent membranes that I was never dumb enough to ask about. She'd been a good captain but didn't suffer curious fools lightly. I found myself humming as I worked, letting the rhythm of a sea shanty set the pace of my cleaning.

Sloan's cabin was organized and neat. Each item had a bracket or pin of some sort to hold it in place and ensure that it always went back to the exact spot it had started from. He had cleared away weapons and munitions prior to my entry into the room. There wasn't so much as a hairbrush that I could use to whack someone with if I had the urge. I could have used the bucket, I supposed, but it wouldn't have given me much satisfaction and probably would have broken the worn, wooden shell.

I thought about Smitters and the pirates in the hold below. I wondered when they would attempt their escape. No pirate crew ever let themselves be taken in without doing at least one stupid thing to escape. It was almost an unwritten rule that pirates either escape the hold or die trying. We weren't much for the long game in life. It explained why pirates were rarely wealthy or old; we gambled everything we had on a whim or a good time.

I'd heard of some crews that decided to enact a suicide pact as their stupid thing, but with Smitters mixed in, that would get nixed fast. The Walrusoid had no desire to meet his maker at any point in time. Death was not his way of thinking, though *thought* wasn't always his way of thinking either.

If death was out, that meant that they would either try "dying man" or using meal delivery to try to break free. My bet would be that they would skip trying to play on the heartstrings of an Alliance crew by pretending one of theirs was succumbing to a horrible death and would instead go the sneak-attack route.

But when? I leaned back on my knees and calves to think. I ran the back of my hand across my forehead to brush sweat and stray strands of hair away as I thought.

It was likely that they would let a few meals pass before trying anything so that the crew would think them complicit. It would also be whenever it was darkest in the hold, so they could hide people near the ladder and wait for delivery.

My crew had gotten so used to prisoners trying to escape that we had built a relay door on the hatch just big enough to drop food through and buckets. We never kept prisoners for long, so clean-up and emptying toilet was never an issue. I think we went a max of three days before getting rid of prisoners. Usually we dropped them off on a barren island in Alliance trade routes or one of the pleasure islands where they could barter passage on a different vessel. I'd only commanded the death of a group of prisoners once. They'd deserved death and a great deal more when I saw what some of them did to the others.

Jim ate a few now and then, of course. Better them than us. I usually only gave him officers or initial casualties from battle. One body could usually hold him for a few days if I didn't let him gorge himself. I learned that the hard way the first time he hurled someone else's guts all over the deck.

The prisoners in the hold would likely be given another meal in a few hours; just before most of the crew ate. I would bet that the earliest they would attempt a breach would be in tomorrow morning's meal. Better to get a groggy bunch of Alliance sailors than hungry, tired sailors. Our northeast plot also meant that the sun would be angled to the hold at the stern, thus limiting the light reaching belowdecks.

"Okay then," I nodded to myself.

"Better than okay, Maggy. The floor absolutely shines," Sloan's joviality made me want to snarl. It certainly wasn't the surprise of his presence that had created my sudden bad mood. I shrugged and dropped a wet cloth into the bucket beside me. "Truly. I think you missed your calling."

"As a servant? No thank you," I turned my head to look at him out of the side of one eye. "I do not follow; I command."

"Commander of servants then, maybe? You could certainly teach them a thing or two. I don't think even my deck hands could have done so well." He walked over and threw his coat over the back of a chair. Useless things on the summer seas: coats.

"You have worthless deck hands, then."

"Or simply just not as capable as your charming hands, Maggy."

"Are you done baiting me?"

"Probably." He lifted one shoulder and I could almost feel the grin behind the mask. I rolled my eyes, knowing there was no *probably* about it.

"Why do you wear that," I jerked my chin at the coat, "when it's hot enough to boil eggs outside?"

"The jacket is a mark of my status and station. My men expect to see me in it; it's part of my uniform," Sloan shrugged and undid a few buttons on the matching vest.

"Another reason to be a pirate then," I shook my head. "No silly dress codes. I like comfort."

"And killing."

"That has its moments, too," I rolled my shoulders and shifted onto the balls of my feet, so I could stand up.

"Do you have remorse?" His back was to me, but I knew I couldn't reach where he stood at the porthole from the length of chain. His desk, and under it were the only things I hadn't cleaned.

"About killing or about getting caught?"

He made an odd coughing noise and waved his hand as though telling me to choose.

"I kill because if I don't, they kill me or mine. I don't set sail with the intent of washing the waters red. I set sail to claim what's mine in life and keep my crew strong and fed. You wouldn't understand it even if I tossed you on a deserted island and forced you to try to survive away from your precious Alliance. You're a company man, bought, owned, and kept," I curled my lip.

His fist caught me in a powerful right hook that popped my head up and made me see stars before I even saw him turning. I managed to keep my feet though, somehow. It was an impressive punch, and I knew my words had struck on something in the metal captain's soul. It didn't escape me that he'd used his flesh hand to punch though. It was obviously personal.

"Speak not of things you know nothing about," he hissed. His face was inches from mine and I reflexively jerked my hands up to fight back. The chains only allowed me to raise my arms to chest level. I'd have to stand on something if I was going to choke him the way I suddenly wanted to. I dropped my hands and took a step back.

"Then educate me, Captain Sloan. I'm nothing if not a reasonable woman." I took slow steps, circling the ring that held me in place in his cabin, like a dog on a leash. I had a feeling there was some interesting information to be had, here. I also needed time to quell the urge to fight back lest I find myself bound and gagged in a hold without escape opportunities.

"Do you assume that all Alliance military men are there by choice alone, Maggy?"

"You could have said no, so yes, I do," I pursed my lips and sucked in my cheeks. I dared him to continue and contradict me if he could.

"The disdain on your face just tells me that you're more ignorant of the world around you than I would have assumed," he huffed out a breath and took two backward steps of his own. "I see no reason to educate you just now, Maggy. Perhaps you should take this opportunity to stroll the deck with my men before they tie you in for the night."

"No lines for me to knot? Rigging to repair? I would think free labor would be worth a helluva lot more than securing me." I cracked my neck to one side and didn't move toward the door.

"We'll see what you're capable of if you can keep yourself in check," Sloan crossed in front of me and opened the door. He called out and my two dog walkers returned to resume their hold on my tether. Sloan nodded once to me when they had unchained me from the floor and taken up the slack.

"Only if you behave," I arched an eyebrow at him before walking out ahead of the two crewmen. I heard his rasping cough echoing down the p-way.

Round and round the deck I went with my two little crewmen following behind ready to drop me, tug my chain, or clean up my messes. I ignored them. In my head, I called them Dogsitter 1 and 2. They were almost identical in age, shape, and lack of stimulating conversation. I'd even tried insulting them a few times, but their reactions seemed limited to slow blinks in my direction.

The wind had picked up in the time I'd been playing servant to the captain. Alternating breezes of warm and cold air came in rounds about the ship. I knew that wasn't a good sign. You never mixed hot and cold of anything unless you did it quickly. This wasn't mixing or quick.

"Storm's coming," I looked back at the Dogsitter twins. They just kept pace behind me, pausing when I did, and walking when I resumed. I wondered if they had mastered the robotic elements of nanites to create a humanoid version and I just hadn't heard of it. The two of them couldn't be humanoid, despite how they looked. Jim in his zombie-state had more personality.

I let myself trip to the deck to see what they would do. They played statues while I very clumsily pulled myself to one side and then the other as though I couldn't gain my footing. They stood still. I shifted a little more, threw my weight and jumped to my feet.

"Ta da!" I yelled with my hands spread as wide as I could and a manic grin on my face. I think one of them may have blinked an extra time, but I can't be certain.

"I wouldn't bother, Maggy," Malcolm came forward, winding rope around his forearm and elbow. "Jimson and Jemison are products of Alliance Military Academy. They don't break form unless they have to subdue you."

He paused and leaned toward me a tiny bit. I think he saw the gears in my brain hum to life.

"I wouldn't recommend it," he whispered and motioned to his head with wide eyes.

"They don't look like much," I mused. "It could be fun."

"The crazy ones always look harmless at first," Malcolm shook his head. "I've put some rope near the mizzen mast for you in case you get bored."

I nodded my thanks and stepped past him to continue my walk.

"You may wish to get the crew busy battening down. I think the gale is going to hit us sooner rather than later," I lifted my eyes to the clear sky and the slightly upturned winds. I could practically see the mists swirling the in the air to forewarn of what the seas would soon look like.

"Tell it to the First Mate. Richter's got the Captain convinced that we'll outrun it," Malcolm arched an eyebrow and walked away. I saw darkness flicker over the crewman's features that told me he could feel the shift as much as I could in the wind and seas.

"I sincerely hope that was a joke," I sucked in a breath and tasted the coming storm. It was blowing a breeze in from invisible islands, flavoring it with fruit trees and tobacco plants. This was going to be a mother of a storm and nothing had yet been tied down.

"I'm ready to be tied to the mast, boys," I did not want to be one of the things left loose and helpless when the gale descended. "Let's head over, shall we?"

At the helm, as though he was waiting for the pleasure of my company, was Richter. I noticed that his eyes were the color of coal when they narrowed on me. Either that or I was seeing a blackness growing in his soul.

"Evenin', First Mate," I said as the Dogsitters tied me in for the night. The line had been switched to rope, I guess as another attempt toward goodwill. Of course, it could have also been for faster access to noose material if it came down to it. It would be easier to sleep secured with rope, if I survived the storm that is.

I opted to be upright again. I really did not want to be sitting when that storm came. "Good of you to take the helm and wait for me to come visit. I do so enjoy our chats."

Richter said nothing to me, and the ropes tightened enough that I couldn't shift to see his expression. I could imagine it, though. The Dogsitters finished and stepped back.

"Boys? Could you please tell the captain I'm restrained and that I would enjoy his company at the mizzen mast if he's not too busy?"

They looked at each other as though translating my words in silence before walking away.

"I'll miss you, too!" I called behind them but neither turned to acknowledge me.

"Why do you need to see the captain? Do you have a sudden urge to relieve yourself?"

Richter's voice was rougher than tarpaper and colder than an ice storm. Definitely not my biggest fan at the moment.

"Actually, I have a sudden urge to ask about storm preparations," I paused. "I pissed before the boys tied me up though; thank you for your concern, kind sir." I would have fluttered my eyelashes at him coquettishly, but I'd been secured facing away from him.

Richter grunted which I took to mean that he was very glad that I had taken the lead on my own bathroom schedule and that he was duly sorry for the discomfort of the morning.

"Apology accepted, Richter," I let a smile ride my voice. "You are incredibly sweet for your concern. I could never stay mad at you, though! I treasure your friendship so much that it pains me when we're at odds."

"Why are you worried about prepping the ship?"

"Because it isn't being done yet," I found myself wishing I had been tied to face him, so I could work on dramatic facial expressions and watch his reactions. "The storm will be here in about thirty minutes or so by my estimate -- or at least the winds will be. I imagine we'll get the rain not long after."

"You're daft. We're moving fast enough that we're going to skirt right around the edge of the storm. It won't touch us," Richter laughed. It wasn't a wholly pleasant sound, rather cocky for my favorite blushing crewman.

"Have you seen the chop of the waves? Tasted the wind? There is no way we're going to make it around this storm," I shook my head. "Have you ever actually been in a squall? Hurricane? Strong rain?"

Richter muttered, "taste the wind" and said nothing else. I suddenly had the sinking feeling that the first mate was about to weather his very first storm at sea and he was the one making recommendations.

"Sonofabitch, you're a virgin," I hissed. "Odah does not make a kind and gentle groomsman, First Mate."

"Did I miss something?"

I had closed my eyes to mentally pray to Odah for a blessing to get me through the danger that would quickly overtake us. The captain's voice pulled my attention back to the pending danger. I was ridiculously happy to see him and I think it showed on my face. His eyes went wide as he looked at me before they narrowed into blue orbs in his metal mask. Fear replaced pleasure and I swallowed hard. I don't think I got all the terror down because I saw the captain's eyes widen again. He took a step toward me and the wind dropped, and my skin puckered, all hairs standing on end.

"The storm's here," my voice seemed to echo in the sudden silence. "Call the crew if you want any of them to survive and start tying down everything you can."

"Are you sure?" Sloan asked, and I cussed.

"I might be self-serving, but that might be my saving grace right now as I don't have any desire to die. You now have minutes before this storm starts tearing your ship apart, Captain Sloan." My voice was at growl-level and I was near to having a second round of wet britches. I considered begging him to cut me loose, so I could help but I figured that would not make my case.

"All hands to your stations!"

Chapter 10

"Captain, you can't seriously believe--"

"Richter, this is not the time. Do as I say and get lines secured. Have the crew lower the sheets immediately," Sloan strode over, and I saw Richter scurry forward and pause long enough to give me a dirty look.

"First or second voyage with him, Captain?"

"Third but we've never hit a storm," Sloan answered from behind me. "He knows to read the waves and skies, but his instincts aren't there yet."

"Well, he's about to get a backhand from Odah himself." I closed my eyes for a moment. I wondered if it would do any good to pray, beg, or barter with Odah, the Master of the ocean and all sailors, but I knew that time had already passed.

Wind rose and stole my ability to breathe. The ship began rocking wildly as though the ocean was a massive belly shaking with laughter at the stupidity of the mortals on the *Draconis*. Waves whipped against the port side of the ship as though intending to turn the ship around. I heard the captain grunting behind me as he fought for control of the wheel and his vessel.

The wind dipped, and I drew in a breath, fully intending to scream it out as I saw a wave coming at the ship like a wall. The oceans lifted us and threw us into that wall of water. I heard screams from the deck as seasoned and new sailors alike saw death close in.

When the wave cleared, I saw that the number of crewmen on deck had dipped by at least two. The ship bobbed madly from side to side and I saw another wall of water approaching in the distance.

"Captain! 8 o'clock!" I yelled.

"I see it, Maggy," he grunted. The waves were shoving him for all they were worth to try to push his ship to the side.

I watched the sailors scurrying about, still trying to tie down sails that were now ripped and flapping in the wind. I only saw a few of them holding lines to lash themselves down for the next wave.

"Grab a line, you useless sea scum! The next break's going to take you to the churn!" I screamed. The couple of men that held lines looked up and then yelled at the others who, mostly, grabbed lines to tie themselves in. When the wave hit, two more were gone.

"Fuck me! You're losing crew left and right, Sloan!" I yelled back at him. He continued to wrestle and lose to the steering wheel. If he didn't turn the ship into the waves soon, we'd be flipped, and it would be over for all of us.

"Malcolm!" I spotted the sea dog tying up a younger sailor to keep him from getting swept away at the next wave. "Get yer ass up here and help the captain turn us."

"Belay that," Sloan growled out. "Cut Maggy loose."

"The fuck you say?"

I'm certain my reaction was not what Sloan expected, but I sure as the north star would not let an enemy captain loose on my ship. My mouth flapped and no other words came as a wave hurled in to fill the open space I'd offered in shock. I choked on the churn and spit it out as the old sea dog came up to the bridge after holding on for dear life. Malcolm didn't ask or wait for an explanation but jumped up to draw his cutlass clean through the lines that bound me before heading back down to deck.

"The keys are in my belt, Maggy. Get yer ass back here and help me before we all die," Sloan's metal leg was digging into the deck beneath him, scraping grooves as he fought for traction. I hurried over but didn't bother with uncuffing myself. Rather, I started pulling the wheel with him to turn the rudder.

Hand over hand we pushed the wheel, inching the ship around to face on the squall and tumultuous seas. I again wished for my tattoos because I could have planted my feet and kept the damn thing from moving an inch in any direction I didn't choose.

"A little...further," Sloan grunted beside me and I looked to see the wave heading mostly toward the bow of the ship. It was still a little to port, but not headed to sideswipe us. We tied off the wheel to keep our course and Sloan grabbed me around the waist before clamping his claw down on the railing.

The wave washed down the ship and knocked me loose in his grasp, but he grabbed onto the chains and kept me from falling into the swell. When the ship rolled back, mostly righting under the barrage of wind and rain, Sloan pulled out the keys and uncuffed me.

"Don't assume this means I trust you," he glared down into my eyes.

"Don't assume I won't try to escape as soon as we're through the storm," I retorted and grabbed the keys to unlock my ankles before tossing the chains aside. I gave him a wild grin and he shook his head at me.

"Fair enough. We're short on crew. Get down there and help them before I lose any more," he snarled.

"Aye aye, Captain," I gave him a wink instead of a salute and ran to the deck. If anyone was surprised to see me helping, they kept it to themselves. I secured lines, rolled the sails, and pulled in and tied down rigging that had been broken. In between, I rode out the roar of the storm with a line lashed around my waist and a wild laugh. Odah may have been raging, but I was in my element and the surge of joy inside me, despite the danger, made me want to sing.

The storm raged around us, throwing waves, hard spikes of rain, and flotsam at us. Only a few souls stayed on deck with me, one of which was the captain. I had to admit to myself that I respected the bastard a little after that.

When the storm became less hurricane and more rain with rough seas, Sloan came to collect me from where I'd stationed myself at the main mast. He didn't say anything at first but stood beside me, soaked to the skin and breathing in the cold, salty air that spun around us like a dervish.

"I'm going to have to lock you in my quarters, Maggy," his words were gentle but ruined my serene joy. I narrowed my eyes and glared at him, reaching up to push my ragged, soaked locks of hair out of my face in the process.

"I'd rather go back to the mizzen mast, Captain Sloan," I said through clenched teeth. "Put me in your quarters and I'll slit your throat. I don't share sleep space with anyone but Odah."

Sloan watched me for a moment then nodded once.

"You'll have the quarters to yourself and I'll take my first mate's bunk," he reached forward and clicked the cuffs in place at my wrists. "My quarters are the only one where I can chain you in place without fellow prisoners or risking my crew. Beyond that, there's no place for me to put you lest I want you to die from exposure. That storm's starting to bring in cold wind and rain."

I watched him loop the chains in his claw, but he didn't bother with my ankle cuffs. He cocked his head to the side and stepped away. I took a step.

"If you even think about coming in while I'm sleeping, I will kill you in the worst way I can possibly come up with," I warned as we neared his quarters.

"I have no intention of setting foot inside the room while you're sleeping, Maggy," Sloan pushed open the door and led me inside. He pulled a towel, wash cloth, and blanket from his wardrobe before thrusting them into my arms. He secured a metal cuff around my ankle and locked the other cuff to the slave ring before stepping away.

Again, he let me get cleaned up with his back turned, and I wondered if he was a fool or had a death wish. He couldn't know that I had no desire to kill him just then; that my muscles were quivering from exhaustion; or that I'd started to shiver in the cold and wet sinking into my bones. When I finished, he used the chain to connect my hands to the ring and locked my arms behind me. He took the ankle cuffs away and threw bedding to the floor.

"I lost five crewmen tonight. If you hadn't warned me and helped, I would have lost a lot more," he said when I thought he had already left, and I turned my head to meet his eyes.

I nodded once and lay down on the floor. The door closed, and I found myself unable to rest for the thoughts swirling like a slow-moving hurricane.

Before my eyes were open, I found myself with the chain wrapped around someone's neck. The crewman dropped a bowl at my feet and squeaked out a terrified sound before his air was cut off.

Light cut through a slightly familiar porthole over furnishings that were not familiar to me. I wasn't in my cabin though the size and shape were similar. My brain wasn't making a connection other than the fact that someone had entered while I was sleeping, and I was now choking the shit out of them.

"Maggy, let go of Seaman Sailor so he can get back to helping Cook clean up," a cultured voice raised the hair on my neck with its attempt at soothing speech. I recognized it but seeing the metal face when I turned clicked everything back into place and I released the young man.

"Did you say, Seaman Sailor?" I looked at the blond minion rushing past Captain Sloan. "Seriously?"

"Blame immigration laws and their lack of creative employees," Sloan shrugged and stepped into the room. "Any reason why you were trying to kill your meal delivery? Other than your general dislike of people and enjoyment of killing, of course."

"I reacted," I admitted. "I don't know how much of his entry and movement my mind caught, but when he got close, instinct took over."

"You have good survival instincts, then." Sloan had his back to me as he dug around in a bureau a few feet out of reach from me.

He turned and flung something, and my body came alive as I curved to the side, spun and grabbed the item out of the air to return the throw. Rough bristles rasped along my palm as I let fly, aiming at the captain's head. It bounced off neatly and clattered to the floor. I blinked at the object and looked up at Sloan with my eyebrows in my hairline.

"Did you just throw a brush at me?"

Though I heard the girlish pitch of my voice, I didn't realize how ridiculous it was until I heard an odd rasping cough coming from Sloan.

"Are you laughing?!?"

He didn't answer, but his body shook, and he continued to make the odd noise. I realized that his random bouts of coughing were laughter from within the metallic exterior.

Surprise aside, it was laughter at my expense, but it didn't bother me. I quirked a smile back, I couldn't help it. After he finished, he leaned down and picked up the brush.

"I figured I would miss, but I wasn't going to take a chance at throwing something sharp at you that you could use against me, Maggy," Sloan shook the brush at me and I could practically hear the grin. "I also didn't expect you to send it back at me, so I'm doubly happy I didn't throw a knife."

"No self-respecting pirate throws a brush," I closed my eyes and rubbed at my temple. I couldn't get the smile to drop completely from my face.

"I'm not a pirate. I'm an Alliance captain, remember?"

"Keep telling yourself that," I pressed my lips together and arched an eyebrow. I remembered the bowl on the floor and crouched down. It was filled with some kind of mush and half of it had slopped onto the deck when the crewman dropped it.

I picked it up and used my fingers to eat. Spoons were a deadly thing, after all. I told Sloan as much.

"After your performance with a brush, I would agree," he nodded and stripped away his shirt.

I considered watching since he didn't ask for privacy, but that wasn't a line I wanted blurred in my current predicament. I scooted myself so that I could sit facing away from him to eat my breakfast.

"Not into men?"

I choked and almost put a new splatter of mush on his floor. Damn I was getting complacent around him if his questions could get to me that easily.

"Not into anything but survival at the moment, *Captain*," I told him once I was again breathing more oxygen than mush.

"Fair enough. I figured you'd watch to see if you could get advantage over me," Sloan mused.

"I'm not into that kind of advantage," I growled.

"I meant injuries, weaknesses, or the like."

"I don't need to watch you change to figure that out."

I heard him approach but ignored him. A cloth dropped down beside me, and I looked but kept chewing, not that there was much in the way of anything to chew. The mush was more water than anything else.

"Finish up and clean up the mess. I want you on deck today, Maggy."

I lifted my eyes to him, letting the predator in my baby blues peek out.

"Oh? Planning to let a dog off her leash?"

"Hardly," he drawled, that metal mask impassive as ever. "I *am* planning to make use of having a mad dog on my vessel though. I've decided that you'll be running combat drills with my sailors."

Chapter 11

"C'mon, Knee-high, let's see whatcha got!"

The sailor turned an alarming shade of purple before he lowered his head and charged at me. It was so easy to get under these boys' skins. You'd think they were just bursting for a fight.

I felt utterly alive as I swung to the left and avoided his charge like a bull-wrangler. I kicked him in the ass for good measure and found someone standing behind me trying to take my cuffed arms in a double shoulder-lock, but I flipped him over and stomped on his chest.

The captain had restored all of the cuffs but lengthened the chain between my legs and had the belt removed. It didn't matter because the boys coming at me, and they were boys, were all doing textbook maneuvers. They weren't going to get far when everything they did was so damned predictable.

When I throat-punched a man who looked about my age before giving him a nut-check that made tears come from his eyes, I stopped and faced the captain. None of them tried to take advantage of my distraction. Disappointing.

"Captain, these boys are about useless."

Several growls answered me, and I rolled my eyes.

"You sent me into a den of puppies and want me to bring you a pack of wolves," I sighed. "Trained dogs are the best you're going to get unless something changes fast."

"What would you have me do, Maggy?" Sloan's fingers twitched where they rested on his metal arm and I catalogued the tell in my brain for future reference.

"Other than take off my cuffs and have them attempt to keep me from escaping? Not much," I shrugged. "They play fair; I don't."

"I see that. Johannes still hasn't gotten up from that clip to the jewels you gave him," Sloan's voice was smooth, but I could see the laughter in his eyes. "I won't take off the cuffs, Maggy."

"Then, they're going to remain pups in a dog show. Did you see the one that apologized after stopping my punch?" I stepped forward and picked up the belt to offer him. "There's no point in my continuing with this."

He looked at me, his mask dipping as he took in the belt and raising as he met my eyes and I thought for a moment…

"True enough," Sloan clicked the belt around my waist and went about tightening the chains. My hands were practically locked at my sides when he was done. When the last lock clicked into place, Sloan stood in front of me and met my eyes in silence, watching me. I lifted my chin and clenched my fists as instinct was suddenly telling me to knock the look from his eyes.

"This is for your own good, Maggy," he whispered.

He grabbed me, spun me and kicked me square in the back to send me flying to the deck.

"Keep her from escaping. First man who brings her to me subdued is first off when we make port...with pay," he yelled.

Oh shit.

Hands grabbed at me from all angles as I shifted my shortened limbs to try to find purchase to move upright. Bodies thudded into me as they tried to pin me and prevent me from moving away. One grab had me spinning like a top as it flipped me onto my back like a crab.

Unlike a crab, I can kick like an unbroken horse. I reared back and planted both feet on the chest of the nearest man, sending him airborne for a moment as he took out two crewmen behind him.

A sailor behind me that I recognized as Malcolm, grabbed my arms to haul me away but only managed to help me to my feet. I bowed low and used my shoulder to knock the wind out of him before arching back to bash him with my head. I heard a satisfying crunch and was unable to feel sorry for taking the old sailor down as I grinned.

Two more grabbed my arms, but they seemed more in the mood to play tug of war than to remember they were holding a dangerous prisoner between them. When they shifted to get a better grip and pull, I tugged them in and threw my body weight back so that they bashed together. I bent and hopped forward to throw my weight down, like a kid jumping into a puddle for the biggest splash. My splash was their grunts as I landed hard on their backs. Their breath came out like a gale wind on a sail.

I saw a hefty man drive toward me swinging what looked like a small shovel and realized that cook had waded into the fray. Before I could regret hurting him, a pan came down on his head and he hit the deck. Bree stood behind him and jerked her chin at me, causing me to smile.

"Biting and frying pans? Remind me to add you to my crew," I said with a chuckle. Movement caught my eye and I turned in time to see an arm coming toward me like a wayward mast. I rolled my upper body with the direction of the arm, coming up behind the man so I could use the low cuffs to my advantage and punched him in the kidney. When he turned his head, and let out gasping grunts, I saw that it was Richter. I dropped to punch out his knee and he hit the deck.

Sweaty and invigorated, I danced around as I looked for the next comer. In front of me was a blasted minefield of crew; shuffling or groaning piles of bodies that were trying to find their feet or see a way past me. I gave them a wide grin but shifted back and forth for a moment until instinct drove me to turn just as the captain swung.

He missed my jaw by a hair's breadth, and I dipped to the side as quickly as I could. I smiled wildly at him and took a few steps back as he shifted his stance. He had both hands up as he took me in.

"Now, this is hardly a fair fight." I gave him a half grin as I danced sideways. Up close, I could tell he had close to a foot's height on me and I knew there was muscle under that uniform.

"It is what it is, Maggy. I'm not taking off those cuffs." Sloan moved to the side as well.

"I don't need the cuffs off. I was talking about you, Captain Sloan." I gave him a wink. "I'm about to kick your ass in front of your crew."

"That's a lot of talk, Low. Maybe you're stalling to save face?"

"Nah. Just long enough to get you in the right position," I charged the moment I saw the sun hit his metal face, thinking I had shifted him to a spot where he'd be blinded by the mid-day sun. Sadly, it was more blinding to me than to him as it reflected off his metallic maw. Starbursts danced in my vision as though I had taken to sungazing instead of fighting.

He swung with his fleshy fist and I ducked. His clamp fist came down and landed just shy of the chain but hit me square in the boob. I hissed but went lower and threw an elbow at his stomach. I was satisfied to hear a grunt as I twirled to move behind him. He spun with me and reached as I ducked and twisted, trying for any advantage I could get.

With my arms practically pinned to my sides and my feet unable to go more than shoulder-width apart, there was only so much I could do. His reach, on any given day, was longer than mine. He could kick out and realized it almost at the same time I did.

His leg came up in a side kick aimed for a headshot to knock me out. I saw him coming, jumped, spun, and landed just below him so I could kick up.

My foot connected and should have incapacitated him with a nut kick. Instead, pain jarred up my leg, screaming from little toes up as I broke my foot. I heard the collective gasp around me that followed the dull thwap of my bare foot when it connected. I lay on the deck, howling in pain and yelling out every colorful swear I'd ever heard in my life.

Sloan pulled me up by the chain as though I was on a skewer about to be roasted over an open flame. I couldn't do more than clench my hands to my foot. It was like I'd kicked a steel door.

"Holy steel balls, Sloan! You've got to be kidding me!" I snarled around the tears that leaked from my eyes.

"I play dirty too, Maggy."

He carried me to the mizzen mast and dropped me like a sack of potatoes before sending a bruised and hobbling Richter to set my foot. I didn't bother to try to move, instead lying completely still and waiting for the pain to stop.

Richter did eventually use nanites that time around, thank Odah. There wasn't the all-out rasping from the brush incident, but I heard tiny noises at odd intervals coming from Sloan that I suspected were barely restrained laughter.

Only a few of the crewmen were damaged enough to need nanites themselves. Most just needed their nose set or a shoulder popped back in. It wasn't the best ass-whooping I'd ever given. But it really was hard to get good knocks in when your hands were bound, and your legs hobbled.

That evening, when I was chained to Sloan's floor again, one of the crew, the one I'd called Knee-high, brought me a bowl of fish stew. It was one of the best stews I've ever had, and I inhaled it. Fighting and nanites sapped my strength. The little buggers use the body's fuel sources in order to heal and the extra strain on my overworked system left me ravenous.

Sloan opened the door to the cabin and looked over at me for a moment before leaving the door open. I was drinking the remaining broth and watched him over the rim of the bowl.

"That look is not favorable," he commented. "I was going to ask if you would be inclined to sharing the cabin tonight, but I think you might try to kill me in my sleep from the look in your eyes."

"Possible," I admitted. "I'm not sure it would do any good. You seem to be more metal than man."

I'd never seen a body tense up so quickly as Captain Sloan did in that moment. I was suddenly glad to be on the other side of the room. As quickly as it happened, though, he relaxed.

"Fair enough," his voice was back to that too-smooth quality. It was so practiced that I could imagine him being called in to calm crowds or sooth babies.

"My brain is telling me that I may wish for tact here, but as I have little, I'm disinclined to listen to that little voice. I have to ask -- how much titanium are you lugging around over there?"

"Would you like me to disrobe so you can see, Maggy?"

I knew there was a sensual tone in him, but my nerves rose to attention to scream danger at that loaded question. I swallowed hard and I felt his eyes like pinpoints of death being dragged across my soul.

"Thanks for the offer, but I'll just put my curiosity in check at this point," I set the bowl down on the floor and shifted to give him privacy.

"Early Alliance warfare took my arm, my leg, and... a bit more," Sloan said from behind me. I heard him shuffling around but kept my gaze locked on the smooth, polished wall two feet from my face. "They replaced the parts that nanites couldn't repair and promised me that when the tech was better, they would do better by me.

That was about five years and several revisions to nanites ago."

"Alliance only gives the minimum of what they can to keep their operations running," I muttered. I had gotten several crewmen because of Alliance cutting corners. Most of them were missing body parts or loved ones because of it. "Should I ask you why? I feel like that's what should happen, here."

"Why? Because I have nowhere else to go. If I leave, there isn't anywhere I can go to get the tech to keep me alive." He didn't sound as though he was dwelling on his situation so much as just stating truth. I pressed my lips together to keep from responding.

"There's some damage that keeps coming back. If I don't keep the Alliance happy with my performance, I die. It's an oversimplification, but it's true."

"What about the super-soldier nanites?" I remembered the turncoat reaction in Jim from the super-bugs like a shot of lemon juice to the eye. I also remembered how quickly it had cured him from being a slobbering, cannibalistic zombie and how it had 'healed' my magical tattoos.

"The what?"

I turned to face him and found Sloan sitting in a chair by his desk in a loose nightshirt over his britches instead of his captain garb. He looked almost human and it loosened my jaw. I told him my story. Jim being turned monster by the sirens and my hunt ever-after for nanites to buy him time. I outlined the day that Spinner and Talimuck had fallen into my hands and the nanite cream they carried that had turned Jim into an Alliance minion that seemed fully healed. I even told him about the loss of my tattoos.

"I wondered about that," Sloan was doing that tapping thing on his arm again. "Rumors about you have always circulated, but the tattoos were always a big part of them. When you came aboard and didn't have a single marking on you other than the love taps from the prison, I wondered if it had been just another tall tale."

"It is now, I guess," I wiggled my fingers and imagined the nails growing and the fingers turning into something more solid than a knife-hilt. I craved the feel of that power again. I knew, someday, I would make my way back to see that witch and barter away more of my life just to get the power back. The hunger to be what I'd been, maddened me a little when I thought of it.

"Not that you need them," Sloan commented. He had silently watched me wiggling my fingers for a few moments. "You're a hell of a fighter, Maggy. I've never seen someone who could take down my men like that."

I felt the praise settle like something warm in my bones but shrugged. "I've been fighting since I was a kid. Sometimes, I was the smallest kid being beat on by a crowd of bullies. Sometimes, I needed to escape before I became something I refused to be. You learn a few things, I suppose."

"I'm sure the bullies learned a little something, too." Sloan lifted his head and I saw that he was leaning forward on his knees as we spoke. There was almost camaraderie in that posture.

"Your men are also pussies," I curled my lip at him and watched his spine harden. I lifted my chin and looked down my nose at him despite our differences in elevation. "If it was a lie, it wouldn't upset you, but it is my *honest* assessment of their fighting abilities."

"Lack of fighting skills aside, they're good men for the most part, Maggy. Can you say the same of your crew? Killers and rapists and the dregs of society, all."

His voice had shifted to that threatening tone and it was like music to my ears. There was no perceived intimacy in that tone, only warning, and I welcomed it.

"No rapists in my crew. There was one, once," I lifted one shoulder. "I fed him to Jim."

Sloan shook his head and turned back to his desk. A knock at the door turned out to be Knee-high back to get my bowl and see if the captain needed anything.

"Bring two more bowls of stew," Sloan jutted his chin at me and nodded at the crewman. "Also, tell Richter to take his cabin. I won't need it."

I felt the hair on my neck rise and death roll through my vision. Knee-high gave me a grin. When he went to leave, I rattled my chain and made him jump, cackling at his quick fear.

"The way I see it, you owe me for the nanites," Sloan stood and stretched. He unbuckled his belt and hung it on the wall while watching me. I narrowed my eyes at him and wondered if the blue flame in them could burn him alive if I glared hard enough.

"I don't owe you *shit*," I snarled. "You tossed me to your crew like flotsam for some training that they failed at. I'm thinking you owe me some peace for that."

"Oh Maggy, there's no peace for either of us. You should know that by now," Sloan took a step toward me and I froze as I watched him move. Despite the metal, the rest of him moved with lithe power in his slow steps toward me. I gauged how many steps he could take before I could rip his leg out from under him and, by my estimate, he stopped one short.

I looked up and saw an echo of blue fire in his eyes as he looked down at me. Were we wolves, we would have faced down with raised hackles and curled lips. Instead, neither of us moved.

The door sounded again, and it swung open without the captain calling for it. Knee-high brought in a tray with two bowls of stew and a couple of mugs of something. His face went pale as he saw us facing off. He practically ran the tray over to Sloan's desk before running for the door. I wondered if his tail had already been between his legs or if it went there when he rushed out of the room, slamming the door behind him.

Sloan stepped backwards slowly and lifted a bowl and mug from the tray before sliding it across the floor to me. I made no move to reach for it. My hands had been locked together in my lap since he'd stood up.

"Eat up, Maggy. New surprises on the horizon," Sloan said as he sat back down at his desk. I refused to back down or look away. I wanted him to know that any advances he made toward me to 'repay' the perceived debt would be met with hostility and violence.

Then he did something that threw me off. He reached up and pulled away the metallic mask and dome. He didn't drop his gaze as he lifted the bowl up to his ruined face. I catalogued the burns, scarring, and twisting of his skin. The only thing left untouched by the ravage that was his face was his blue eyes. The skin around them was tanned and at complete odds with the rest of his face.

His mouth was a jagged, half-finished line and it was a wonder his soup didn't end up down his shirt, but I figured he'd gotten used to working with what he had. Even as I watched, the skin seemed to shift and pull as though the damage was still happening, and I understood his comment about nanites. Whatever had ruined his face, head, and neck, was still trying to finish the job.

I knew in that moment of vulnerability that he wouldn't touch me. As sure as I was of the tides and currents, I knew he wouldn't lay a finger on me, even if he enjoyed my reactions from the implication. He had his own demons; he wasn't interested in creating new ones for me.

As I watched the twitch of his skin, likening it to a horse's skin as it's pestered by a biting fly, I imagined the agony of his every day. I wanted to ask but settled for glaring; my gaze was unflinching and unforgiving. It was the only sign of respect I could give him. Sloan finished his stew and tankard of whatever hard ale the ship kept

"Come near me, and I will rip you into tiny pieces and rain them down on your crew," I growled. I swallowed, hearing the loss of some of the menace in my voice and sincerely hoped he didn't note it. I wouldn't give him my sympathy, only the same bitch he'd had to deal with from day one.

When Sloan put down the dishes on the tray, he eyed my untouched bowl and mug with a shrug. He stood, took two steps toward me and then shifted to walk to his cot. He tossed me a blanket and lay down. I heard the rumble of his snores through the long night.

Chapter 12

I woke to buzzing that shook my whole body and screamed that the world was turning inside out. I rolled sideways before pushing myself back into a sitting position. The roll of the ship had me striking the edge of the chair near Sloan's desk. I remembered him moving around at some point a few hours past and checking the chains, but I didn't realize he had loosened the constraint before leaving the cabin.

I stood up and stretched as far as my bound limbs would allow before another shift had me sliding across the deck toward the captain's wardrobe. It wasn't the normal shift and fall of a ship, even in heavy storms. It felt closer to a ship in port being pushed sideways by the lack of forward momentum and the pull of the lines. My legs weren't used to the almost-organized shift and roll of the deck beneath me. The buzzing clued me in a little to the unusual aspect of the ship's movements.

The door opened, and Richter stepped in wearing a frown that was, surprisingly, more jovial than I remembered seeing him. He unlocked the chain from the ring on the floor before giving it a tug.

"If I come, will you toss me a treat?" I rolled my eyes and stalked forward until I stood just in front of him. I jerked my chest forward and snarled at him, but he didn't jump. His eyes widened slightly, but not enough to give me satisfaction from scaring him.

"Captain wants you on deck," he stated unnecessarily.

"Oh? I would've never imagined that's why you're here," I walked past him into the passageway. I tugged him forward from where the chain was clipped at my waist. If he was going to be my sitter for the moment, I was going to make him work for it.

I heard a slight misstep and grinned.

"Come along, tagalong," I shifted my gait to roll forward. I wanted him and everyone else to remember that I was the predator here, baring my teeth. When I reached the main deck, however, what I saw left me toothless.

Just above the water to the starboard side hovered a ship. The sky above it was filled with a massive balloon and a clanking piston that chugged steam, creating clouds around it. Lines in the process of being secured to the cleat on the *Draconis* from the visiting vessel floating on an ocean of air to starboard. A plank was also being lined up and secured between the two vessels.

Shouts were called between Sloan's crew and the crew of the visiting vessel. I stared at the hurried, ant-like movements as though I was locked in place as my stomach filled with rocks. Some part of my consciousness heard my name being called and I was unsurprised when a clamp-like hand settled on my shoulder.

"Tighten up her restraints, Richter," Sloan said, his voice either unnaturally soft or overwhelmed by the noise of the chaotic movement around us. I knew what I was seeing and equally knew that it wasn't good for me. The starched Alliance uniforms of the visiting ship made the rocks in my gut roil like lava.

"Permission to come aboard, Captain?"

At some point in anyone's life, they will come across a person that, upon sight, they will hate with a fiery passion that makes homicidal tendencies seem reasonable. I wouldn't say this was my first time feeling that way, but it hit me hard when I saw the woman crossing the gangplank in her crisp blue and red uniform.

A *woman* in Alliance blue.

She wore officer garb and called to Sloan with a lifted hand and a friendly smile. She stepped forward with confidence that bespoke of someone who knew her place in the world. I couldn't guess yet if it was due to her commission and experience, but she was within a year of my own age. I wondered how much of her experience was from hard work and how much had been given as the right of a commissioned Alliance stooge. I hoped she was some sort of gentry, so I could hate her even more.

"Captain Aerillias, please," Sloan motioned forward but did not take his clawed hand from my shoulder. Apparently, the wild dog on his vessel needed to be kept at a short leash for visitors.

"This must be Magerious Low?" The woman's grey eyes traced me from head to toe with a North wind chill. She had an olive tone to her skin that said she was from one of the Mediterranean areas, but her hair was the white blonde one would expect from Northern climes. She reached forward to take Sloan's hand and I saw smooth, uncalloused skin and carefully tapered nails.

Not hard work then. So much for dedication among officers. I wondered if dirt or blood had ever directly touched her pristine, pampered skin.

"I *am* Captain Maggy Low," I inclined my head and jerked her gaze back to my face from where it had warmed on Sloan's metallic exterior.

"You *were*, you mean," Aerillias arched an eyebrow.

"Let's meet in the middle and say I will be again," I let all my teeth show in a wide smile. "It's only a matter of time."

"Time you are almost out of, I would say," the woman rolled her fingers as she spoke as though turning the globe by herself. "I would think, with all I've heard, that you'd be smart enough to realize that my appearance means you've almost reached the end of your journey."

I had made the connection but kept it from my expression. I jerked my chin in the direction of her ship. "Let me guess? You've brought air-engines and balloons to hasten the journey for Captain Sloan and his crew?"

"Of course. The chancellor has decided that you are needed at auction sooner rather than later. Let's just say the pre-auction bidding had piqued his interest in getting you to the Continent Alliance holding a little faster than our normal slave transport." Her soft smile was all condescension and no sympathy. "You should feel honored at the special care being taken. There's a chance the sale of you will fund a good portion of the fleet for upcoming battles."

"Thrilled. I have to wonder whose birthday gift I'm about to be."

I didn't wonder. I knew exactly who she would name in her next breath and at the contempt that curled around her like a ring of smoke from a pipe.

"Your *father* is most anxious to see you and purchase your bond, it seems," Aerillias inclined her head. "Family vacations and happy reunions seem to be in your future."

"I prefer death and throat punches," I quipped. "But if this goes the way you think, I guess we'll both be right."

"Charming," she turned her face from me, dismissing my presence. "Jonah, how about a drink as the crew outfits your vessel with the upgrades? I brought a bottle of Songhai bourbon. I remember how much you enjoyed it."

"Of course. After you?" Sloan released me and motioned the pseudo-captain forward before following her in the direction of his state room.

Richter jerked at my restraints. I bared my teeth and growled at him. Thank goodness for the first mate reminding me that I'm a vicious woman. Sadly, he didn't look ruffled, so I followed him to the mizzen mast where he attached my chain but didn't wrap a rope around me.

"I'm almost hurt at the lack of precautions you're taking, first mate," I tried to give him puppy eyes. He rolled his eyes and walked away.

I tucked my fists under my chin, leaned against the mast, and started humming a dirty sea shanty as the two crews shifted around the main deck. Lines were unfurled from cubbies belowdecks, telling me that it wasn't the first time the *Draconis* had been outfitted with balloons and a steam engine.

Steam power had been part of the Alliance's subjugation of the world. When they rose to power as the governing power, around the same time as the French finished chopping off the heads of their monarchy, new technology started coming from everywhere and new creatures crawled out of every cave, crevice, body of water, or mountain range. The Renaissance ended with a bang that changed everything and nothing. The amount of new technology and change was faster than the world seemed capable of keeping up with. Steam was just one of many new technologies that the Alliance introduced.

Steam engines, though powerful enough to move large conveyances and lift them into the sky, were also very dangerous with their tendency to overheat and explode. Scientists came up with ways to make the engines safer and more efficient, including pulling moisture from the air or through stores of rock. The airship technology remained predominately Alliance property, though. Ships outfitted with steam engines had to be registered with the Alliance and could, therefore, be required to hand over their ship to the governing body at any time for any reason.

The *MadCap* had a scavenged engine pulled from a downed vessel and barely pieced-together scrap. I knew Jim had likely given up the information about where and how it was hidden in the ship if they'd asked. I wouldn't be surprised if he'd already flown her to the Alliance holding I was being taken to. Damn him and his nanite-entranced brain.

The Alliance is also who brought nanites into the world. Unlike the steam engine that had been created a few centuries earlier as failed technology, no one seemed to know exactly where the first nanites came from. The only thing I knew is that it had given the Alliance a major advantage in their global takeover; making their military harder to kill and cementing their power that much faster. In less than half a century, the Alliance had taken charge, subverted attempts at being overthrown, and continued to change and update the different technologies they seemed to have pulled from thin air, like the engine they were attaching to the *Draconis*.

The ship continued to shift from side to side as the airborne vessel moved against the plank and was pulled by the heavy lines that joined them. It was a strange feeling to move sideways. Ships don't go side to side in smooth shifts like they're being dragged over land on wheels, but the odd rigging and maneuvering made it feel that way.

I couldn't say exactly how many hours it took them to set up the rigging, but it certainly wasn't long enough in my opinion. Days would have been better or even weeks. I didn't like seeing this side of efficiency in the Alliance.

Captain-in-title bitch-face walked onto the deck with her arm linked in Sloan's. She was gesturing with her perfect nails and soft hands to various rigging that had been set up as though she had done it all single-handedly. I heard a little of what she was saying about upgrades and stronger materials. I found myself mirroring her gestures from where I stood with emphatic head movement and eyelash batting to fill in what I couldn't see. Her voice annoyed me and didn't seem to stop. Blah, blah, blah.

The *MadCap* hadn't needed anyone to come and attach some rigging and air balloons to her. My ship had all of that tucked into a top hatch near the helm and a second smaller one near the forecastle. No one had ever needed to bring my ship steam engines to attach behind the steering with rigging that ran to the wheel. Stupid Alliance. Stupid Captain Aerillias.

"...almost done."

I snapped to as I realized that Sloan was striding toward me and had said something to me. I shrugged and gave him a dirty look. It seemed like the best approach.

"You didn't hear me over your brooding internal dialogue, did you?"

"I heard," I snapped. "You said we were almost done."

"Close. I asked if you were relieved to find that your journey was now almost done. I imagine you'll have an easier time attempting escape once you're off the *Draconis*?"

I peered at him, trying to gage the sentiment behind his words. Was he trying to piss me off or just telling me that he would be happy to be rid of me?

"Yes. I've always wanted to visit a slave market as one of the items up for bid. I can check it off of my to-do list," I drawled.

Sloan watched me for a moment but said nothing in response. I half expected him to apologize for a moment with the way his stance shifted.

"Oh, Captain Sloan?"

The blond bitch was calling from the plank being returned to her vessel.

"You *will* come see me when you reach port, won't you? We have so much to discuss," she gave him a little wave and stayed on the plank as it was pulled back onto her ship. The airship lifted and turned starboard before heading off into the sky, puffing steam like a happy opium junkie into the sky.

I faced Sloan and gave him a simpering smile as I fluttered my eyelashes. With my tight restraint, I couldn't lift my hand above my waist, but I gave him a little flappy wave and flashed my teeth. Sloan let one cough escape before controlling himself. He turned to watch the ship depart before shifting his gaze back to me where I was still posturing. A harsh bark of a sound came from him that he turned into a cough before quickly walking away. I couldn't help it: I grinned at his back as he headed to the main deck.

A few hours later, the captain was calling for the mast to be brought in and everything to be tied down. The massive balloons sat like dried out jellies on the deck of the ship in bright, golden hues. Leave it to the Alliance to decide that butter yellow was a good color for air balloons.

The engines had been primed and tested. The sound that came from them was blusterous and left my ears popped for several minutes after the test run. I hoped that I would be moved to one of the other masts before we took off.

Sloan and Richter moved around the deck, calling directions and preparing the crew. I was ignored; just the way I liked it.

One of the crew from the airship had dropped a screw near the wheel when they were setting the engines in place. I didn't know if it was one of the screws that should have been holding the steam motor in place or if it was just an extra, but I saw it as the gift that it was.

It took me a bit to reach it. I had been given enough chain to circle the mast which I did as though pacing. No one bothered to talk to me, assuming rightly that I was agitated and trying to walk off excessive energy. After about three careful swipes with my leg and finding the screw just out of reach, I plopped down and stretched my legs out as far as I could to pull the tiny piece of metal close to me.

I kept my head flopped to the side the entire time. I was hoping anyone who looked would assume I was having a tantrum of some sort. When I finally got it close enough, I turned to watch the movement on the deck for a bit. I made eye contact with Sloan and glared at Richter before lifting my chin and turning away. I jerked my legs in quickly and made myself fall over so I could get the screw in hand before shifting and pulling myself to my knees. I jerked my head back with an angry glare as though daring someone's amusement.

Richter dropped his eyes, and I knew, he at least, had seen me as a klutz worth laughing at and nothing more. *Good.* It meant that if anyone else brought it up, he would use it as a point of mockery.

I stood and paced around to the front of the mast to lean again. I tucked my hands to my waist as though trying for a hands-on-hips pose. It was the closest I could get to the base of the chain that held my hands locked to my sides. I couldn't reach cuffs or wrists, but I could reach the leather of the belt that held the chains in place.

Each side had a tiny lock that kept my chain drawn in and I started there. I could feel the round keyhole and worked the screw inside with my first finger, middle, and thumb. I made the movements as tiny as I could so that I would just look like I was fidgeting.

I knew I would only be able to unlock one wrist and, if luck was smiling on me, the lock that chained me to the mast. If I undid any other part of the restraint, it would be too noticeable. Just the act of undoing my other wrist or even putting the screw in my other hand would be visible. One wrist and the main chain would have to do.

Sloan walked toward me about a second after I got my wrist unlocked from my waist. I leaned back against the mast and watched him come with a cold glare. His blue eyes rested on my face for a moment before he went to stand at the wheel.

I rolled my weight to the side and looked back at him.

"Are we about to lift off?"

"Yes. You might want to sit on the deck, Maggy," Sloan told me, and I shrugged.

"This isn't the first lift-off I've ever done. I'll be fine standing," I told him and jutted my chin in the direction of the steam engine. "If that Alliance crap is going to kill me, I'd rather die on my feet anyways."

Sloan shook his head.

"I know you're worried about reaching the Alliance--"

"I'm not worried about anything," I snapped. My nerves were frayed but not from what he thought. Adrenaline was rushing through my body like lightning.

"Always about bravado, aren't we? You are allowed to be human, Maggy."

Sloan's words were clipped and sharp as he responded to my tone.

"Humans die faster than anything else on this planet. Haven't you noticed? Not that you would know what that's like."

He stiffened. For a moment I thought he'd walk over and clock me from how rigid he went.

"I'm human," he said softly.

"You're more than half machine from what I can see," I hissed. "And an Alliance pet to boot. You've no clue what it's like for everyone else."

The bitter taste of my own truth flavored those words and the misplaced venom I spewed at him. I swallowed. Part of me wished he would step over and strike me for that comment. After what he'd told me, and what I'd seen, I deserved it for taking such a cheap shot.

He gave me a sharp nod and walked back down to the main deck. I got him to do what I wanted, but damn...I actually felt guilty. I cussed at myself both for the words and the fact that I felt a damn thing about hurting his feelings. Fuck feelings, that was the quickest way to die.

I continued working at the lock holding me to the mast. The captain called orders and Richter came up to the helm to take the wheel. I leaned into the lock and gave him a wide smile. He glared back and then did his damnedest to ignore me. Predictable.

The balloons began to inflate, and Richter powered up the engines that would direct the ship once we were airborne. I popped the lock loose and the noise from the steam motors covered the sound nicely.

I knew that the best time to make my move would be when the ship was pulling free from the water. Everyone on deck would be running around in the mayhem and their footing would be less sure. I could use the distraction to take out Richter, yank the wheel and send the crew and captain flying. It would be easy to take prisoners and secure the ship after that.

I hoped. I knew a lot could go wrong, but it was the best shot I had. I also knew this crew would be unwilling to let me kill anyone if they could comply; something my own crew wouldn't have cared about. There were benefits to valuing life at times, at least on the enemy's side of things.

A sucking, sloshing noise was my first indication that the ship was being pulled up. I bunched my muscles, again missing my calf tattoos. It would have been so much easier to crouch down, get angry, and launch to send a shockwave out against Sloan's crew. I rolled my shoulders to push the thought away and concentrate on the present. I could feel my anxiety shoot adrenaline into my muscles; it was no rage magic, but it would help.

Before I could take a step toward Richter, a roar cried out from below decks like a beast had been released in the belly of the ship. Men all over the deck froze amid what they were doing and turned to face the passageway. A horde of running shapes like a hornet's nest had been cracked open on the ground, surged forward.

Smitters and the pirates had finally made their move.

I grinned, grabbed the mast with one arm and swung my legs at Richter, knocking his head to the side. His face hit the deck before his body could follow. The noise he made on contact meant that he was going to be in a lot of pain when he regained consciousness.

I pulled the keys from his belt and worked at my other cuffs before unfastening the belt at my waist. There was no need to yank the wheel and send the crew to portside; they were too busy dealing with the agglomeration of angry teeth and limbs coming at them. I did crank the wench to stall out the steam engine filling the balloons to stop our ascent into the air. The ship shuddered and plopped back down into the water. I heard shots fired and kept low as I untangled myself from hitting the deck, only hazarding a lift when the chains had been completely separated from my person.

Amid the writhing mass was Captain Sloan holding his own against the insurgency. He'd killed a couple of pirates before he'd run out of ammo with no time to reload. Damned steam cannons could only hold two shots, but at least he'd made them count. His cutlass gleamed in one hand while his claw grasped and flung bodies from his other side.

I felt my lips curl as I watched him for a moment. He was truly a sight to behold, a pirate out of legend. I half wanted to cheer him on except that he was in the way of my freedom.

Other than the initial shots, Sloan was mostly holding back the couple of pirates dumb enough to face him. The others were busy subduing the crew of the *Draconis* while those facing the captain seemed almost more intent on harrying him. Could be that they figured they couldn't take him, but that he'd surrender for his crew like a good boy.

I wiggled my legs to get full circulation back into their stiffened lengths before running at the stairwell to the main deck and leaping the distance. The shock of the landing on my bare feet was like a hard slap, but I was too damned happy to have my freedom to let it slow me down.

I swaggered forward and batted the pirates away from Captain Sloan with my bare hands. They looked surprised then annoyed. One even tried to swing at me before I gave him a glare that turned into an evil grin.

Apparently, recognition didn't kick in, but instinctual fear did when he glimpsed the predator in my eyes. Even sailors with addled wits came to their senses when they met my eyes. Crazy had a way of stopping people.

"I'll handle the captain, gents," I turned.

"Oo the fuck err you?"

"That's Captain Maggy Low," Smitters called from somewhere near the forecastle and the pirates closest to me stepped back. Some muttered and others just shut up.

"O, yer tellin the truth for once, Smikkers?"

I saw that the pirate speaking through a set of protruding mandibles and something that looked like a straw waved as he tried to form words. Antman? No, that's too ridiculous to even conceive.

"And ye better show her some respect as yer new captain," Smitters jutted his chin at me and I grinned. I turned my eyes back to Sloan whose gaze could have frozen the Bermuda triangle.

"Hear that, Sloan? I already have a new crew," I motioned for him to put his cutlass down. His eyes roved from his subdued crew and back to the couple of sailors beside me.

"How long have you been planning this?"

"Escape? You shouldn't need to ask…"

"No. When did you set up this crew to come rescue you? Did you do it during prison, somehow? Did an Alliance agent help you?"

"Hell no. Do you think I'd truck with those...or rather, you bastards? This was just good luck," I looked at the ragged crew around me. "Smitters, what happened to the captain of the ship you met the *Draconis* with?"

"Dead. Waste of space, that one. No captain out there like you," he spit to the side and a bit of tooth and blood came out.

"Well, what say you, crew? I promise to chase down and make as much of the Alliance as miserable as possible. I promise glorious adventure sometimes spiced with glorious death. Will ye follow me?"

"Aye!"

Most of the crew responded immediately except for the strange, ant-like sailor near me.

"I wud shtep in ash cap-in," it said to me and I shrugged. I turned to a nearby sailor who'd outfitted himself in every weapon he could find, grabbed a cutlass and bowed to the opposition.

"Best me and it's all yours," I grinned.

The sailor made a clicking noise and charged me. Several additional appendages popped up on its side as it came toward me. I waited, slid neatly to the side and bashed him on the back of the head for all I was worth. Predictably, his exoskeletal limbs prevented him from gaining quick purchase when he dropped low and I was able to kick out. One of his mandibles cracked and a sound like a pierced balloon came out of him. I cringed at the pain the noise caused but watched him as he shifted and writhed, his head swinging back and forth madly.

It lasted for longer than I was comfortable with and I stepped back to watch him with my hands on my hips. The writhing didn't stop, nor did he take a step toward me. I looked back at the weapon-mule sailor and motioned at his hip. He looked down, pulled a club and tossed it to me so I could turn and whack the sailor squarely in the center of its heavily shelled head. The sound he was making thankfully quit as he dropped to the deck and didn't move.

"I didn't kill him, did I?" I pursed my lips. "We need as many crewmates as we can get to man this vessel."

"I don't think so, Cap'n," Smitters walked forward and nudged the fallen crewman with his foot. "Looks like you just gave him an early naptime."

"Good." I turned and popped Smitters square in the face with the club, knocking him back a foot in surprise. I curved into a side-swing, letting the cutlass drop so I could hold the club in both hands before I popped the swing up and got him square in the chin. He dropped like a whale cut from a hook and the deck shook with the impact.

I leaned down and scooped up the cutlass again, striding forward to stand over his dazed form where he lay and put the tip of the blade directly under his fat chin.

"How the fuck did you escape the Alliance when they took our ship, you rotten, yellow bastard?"

Chapter 13

"Ya see, Cap'n--"

"Nope," I shifted and kicked him hard in the side. "I'm not feeling in the mood for lies just now, Smitters. I'm thinking you're an Alliance spy and I'm not sure there's a force in this damned world that will make me trust a fucking thing you say."

Pounding sounded to my right and I whipped my head to face the passageway below decks in time to see a slew of dirty, half-naked bodies come forward. They paused in the opening to blink at the bright light from the sun in a daze that I knew would not last long.

"Fuck. Did you let out the other prisoners?"

"No Cap'n," Smitters gasped out from my feet.

"Someone did," I tossed the club away and reached down to grasp the Walrusoid's hand to help him up. "Never mind. I trust you for right now. We've bigger things to deal with."

As I'd figured, the mass of feral slaves did not hesitate long. Growls rose up from them as they hunched forward in tandem like a pack of wolves. Spittle dripped from the edge of their mouths just before they charged. I may have yelped like a little girl for a moment as I saw them coming at me.

Deranged, angry pirates have nothing on a feral pack of humans who have devolved to their basest nature, I kid you not.

"Arm up! Keep to groups or they'll tear you apart!" I motioned and screamed, staying close to Smitters. I figured his bulk would slow them down if nothing else. I didn't discount the thought that I might have to run and trip the fat bastard to be successful.

As I was shifting to a fighting stance, I saw movement out of the corner of my eye. Tied to the masts were the Alliance sailors. I cringed and swore under my breath. Death to able-bodied sailors via vicious pack of humans was not something I was okay with.

"Cut the captives loose! This isn't the way for anyone to die. Let 'em die on their feet defending themselves!"

A few of the pirates looked at me like I'd gone daft. The feral humans descended upon the ant-sailor still passed out on the deck and ripped apart his form with their bare hands before moving in a wave toward us again. I shoved a few pirates up to Smitters and pushed the two guarding Sloan away.

"Sloan, you're going to need this," I pulled a cutlass from the walking weapons-hoard and handed it to the *Draconis* captain. "Either help me cut your crew free or fight off the mob but stay the fuck out of my way."

I didn't wait to see what he'd choose as I ran and hacked through the lines wrapped around the Alliance sailors. Several of them cowered back as though the assumed safety within the restraints. The men's eyes locked on the horde biting and clawing their way through seasoned pirates.

"Stand and fight, you useless boyos. Defend yourself or feel what it's like to be torn apart by a mob of madness," I growled, flinging one after another forward as I continued to cut and hack at rope.

Movement caught my eye and I saw Sloan standing near the railing doing the same for Malcolm. The old sailor had a bloody gash across his forehead but rose to fight with fists and what looked like an oar. The captain moved on to Knee-high, who looked less-than aware and was probably in shock.

Sloan met my eyes as I cut loose the last of his crewmen and we turned in tandem to face down the savages. The pirates had lost about three and only taken about five of the charging masses. Several of the former prisoner-slaves had cuts that should have stopped or at least slowed them, but they kept coming.

"You're going to lose your payday, Sloan," I called as I took the head off one of the mindless beasts. "The alternative is to end up like that one."

I pointed at a mass of goo that had once been a sailor. There was no way to tell if it was a pirate or Alliance; it was just gore ripped into tiny pieces and possibly gnawed at. It was hard to tell. No weapons and that pack was still vicious and winning.

"I'm thinking that's only part of our problems, Maggy." Sloan was hacking and slashing his way through the charging fiends as though scything a field. "We're losing crewmen left and right."

I saw what he meant as two more of his sailors were downed and another pirate was overrun. For a bunch of sailors, the group certainly did not understand the value of working together. I grabbed a fallen cutlass and cut apart one of the mob in my way, swinging like a weaponized tornado. I'd seen teeth connect once or twice, but they found Sloan's metal claw-arm and he just shook them off.

"Can I help?" I gave him a wild grin and a wink as I stepped in behind him. I felt him shift and press against my back. The pressure of his body against my own as we faced the throng was comfortable as though we'd done this a million times. My blades were a blur of curving death that took limbs, heads, and chunks of flesh for anything that came close enough to risk it.

Sloan and I locked ourselves into position as the group closed in around us like a gaping maw that planned to swallow us whole. Too bad they hadn't thought to kill their meal before trying to ingest it. Our blades bit back, keeping the clamp of death opened by savage force of will. Neither of us gave an inch, offering no opportunity for that mouth to close on us.

When I hacked apart the last figure to approach me, I slid to my knees in the carnage of body parts that surrounded us like we had dug a hole. I heard Sloan's heavy breathing behind me and turned my head to see a similar mound on his side.

"Mine's bigger," I muttered and heard him cough around the heavy huff of air.

A few feet away, Smitters and two others stood dripping with blood and viscera. I heard a clacking and lifted my eyes to see another sailor had climbed the main mast and was hanging on for dear life, his body coated in blood; some his own.

"Well," I huffed. "Your payday has been destroyed as has most of your crew and the pirates you took hostage."

I took a breath.

"I'm thinking you owe me," I choked out, coughing on saliva tinged with something I'd rather not identify.

"How do you figure that, Maggy?"

His breath was just as ragged, and I turned to offer him a hand up before taking a wide, side-step over the pile of death.

"I saved your life, of course."

Rasping and hacking doubled Sloan over as he stood beside me and we both avoided looking at the nastiness of our own making on the deck. I cocked my head at him and let my lips curl into the hint of a smile.

"I think you have that backwards, Maggy," Sloan said once he got his laughter and breathing under control. "Malcolm, man the wheel, if you would?"

"Oh? How do you figure?" I leaned over and ripped away fabric from a piece of a crewman near my feet before wiping my blade down. "Malcolm, belay that order. Smitters, take the wheel."

"Malcolm, please keep the wheel and ignore Maggy. Do you not remember the battle? Have you blocked it out? I saved you from at least half a dozen of those...they were human, weren't they?"

I shrugged. Malcolm at the helm was probably preferable to the questionable motives of the walrusoid. I waved the old sailor on.

"Once, maybe. Alliance prisons have a bad habit of undoing evolution in humans through torture and deprivation," I tossed the fabric aside and frowned at the still-dirty blades of my borrowed cutlasses. "I've seen them use their own prisoners to hunt down attempted escapees. It wasn't pretty. It also wasn't something I ever hoped to encounter again."

"When would you have seen such a thing? If I recall correctly, this was the first time you'd ever been captured and taken in by the Alliance," Sloan was looking at his own blade, or the rough-hewn one I gave him at least, as though it was an insect.

"You assume they keep the prisoners at Alliance facilities instead of taking them out into the field to fill their purposes," I gritted my teeth. "That lovely organization that gives you your paycheck has no qualms about testing weapons on various 'wild' areas: islands, continents, ports of call…"

I looked into his eyes, but I wasn't seeing the metal-mawed captain for a moment. I was remembering crouching down in the flats outside Plymouth on Montserrat, where I grew up. I could hear the crash of shrubbery being trampled and the terrified squeak of the old man just before the mob started in on him. Alliance officers, Spinner among them, stood by with whips, dressed in armor and watched for longer than was necessary as the prisoners ripped into him. I'd spoken to the old guy, whose name was Everret, and he'd been thrown in jail for taking food from a downed convoy. Some of the food had already grown mold from being left to the elements for so long and yet the Alliance took him to prison.

"Well, no matter who saved whom," Sloan dropped the weapon with a clatter and looked around in the fallen friends and foes before lifting a familiar-looking cutlass. "We are at a point of reckoning, Maggy."

"Oh?" I tugged a belt loose from one of the dead and proceeded to tie it at my waist to hold the two cutlasses.

"By my estimate, there are a total of nine crew to man a ship that needs almost twice that," Sloan waved his hand around me and I nodded, tightening the belt so it hung better at my hips. It was too wide for my frame, but it would do for now. I set about finding a set of boots that would fit. I suddenly missed my wardrobe. It was such a little thing to hit me, but I wanted *my* belt, and *my* weapons, and *my* boots. I huffed out a breath that made my scraggly hair shake.

"That's enough to man the ship," I shrugged and gave up looking for the moment. The boots I was finding were in singles. As in, single legs scattered around. Finding a match was just getting annoying. Was it even possible that there were that many left feet and no right? Did one of the mob eat all of the right feet before dying?

"Barely. That count includes myself and the three members of my crew that I can account for," he pointed at the one still up the mast, Malcolm at the helm, and another crewman being glared down by Smitters.

"So, you work for me now, then," I shrugged as though it was that easy. I knew it wasn't. Sloan stood still and watched me for a moment. I heard a low whistle roll out from Malcolm at the wheel and lifted my palm to Sloan in equal parts cease and peace. "Okay. You want to hash this out, but you should see that this is never going to play out in a way that leaves you looking favorably."

"To a point, I suppose," he inclined his head. "It wouldn't be hard to claim that you took advantage of the change in status quo and forced my remaining crew and I to help you man the vessel."

"That's assuming you feel that you, and your crew, would be better off continuing as you are," I couldn't help the smile that played across my features as I remembered some of what had been said between us.

"I've a feeling your crew might be willing to change allegiance with the right motivation."

"Are you telling me you plan to buy my crew?"

"Why don't we ask *them*?"

I took a step toward the two remaining Alliance sailors on deck, looking them up and down and taking in their injuries. The one who'd come down from the mast had some nasty bite and scratch marks, but they were mostly superficial. The one being glowered at by Smitters and another pirate had nasty slashes across his waist and chest that caused his shirt to cling wetly to his skin. His injuries looked pirate-given, not hysteria-caused. I eyed Malcolm who was bloodied, but otherwise seemed good. I did a mental count of the various crew that I knew who'd been lost. Too bad to waste working flesh this way.

"Smitters, what've we got left?"

"Johannsen, Stuart, Skokus, myself, and three worthless Alliance and their captain it seems, Cap'n Maggy," he pointed out the remainders.

"Skokus?" I inclined my head to the snake-like pirate whose skin seemed to slither and crawl even though he was standing still. "Take Johannsen and go check below decks for any survivors. Someone had to have let the beasties out. If they're alive, you have permission to make them regret it, but I want to speak to them. We need crewmen if possible."

The two pirates bobbed their heads and hurried away.

Stuart was a short, blond, leggy woman with various map tattoos covering her exposed flesh. She had a black eye and a bloody side but seemed otherwise intact. She also had the expression of a tough bitch that went at odds with her otherwise pixyish attraction. I immediately liked her for the look of thinly held aggression in her eyes.

"Stuart is it?"

"Abby," she nodded. "Former First Mate to the *Scourge*."

"Good. We'll need a tough bitch like you helping at the helm," I nodded, and her mouth quirked for a moment. I turned to the Alliance men. "And you lot? Do you want to go down and await your fate in the hold or would you like to face a life of freedom and glory?"

"You forgot death," Sloan groused.

"Oh right. Do you want to die or have a life of freedom and glory?"

"That's not what I meant," Sloan's voice had gotten tired and it made me smile.

"I have family," one of the sailor's started, "how do I know the Alliance won't kill them if I help you?"

"Good question…" I looked at him to fill in the blanks, motioning with my hand.

"Robert Hammons, ma'am."

"Good question, Bob. For all intents and purposes, you will be dead. The Alliance does not seek vengeance on dead sailors' families. Is there a wife?"

"No ma'am, my folks."

"Then they will live out their lives, possibly collecting your pension if you have one--"

"No pension, ma'am."

"Okay, they will live out their lives in the manner which they currently do and," I raised my hand to stop him from interrupting again. "If you call me ma'am one more time, I'm going to throat punch you."

Bob swallowed and nodded.

"...AND you will be able to send them earnings you make as part of my crew while keeping yourself free from Alliance goons and the skewed sense of justice at their hands."

"You forgot the part that he might die or be captured," Smitters mumbled as he returned, hauling the cook and Bree.

"Or he could go yellow and sneak away while his captain is being hauled off to prison," I said, my voice low and threatening. "I haven't forgotten our need to have a little tête-à-tête, later."

"We found these two hiding in the galley and the remains of a sailor outside a smuggler's hold," Smitters pushed Bree and the cook forward. I nodded at them.

"At least we won't starve," I was glad to see the girl. It bothered me to think that she might have become a practice round for the wild animals escaping from the zoo. "Any markings on the sailor to identify him or her?"

"Not one of ours, probably one of his," Smitters pointed a broken tusk at Sloan.

"Bring up the body so we can dispose of it with the others," I frowned. "We need to re-prep the ship for air travel once we're done. I can guess at the kind of critters we're going to attract with all this rotting meat."

A couple of the sailors went white and Stuart didn't look much better. I knew which of my new crew had seen some of the deep feeders in their travels. I directed them back toward checking the lines and making sure that the balloons were still intact. The steam engines had fully cut off when no one had been around to prime them for finishing the lift. We were lucky that they didn't do more than choke out after being left on a low gear for so long.

"Sloan, do you think you can play nice and work with me?" I cut my eyes to the captain who'd been surprisingly silent while I worked out the semantics of our next moves.

"That depends on you, Captain Low," Sloan said slowly. My ears caught the respectful title, and I narrowed my eyes at him. "I think you're going to need me a bit more than you think if you want this to be a success."

"I'm all ears, Sloan."

"The Alliance is going to expect us to make the holding within the next 48 hours. If we don't, they'll likely send a fleet of airships to find us and probably a few small boys equipped with steam engines.

"Hiding isn't going to do us good, though I would recommend you do what you can to dump my remaining crew and anyone else you have...mixed feelings about...on an island and ditch the ship. Sink her, probably."

"That's a sad state of affairs, Sloan," I tsked and shook my head. Though she wasn't my ship, the *Draconis* had grown on me a little. That and I hated sending any ship of good bones to the bottom of the ocean if I could avoid it. "I'm thinking of selling her."

Sloan didn't speak, but I felt fury radiating from him and knew I wasn't the only one who got attached to my things. Sinking was one thing but having someone sell off your favorite toy was very different.

"However, you see fit, but you'll want to do it quickly if that's your plan."

"I sense a *but* in there, Sloan," I arched an eyebrow. "Don't keep me in suspense, spill it."

"I'm still working it out," his eyes through the mask were heavy on my face and I nodded once.

"Why don't we let the crew get things set up. I don't suppose that bitch captain left the bottle of bourbon with you?" I motioned in the direction of what would now be the p-way leading to my cabin.

Sloan inclined his head, and I could feel the smile coming from him as he took a step toward the cabin. I gestured at Stuart who handed me a blaster with a nod. I was really getting to like this girl.

"Make yourself at home," Sloan gestured as I flopped down on his bed.

"For now, this is my home, Sloan. This is my cabin. This is my crew," I paused. "You're my crew, lest you forget."

"Of course not," he poured us both a hefty portion of what looked and smelled like good bourbon.

"I prefer rum, of course," I lifted the glass to take a small sip to test the flavor. It was a pretty good bottle, I had to admit. I downed half my glass. Sloan eyed me for several long moments. He then reached up and pulled away the metal plating that covered his ruined face and head, so he could take a sip. It was bad manners not to drink when the captain asked you to, after all.

"Of course. Don't all pirates?"

"Are we really going to fall into stereotypes, Sloan? I was just starting to like you," I lifted my glass. "Alcohol always helps with that though, doesn't it?"

"You need to let me take you prisoner."

I held my glass to my lips and lifted my eyes to the metal majority man across from me. His ruined face didn't bother me, and I saw no challenge in his eyes, but it didn't make me feel better about what he'd said. I blinked slowly, sipped my drink, and waited for a rasping laugh or an uncharacteristic "just joking" that didn't come.

"I'd hoped we were past nonsense, Sloan," I sighed and lowered my glass and raised the blaster that I had settled in my lap. "I'd prefer not to kill you and your able body before we're off."

"You don't look or act like a normal pirate, Maggy," Sloan sipped at his drink.

I tried to keep my hackles down, but comments like that were an easy way to get under my skin.

"What do you mean?" I was pretty sure my voice didn't betray me.

"You're a young, beautiful woman, healthy, strong, and you have all of your fingers, toes, and teeth," Sloan gestured, his hand curled and just short of pointing at me as though I needed him to point me out.

"There are few women captains, yes. That doesn't mean there aren't women like me on other ships. Pirate vessels all of them, but they're there," I sipped.

"But you're unmarked...perfect...ly intact," he stumbled, and I arched an eyebrow at him. "How is that possible with all of the skirmishes you've had and ships you've overrun? I can't imagine you sitting back and letting the crew do the work."

"Never," I growled. "I was front line for each and every boarding."

Sloan didn't say anything. He watched me, glass in hand, his ruined face the color and look of the insides of a tomato. I reached for the bottle and topped off my drink.

"If I were to disrobe- "

"Do you want to disrobe?"

"No." I lifted my eyes slowly to him, giving him a heated look that told him I would find every soft spot on his body to hurt him if he asked again. What was left of his lips curled.

"As I was saying: If I were to disrobe, you would see that I'm not unmarked. I have knife wounds, scarring from a hook and a few bites from enemies that chose to embrace their less-than-humanoid traits. Hell, you've seen the whip marks on my back from prison," I downed the drink. "I have my battle scars, but I've never let them be something that would disfigure me completely, lest I lose my most valuable weapon. I've always kept nanites on hand for healing. The scars on my body are mostly from my life prior to pirating, though even some of those were wiped away when they took my tattoos."

"I'd never thought you might be vain," he mused, his tone low and his eyes on the contents of his glass.

"You commented that I'm unusual because I'm a woman, a pirate captain, blah blah blah, correct?"

"I don't recall saying blah blah—"

"Sloan."

"Yes, you are an anomaly."

"Good word for it," I nodded, considering. "Women in this life are rarely expected to take a place of power unless they have wealth or beauty. Wealthy women buy what they need, beautiful women do it through manipulation when they need to. My mother was a whore. Her beauty was the only thing that put food on the table for her because she couldn't think beyond hand to mouth.

"I refused that life. I could see beyond what was directly in front of me and decided that I wanted more," I refilled my glass. "Men look at me and assume that I'm a beautiful prize lucky enough to fall into this life. They underestimate me. They assume I'm dumb and that there's a man nearby pulling my strings. I use that to my advantage.

"The *first* time I got a knife to the face," I paused to let that sink in. "I considered letting it heal slowly and scar just so I would be taken more seriously. Then, I came to the realization that not being taken seriously was one of the best weapons I could possess.

"Being an anomaly, as you put it, is what's helped me be as successful as I am. A dagger can be both beautiful and deadly," I downed the drink. "Now tell me your plan before I decide to spend the day getting toasty on fine bourbon."

"There's something going on in the Alliance headquarters that I need to get information on and taking you in is the only way I can do it," Sloan huffed out.

"Are you telling me you're a spy? I don't buy it."

"I am a spy, for the Alliance, but not the Alliance you're so familiar with," he rubbed his fingers down the side of his face. I could practically see it bruise and welt under his touch.

"I was sent to get you to assess where your loyalties lie. The belief was that either we could sway you either fiducially or if you have some sense of doing the right thing."

"Money is the right thing," I refilled my glass.

"That's what I believed at first…" Sloan said the words slowly as though expecting an interjection. I was just waiting for him to get on with it. I held my silence, barely, and traced the glass with one finger but didn't take another drink.

"No matter the reason," Sloan handed me his glass and began pacing the room, "I think that there's something to gain here, but only by working together. There is something much worse going on inside the Alliance and we need to find out how to stop it."

He stopped to touch the mask as though he was going to put it on but stepped back and began to tap on the edge of his metal arm.

"I believe you," I saw the tell and knew that he would lose if we ever played cards. He showed his nerves by scratching or tapping at skin that was no longer there. He'd done it every time he'd been about to do something I didn't like or when he was trying to make me believe him. "That doesn't mean I should trust you. Hell, why would I *want* to help you? You've beat the shit out of me every chance you've gotten."

"Yes, because flowers and chocolates wouldn't have made you suspicious of me from the get-go," he drawled and took most of his glass in one drink. He had a point.

"Okay, but why is taking me in the key to this?" I dropped back the rest of my glass, savoring the burn as it made its way to my gullet.

"Because the information is with Ned Low."

Chapter 14

"Fuck off," I snarled and hurled the glass at him for good measure.

Sloan ducked, and it bounced off the wall behind him. Either I'd lost my touch or...

"Clear aluminum glasses," he shrugged. "I'm telling you the truth, though. I need to get you to Ned Low, so I can get the information. It was lucky that you were caught, actually, or there wouldn't be an auction; there wouldn't be a way to get close to him...hell, there wouldn't be a way for any of this to happen."

"So, you're trying to tell me that former-pirate-turned-backstabbing-Alliance-crony, aka the man who contributed the sperm of my creation, is going to help you take down the Alliance?" I paused, lifted my hand into the air and stared up to the ceiling as though divine intervention was required. "I call bullshit."

"Well..." If he dragged out the word any more, it would have become a song.

"Spit it out."

"I can't guarantee that Low is trying to help, per se. My source said that he would have information that would be crucial to our ability to restructure the Alliance," he poured himself another cup of nerve-dulling happy-juice before scooping up the glass I'd thrown at him. "It was a short missive with limited information in case it got intercepted before reaching me." Sloan motioned toward me with the bottle, the skin above his eye arched up but eyebrow-less.

"Yeah, hit me again," I shook my head. "I feel like you might just need to pour the entire bottle down my throat for this conversation to make any sense.

"So, your source said that you needed to get close to Nutless Ned for information and that you would need to sell me off to do so?"

"That's the gist of it, yes," Sloan handed me a full glass. I didn't bother at sipping it. I poured it down before letting out a satisfied belch.

"So, kidnap the bastard and get him to tell you everything that way," I shrugged, stood and refilled my own glass. "If I don't show, he's bound to head off and make someone's life miserable. Snatch him then."

"One, it isn't so easy to just up and kidnap one of the most notorious pirate lords in the world who also happens to be a favorite with the Alliance."

I went to interrupt on the grounds that I refused to recognize my father as more notorious than me, but Sloan lifted his finger and nodded as though he knew my argument.

"And two, my source believes that Low will only share the information with you. We were planning on planting someone to stay close to you, so we could find out; maybe a love interest, or…"

"Hold on," I started laughing. "Why do I get the feeling that you were going to be put in for the 'love interest' in this endeavor? Did you plan to appeal to my kindness and show me you were a big softy, so I would roll over?"

"Actually, I planned on pissing you off enough that you'd try to beat the shit out of me and go off the adrenaline for battle," he lowered his chin just a bit and I blinked at him in silence for several heartbeats as what he said sunk in.

"Huh. That probably would have worked," I admitted. I wanted to be pissed, but I knew that would probably be the best way to get into my pants. It also wouldn't have meant shit to me, so I wouldn't have cared who he was. I stood and paced the room.

"We did research long before we ever considered trying to use you," Sloan drawled.

"Okay, well that plan is jacked to shit. What's the new plan?"

"The old plan is the new plan," he sipped at his drink.

"You mean sell me off, pretend to be my boy-toy, and get the information?" I laughed but Sloan's eyes didn't change, and he just kept sipping at his drink. "The hell you say. I'm not going to be paraded and sold to my father for *anyone*."

"Even if we can find a way to keep the Alliance off of your back, get back your ship, and get you your first mate, sans mind-control?"

Either the alcohol was getting to me or Sloan was incredibly clever and armed with exactly the right motivation to put me in his pocket. I hoped it was the alcohol because I hated the thought of being so transparent. I stopped pacing a few steps between him and the door. I had a brief thought of locking him in and just sailing for bluer seas. There was so much wrong with this plan even if the carrot being dangled was exactly the stuff I wanted.

I was losing my fucking mind. That's all there was to it.

"Okay, but I don't know how you can guarantee me a way out when things go bad," I set the glass on his desk and leaned forward to poke him on the chest.

"You're right. There's no guarantee of anything in any of this," he set his glass down beside mine on the desk and reached up to scratch at his cheek.

I reached forward and pulled his hand away. I had a strange urge to touch his skin to see what it was made of because it no longer looked like human skin. I dropped my hand to tap the side of the faceplate where it lay on the desk. The metal was still warm to the touch and it looked like one smooth piece -- almost skin-like in its design. I shrugged and stepped away from him. Understanding the metal face of the man who wanted to use me wasn't appealing despite my growing curiosity.

"You're really not very good at making me feel better about your fucked-up plan."

He sighed. "No, I'm really not."

I walked to the metal ring embedded in the floor that I had spent time chained to. I paused over it and considered the events up to that point. Little things ticked into place as I stared at the ring and thought of what it symbolized but what it hadn't really meant while I'd been attached to it. I took a breath and wiped all emotion from my eyes before I looked back at Sloan, who hadn't moved. He looked as though he wasn't breathing but he blinked slowly at me. I lifted a shoulder at him.

"So, why the hell would I risk it, then?"

"Because you want your freedom as much as I do," Sloan's voice came out rough as though he'd swallowed nails instead of fine bourbon. "If you take off now, like you're considering, your first mate will stay in Alliance hands and you'll never get him back."

"Stuart's good," I looked away and rubbed the ring on the floor with my big toe. "She'll make an excellent first mate. Maybe better than Jim since she won't try to eat a crew member."

"You'll run forever, and they won't stop coming for you, Maggy," Sloan said softly. He cleared his throat and some of the smooth, casual tone I'd come to expect from him came back. "Just think how you'll be able to stick it to them when you escape from within one of their compounds, a captain as your hostage, and your own ship under your feet?"

My eyes cut to him, the room fading around me.

"My ship? My ship is AT the compound? You know this for certain? It isn't just Alliance bullshit? This plan will take me to where they're keeping the *MadCap*?"

"They've offered it to Low for refitting as part of his own personal fleet."

I've heard that in moments of black rage, the person experiencing it will go blind just to wake with blood on their hands and a strange taste in their mouth. I came very close when my brain absorbed Sloan's words.

"*Low. Has. My. Ship*?" I saw Sloan's eyes go wide either due to the demonic voice that came out of my mouth or the fury that flowed off of my body in fumes. I half felt the familiar itch of my bloodlust heating my skin and energizing my body like a phantom limb.

MadCap was my salvation. It had taken me away from the island where I had practically been beaten to death as a child and almost whored out. It had been my first real place in the world and had given me a new life and family in Jim and some of my lost crew. Though the people that I considered family were gone, the ship was still out there. Still mine. I had failed Jim thus far, but with *MadCap*, I could save him and start again. I could find my freedom again. No one would stand between me and that hope for freedom.

"Yes, but we can get it back for you, Maggy. One little plan and we can get into the compound and put you back on your ship." Sloan lifted both hands to me and took a slight step to the side. He picked up the bottle and handed it to me, which I downed.

Don't get excited, there was barely more than three fingers of bourbon left in the bottle. I tossed him the empty and jerked my head for him to follow me.

"Let's get this pile of driftwood into the skies and get me my ship back. No fucking way it's being turned into an Alliance vessel," I stomped out of the room and onto the deck to start calling orders to my crew.

"I'm not sure a prisoner would be armed and have boots on," Sloan said from the helm.

"One that's been lulled into complacency...okay, maybe not the armed part," I unbuckled the belt and handed it to him. He reached for it, but I didn't let go right away. I wanted to tug it back and did for a moment before letting out a rude sound and letting go.

"Smitters looks ridiculous in that coat," I groused. I really wanted the weapons back.

"He looks more comfortable than cook does on deck or Malcolm does in Richter's gear," Sloan remarked, and I shifted to eye the hefty man standing near the main mast twiddling his thumbs. Richter had been the remains of the sailor we found outside the smuggler's hold and the one to let the feral humans loose. I liked his gumption and at least he'd tried to win the ship back. Too bad he'd been stupid and ended up killed for it.

Malcolm had donned a set of Richter's clothes to fill the missing spot. Cook was playing deck sailor with Stuart down in the kitchens. Alliance didn't hire women to work on the ships; we'd dressed her as a man and left Bree as the captive put to work. Even putting Stuart in the kitchen with Bree was a risk, but the alternative was to throw one or the other overboard. Hopefully, they wouldn't be looked at too closely.

"Malcolm's a better first mate," I chewed the edge of my mouth, watching the old seadog maneuver around the deck, keeping the men on their toes.

We were coming up on the forty-eight-hour deadline and were starting to cross paths with other steam-outfitted airships that were all flying Alliance colors. Pirates and crew alike on the *Draconis* were playing nice in their borrowed gear.

Sloan had taken the couple of crewmen aside and had words with them. I'd heard a bit but not all of what he told them. What I did hear was talk of how they were "crucial" for the mission and "greater good" was spoken with a few more chest-thumping patriotic catchphrases. Sloan knew how to stir the hearts of his crew.

I told the pirates that I'd rip out their eyeballs, stuff them down their gullets and use their entrails as bootstraps. I had a way with words, too.

My familiar chains were hanging loose, and I fought the urge to rattle them at anyone who looked cross-eyed at me. We were moving into the lion's den, as it were, and we needed to look the part, but I didn't have to like it. I kept reminding myself that putting myself in this position would lead me to my beloved *MadCap*. And Jim. I would get Jim back. But, the *MadCap*...

"I hope you're prepared to act, Maggy," Sloan leaned near me with a posture that seemed to speak menace. "We're about to be boarded and inspected."

I curled my lip at him and jerked my chains like an angry mutt. I saw his head incline slightly in acknowledgment before he motioned Malcolm over to take the helm. The salty crewman had been one of the few to remain quiet throughout the entire thing.

"Alright there, Maggy?"

It was the first thing he'd said, and I cocked my head at him.

"You've a place in my crew after this if you keep steady to the course, Malcolm," I whispered. He eyed me for a moment, his eyes squinted and lined with years aboard a ship. He had the years I always looked for in a sailor even if he didn't seem to have the heat and ire to make the best pirate.

If all went well, I wouldn't need a hateful crew so much as a skilled one, so Malcolm would fit right in.

MadCap. MaddddCap.

Repeating it over and over in my head is the only thing that kept me from losing it. My ship was somewhere ahead waiting for my return.

A small Alliance air vessel lined up beside the *Draconis*. I assumed they were checking the credentials of the ship or just logging her entry to port until a gang plank slapped over and I heard a familiar voice.

"Permission to come aboard, Captain Sloan?"

Oh fuck, it was Captain Softhands. I lifted my eyes but kept my face locked in the scowl that had become my natural expression the moment the chains were returned to me.

"Permission granted, Captain Aerillias," Sloan called and stepped forward to take her hand as she stepped down onto the ship. He made to step back, but she kept hold of his hand and walked forward.

"You're late," she stated simply as she looked around the bare-bones crew. "What happened?"

"Pirates tried to take the ship and let loose the human cargo," Sloan made a noise. "It was rather bloody."

"Yes, I'd heard there was a group of bloodhounds in your cargo."

"Bloodhounds?"

I could imagine Sloan's eyebrows reaching for the sky at the term Aerillias used so casually for the feral prisoners.

"They're broken prisoners used to root out escapees or sold off to guard caravans and such. Brutal creatures, but useful," she motioned with a curving of shining fingernails and long-fingered hands. Her nails had an odd sparkle to them that drew my eye and I wondered if she was so daft as to put gemstones on her nails. I could imagine members of my crew spotting that and biting her fingertips off just to take the gems.

"I see," Sloan sounded calm, but I could detect just a hint of his ire. He truly hadn't known that the prisoners were turned that way on purpose. Maybe I hadn't been clear enough, but more likely he just hadn't wanted to believe me. "Well, they managed to take care of each other and several of my crew in the process. I had to put many of them down myself."

"But I see you managed to keep the prize safe," Aerillias' gray eyes lit on my face and she looked me up and down in appraisal. "Amazing that she's unharmed."

"She was chained in the cabin at the time," Sloan replied.

"Didn't I tell you installing that ring would be useful? Of course, I had other plans for it," She leaned into Sloan and made a low noise that made me want to gag. "Perhaps after the auction you'll get a few days furlough and we can try it out."

Sloan's eyes shifted to me for the barest heartbeat and he swallowed hard. Aerillias gave a throaty laugh and tapped her nails on the side of Sloan's face.

"Well, I suppose the report will be much smaller than planned," Aerillias pulled out a pad of paper and quill.

"Cargo consists of one prisoner and... oh wait. Didn't you say that there was another who took to helping the cook?"

"She was killed as well," Sloan said quickly, and I turned my head. He'd just freed Bree from being auctioned off and hadn't even hesitated. There were moments when Sloan made it difficult for me to remember he was Alliance.

"Pity. I'm sure she would have done well in a pleasure house. I'd heard from Spinner's missives that she was a nasty piece. I'm sure she would have fit in at Delilah's."

I bit down to keep my thoughts from spewing out of my mouth. I'd heard of the pleasure house she was speaking of. It's where the wealthy could go to beat the shit out of men and women who couldn't do a thing to protect themselves. It was basically free reign to murder if you had enough coin or status.

"Yes, we lost quite a bit on this trip. I'll be glad when we're in port and can put this behind us," Sloan attempted to steer Aerillias away from the helm, but she released her hold on him and stepped back to me.

I felt her gaze and slowly raised my eyes to meet hers. Sloan had told me to hold the chains tight and pretend to be fully bound. He couldn't have realized what pressure that put on my restraint when facing the useless flesh that looked me over.

Aerillias leaned in and ran a fingernail down the side of my cheek.

"I do hope that Low lets me have a turn at you, Maggy," she breathed, and I could smell the salty brine of a seafood lunch on her breath. "You'd be a fun distraction, I think."

I stayed very still as she leaned slightly closer and I jumped at her with a snarl and her head jerked up while she pulled her fingers back from my face. I should have bit her. She would have been a more believable captain if I'd taken one of her fingers off.

She laughed in a bell-like sound that rasped my nerves like a dull blade. I curled my lip and spit at her.

"Maybe I'll wait until you've been broken a bit more," she remanded. "Not too much mind you, but a little."

I turned my face from her in dismissal. Part of me wished she'd be stupid enough to reach out again or that I could just ignore the slack on some of my chains and kill the stupid chit. It would ruin the plans we had in place though, and that was more important now.

MadCap.

Oh, my lovely ship, I would do this and so much more for your return.

I heard Sloan and Aerillias making banal chit chat as he walked her back to the plank that led to her vessel. I watched through my lashes as she stroked down the side of Sloan's metal face before letting her hand drift to caress his claw-like arm. She gave him a satisfied smile and turned to walk back to her ship.

When the plank was withdrawn, Sloan gave a wave and the airship chugged away and down. The captain turned and saw me watching him. He paused and then strode toward me with a visible sense of purpose that caused a swell of anxiety at the base of my spine for a moment. I reminded myself who I was, and I stood straight to look him in the eye.

"No matter what they do, Maggy. You will not be given to Low permanently. I promise you," he stood a foot from me and glared into my eyes as though I'd made an accusation. "I swear to you that I will do everything in my power to keep you from that fate."

I pursed my lips at the starkness in his eyes and wondered at the captain that stood before me. I wanted to ignore him, but I couldn't keep my damn mouth shut.

"Who are you that you care this much? What was done to you that you would make a promise such as that to the likes of me?" I dropped the slack on the chain and raised my hand, palm out to him before he could respond or walk away. "You do know that, for my ship, I would kill you and anyone else who stood in my way. That's the easiest thing I would do for my freedom and my ship. I would have no hesitation. You need to remember that."

Sloan said nothing, but I saw his chin rise a fraction of an inch.

"Don't tell me," I shook my head. "It's better if I don't know who you are or why you are this way. As soon as you get your information, I'll be on my ship and on my way, so there's no point in knowing any more about you than I have to."

Sloan stood stock-still and stared at me, the skin just below the lip of his mask bobbed as he swallowed once. I shook my head and paced away from him as far as my chain would allow.

MadCap.

MadCap

Chapter 15

My stomach can handle hurricanes, mad otter attacks --don't ask -- even the *MadCap* cook's "Stew Surprise," but coming down in an airship will never feel right to me.

Briny air rose up off the ocean to greet us as the ship dipped down. Air was let from the balloon-like bladders above our heads to give a slow descent. The steam-engines were running on low with a canvas flap extended behind like a fin to allow greater control to head into port.

Unlike the two times I had flown the *MadCap*, the *Draconis* was heading for a shore landing. Lines were dropped and massive men and women who were part of the docking crew reeled in the ship like prosperous fishermen. Arms bulged, and forms shifted as they pulled the mass of the ship in through a combination of pulleys and brute strength that I envied.

Sloan had attached the chain to his person and was standing near the guardrail or I wouldn't have been able to see what was going on below us. I think he saw me go a little peaked and decided that the rush of air from beside the ship might be a way to keep me from hurling up the contents of my stomach. There would be no end to the ridicule if I lost my lunch.

We inched forward, and I felt dread slide up my spine like an unwelcome touch. Part of my brain railed at me for agreeing to be part of this thing while the other half just wanted to cause mayhem. It's sad that the latter made me want to smile despite the fact that I had no clear view of what could happen. I settled both with a scowl that, I hoped, nicely blocked my nausea and made me look like the fierce predator I reminded myself that I was.

Several Alliance officers and lackeys were waiting for us the moment the ship was lowered so they could attach a sturdy-looking gangway. Sloan twisted the chain around his hand, and I was again the dog on a leash.

"I'll take her to a cell to await auction, Captain Sloan," a rotund man reached his hand forward. Sloan looked down his nose at the man and didn't release me.

"This prize has been a hard transport. I'll deliver her myself, thank you." Sloan tugged and walked me past the man who opened his fleshy mouth to protest. Sloan made eye contact and the other man clapped his mouth shut.

He walked me down the platform and I turned back to look up at the *Draconis*. I loved the view of any ship that was seaworthy, but seeing it set up on a drydock sort of landing made the vessel seem even more massive. I had the urge to go back over and pat her and tell her she'd done well by getting us this far. I was feeling sentimental, but I'd almost claimed her for a bit and that was enough.

We passed through doors with sentinels on either side. Both wore the familiar jackets of a marshal and I had the urge to kick out at them simply because it reminded me of Spinner. I found myself looking forward to the next time I saw that bastard sans chains and restraints. I would make sure he regretted every breath he'd ever taken. I pondered the sidearms of the sentinels while I wondered where I might commission a whip.

Once inside, we were shadowed by two more Alliance stooges. I turned and gave a young blond man a lip curl. He watched without reaction and kept pace a few lengths behind us.

"Just keep being your charming self, Maggy," Sloan said in a low voice beside me. "It's time to parade you around and get the bidding war started before we even put you up to auction."

I lifted my eyes to find him watching me from the side of his metal face. His posture was directed in front of us, but I could feel that wasn't where his attention was locked.

"You realize that the moment they unchain me, I'm going to tear you to pieces, don't you, Sloan?" I let my voice take on the smooth tone that he generally used.

"Whatever you say, Maggy," Sloan inclined his head at a woman we passed who wore so many jewels that she should have been lying on the floor, unable to move from the weight. The woman fluttered a fan at her powdered and rouged face. Her hair was done up in the white curled wig that still seemed to be popular with the landed gentry. All it did was underline her age by filling in the creases on her skin.

A young man stood beside her with carefully curled hair that hung loose around his collar in what was likely an attempt for rakishness though was obviously the long work of mistreated servants. He lifted the woman's hand to his arm before giving me a wink and leading her away.

I ignored him and all of the others who stared at me like an exotic exhibit. I held the steel in my spine despite an urge to curl in and skulk. I felt like an animal, but I didn't want to give them the satisfaction of seeing it. Ruse or no, I wanted them to see me as who I was: Captain Maggy Low; the terror of the seas, vicious pirate lord, and death to any I chose. I wanted to promote fear despite my restraints, as it should be, instead of displaying the captured and beaten woman they thought I'd become.

Sloan tugged at the chain. I slowed to stare down a dandy in a suit so fluffy it could have been a dress. He stood leaning against a titanium-inlaid cane that had wood wrapping around its length like vines with gemstone flowers. It made me want to beat him to death with the ridiculously ostentatious accoutrement before choking him with his cravat.

I turned to snarl at the captain holding my leash but settled for a lip curl. I was caught between the urge to strike out at him or reign in my dignity and stand tall. I settled for yanking back and then setting a pace equal to Sloan's but a few steps ahead as though leading the way. I sensed the shift in Sloan's grip on my chain about a second before I saw what caused it.

"Chancellor Willett," Sloan's voice called, and he stalled to bow. I did no such thing, choosing to lift my chin and look down my nose at the man who stood before us.

The man had style; I would give him that. Dark hair was neatly combed with the slightest hint of curl at the locks nearest his brown eyes. No make-up or wig touched his youthful power. His skin was bronze like some sort of ancient statue casting a sharp relief to the starched white collar of his shirt. The beard and mustache on his face were immaculately groomed without a single hair out of place. His face was unlined with mirth or anger over broad shoulders that tapered down to a narrow waist and muscular build. I could imagine him on deck with the muscles to pull lines and steady masts despite the heavily brocaded jacket that adorned him. I could see that his hands had the roughness I would expect of deck crew despite the perfectly trimmed nails and clean skin.

As I looked at him, I found the starched, clean perfection funny considering how much blood I knew was on his hands.

"Captain Sloan. You're late."

It was no wonder his face was completely unlined. There was no tone shift or inflection of any sort when he spoke. It didn't mean that we didn't understand the chancellor's displeasure at Sloan failing to bring me to the holding at the predetermined time, though.

"Apologies, Sir. I won't waste your time with explanations that the customs officer probably already briefed you on." Sloan didn't come up from the bow until the Chancellor motioned him with a tiny wave of his hand.

Chancellor Willett's eyes drifted to me and I felt the press of power in the man's gaze. I had no plans to capitulate here any more than I had when I'd met Sloan. The man was at the top of his chain and trying to cow me with a look. Power games were something I was familiar with and didn't shy away from; that was something I couldn't say about the political maneuvering I knew I was going to witness while a guest of the Alliance.

Yes, I know I'm heading into slavery, but it was being done mindfully and I figured I'd be able to leave any time I wanted. Ergo, *guest*.

"Magerious Low. I would welcome you, but your stay will be brief, and you don't belong here, so it seems like a moot point."

The words blended together in his non-tone, so it took me a moment longer than it should to come up with a response.

"It's Maggy. Captain Maggy Low." I gave him a winning smile that didn't reach the dark fire in my eyes. The urge to jump forward and put my hands around his neck was almost overwhelming. Leave it to an Alliance holding to bring every rage-induced fantasy to the fore of my being. My hackles had been steadily rising since we'd started the leashed walk down the hallway and I imagined my hair was standing straight up by now. The urge to attack was so strong that I could almost feel my teeth sharpen despite the fact that they could no longer do so.

"So you say. I think you'll find that those around you would call that assumptive title debatable, Maggy," the chancellor inclined his head and turned back to face Sloan. "Why is she here instead of in a cell?"

"I thought that the bidders might want to see what they were purchasing," Sloan tugged at the chain in an absent way. "It might whet their appetites."

"Looking to line your pockets a little further? Predictable. Of course, with the loss of the rest of your cargo, I suppose this is your only chance for a payout, so it makes sense," Chancellor Willett nodded once and motioned for one of our shadows to come forward.

"Parading the merchandise is so blasé. Richards will take her to a cell and prepare her for auction, Captain Sloan."

He looked down at the chain in Sloan's hand and waited.

"Yes, Chancellor Willett. Might I recommend that the other marshal assist? She's known to get a bit...feisty," Sloan handed the chain to one of the shadows as he spoke. An equally youthful marshal came forward at Sloan's beckon.

"Of course. Marshal Simms?" Chancellor Willett waved my new leash-holders away. "Captain Sloan, perhaps you'll join me for a drink before you head to your accommodations?"

Sloan inclined his head, and my chain was tugged to turn me away. I caught a flash of blue eyes just as I turned. That man needed to be more careful. His sudden need to check on me or keep me close was bound to get him in trouble if he didn't play his hand right. Sloan in trouble would equate to increased difficulty leaving this miasmic government holding. It would only take one of the barracudas to notice that he checked on me before they'd try to figure out why.

I followed the two marshals down the hallway. At first, I thought they were taking me right back out to the *Draconis*, but they veered left just before the double-doors that led out. We walked past immeasurable luxury for several minutes. Everything was decorated in rich red, bright gold, and midnight blue, Alliance colors. It made me want to break things, but I remained in outward control despite inward ragings.

They lead me through another hallway and down a few flights of stairs. I began to notice that the hallways were no longer lined with windows. The colored decor shifted to paint and brick instead of velvet and precious metal. The hall started to smell of must. As the unpleasantness increased, I knew we were headed down even if the number of stairs had been negligible.

Richards or Simms, I had already forgotten which was which, tugged at the chain with enough vigor to almost send me to the floor. I turned my head to see one of the marshals smirking at me and I wished for a moment that my chains were a touch looser. I tugged back, it was to be expected that I would be an angry, uncooperative captive, after all. Resistance was the soup du jour. I like soup.

Resistance was nothing really. What I wanted and was fighting against was the desire to kill, maim, and torture. I wondered if Sloan had seen half of the evil I had within the population of the Alliance. My hands were red but theirs were dripping blood in a never-ending stream.

I knew Sloan held his own demons, some invisible and some written plainly on his face, but had he seen murders? Torture? The sheer demon face in powdered wigs and sparkling jewels?

I was inside the snake's nest of all of the evil I'd seen in the world and all I could do was play leashed puppy. At least puppies don't always obey especially when you tugged them for a walk instead of letting them lead.

I slowed my pace, dropping my eyes to the ground. I heard them whispering something that sounded suspiciously as though they thought they'd have a chance to torment me. I slowed a tiny bit more until the chain grew taut between us.

My captor gave a slight jerk, and I took a shuffling step as though tired. The other marshal hadn't taken in any of the slack despite Sloan's hints. My leash-holder tugged again, and I shuffled again. They probably thought fear was keeping me from coming along. I felt the laxity in the chain as the young man loosened his grip to give a massive heave on the chain and I grinned.

I looked up and dove forward, hitting the blond marshal square in the chest and knocking him to the ground. I dropped my head in a mighty swing and connected with his face. I loved the sound of someone else's bones crunching.

The dark-haired marshal grabbed me from behind and tried to haul me off his compatriot. I threw my weight to the side and unbalanced him, throwing us both into a roll with my back to his chest. It was a good angle to bend my knees and stomp backwards. Unlike Sloan, I wasn't knocking on steel balls this time.

The sound of a grunted yelp was pure artistic symphony. I shifted my weight, curling my legs up for a rocking sort of leverage and landed on my knees beside him. When I swiveled to gain my feet, I grabbed the belt, bent into a bow and hurled myself forward. My first captor found himself rammed the moment he got to his feet. Blood came in a steady flow from his nose and he doubled over. My skull connected with his stomach just before I drove him toward the wall like a charging bull.

He grabbed for my waist and I didn't bother to try to stop him. The momentum of our movement caused me to topple and took any chance at his getting a grip on me.

Sloan had been nice enough to use the oldest restraint belt he could find when he chained me up before we landed. I had a moment's thought of how annoyed he was going to be if I managed to escape just before the belt chose to pop loose.

My hands came up with a leather expanse of ragged belt chained to them and I clapped it under his chin, knocking his head up. I brought it back down and slapped it over his face, wrapping it around his head until I boxed both ears with the rough leather. I pulled back one more time, striking him in the throat, holding it there while I listened to him choke.

I heard movement and knew it was the other marshal coming to help. The sounds of dragging and scraping cloth told me he was crawling on the floor behind me. Just the same, I was impressed that he managed to move so soon after I'd squashed his testicles with both of my booted feet.

Blondie blacked out before his buddy could help and slid down the wall. I turned to swing down hard on the back of the other marshal's head with my belt-turned-paddle. He hit the ground face first and I was pleased to hear another crunch.

Ah, it's the little things that make my heart skip a happy beat. I was grinning wildly at the two unconscious marshals when I should have been paying attention to what was around me. Or more precisely, who.

I distracted myself further when I remembered how escaping was bad for the plan. A moment later, the solution found me as lightning shot through my body, and I seized before dropping to the floor in a heap.

Chapter 16

For a moment, my brain didn't register the smells and odd echoing of the room that I was in as it tried to send me to a happy place. I imagined that it was morning on the *MadCap,* and I was getting ready to crawl out of my bunk and raise hell for some unsuspecting vessel, Jim at my side and war in my blood.

Unfortunately, I only had the fury in my blood, and it was being held down by straps over my arms, legs, torso, and head.

"Oh good, you're awake," an unfamiliar voice said as I opened my baby blues. I couldn't turn to see him, and the sound of his voice came from somewhere off behind my head. The sound of movement hit the cement walls and bounced around the room before it struck my ears with misdirection. I swiveled my eyes trying to pinpoint the other occupant of the room before a rustling near my head drew my attention.

The youngest face with the oldest eyes I'd ever seen appeared above me. He looked like someone's toddler wearing a ragged, white wig that flowed down his shoulders and beyond. His eyes were a startling shade of green; almost more startling than the sweet smile that played upon his lips. I didn't know whether to pat his head or punch him.

"Miss Low, I can't tell you how happy I am to meet you! I've heard so many stories about your adventures!" He nodded his head and shifted so that I could see him directly instead of at an odd upside-down angle.

The new angle cleared some of the confusion at my first glimpse of him. The skin on his face was stretched tight, creating the initial impression of youth. It was so tight that it resembled raw pastry that had been pulled and draped across the bones of his face like the start of a meat pie. His nose was an angle with tear-drop holes, his lips a bare curve with a sharp line between them that curved merrily in his smile, and his eyelids smoothed into his hairless eyebrows like rolled bread dough.

The hair stuck out at odd angles and I realized that he had no ears, at least not the human sort of ears. When he cocked his head, I could see that he had ear holes, just not shells of flesh that curved around the orifice. My brain scrambled to think; to remember what he was. Nightmarish images fluttered through my brain as I grasped for the word I needed.

"Voyag," the word shot from my lips of its own accord when the random jumble of thoughts that was my memory made the connection. The creature frowned at me.

"Let's not call each other names, now. I am Vanyik, and I will see to your implant today," his mouth split wider and I cringed. I knew there was a longer, more technical name, but I couldn't remember it, much less pronounce it. To call Vanyik a voyag was akin to insulting his parentage in his native tongue.

I had learned about them from fairy tales. His species were the frogmen in children's stories that started as a man but was turned amphibious by some spell. The stories made it sound pretty by marking their kind as a sort of victim who only needed a kiss from a princess to be restored.

The reality, however, was a creature that was only ever born male who required a humanoid reproductive partner. The voyag would lick the woman's skin, leaving spores that would erupt several months later with babies. The woman would die as all her skin broke apart and was eaten by the offspring. Thankfully, they could only apparently reproduce once in a lifetime, but that didn't make the spores on their tongue any less toxic to humans. Being licked by a voyag that wasn't in a mating cycle usually resulted in the production of acid from pores that ate away at a person's skin and killed them.

Despite fatal methods of procreation that tended to limit interactions, they were clever creatures with an adeptness with technology and ridiculously long lives. Most of the steam engines that graced airships had been improved upon by Vanyik's race to the point that, instead of requiring the space of an entire stateroom to operate, they only needed a tenth of the space. Rumor had it that the creatures were also working with nanite technology to create something that might help with their limited population.

The Alliance was a logical place for them to find employment. I doubted the Alliance had any qualms about awarding Vanyik's ilk with humanoid hosts in exchange for the advances in tech. I shuddered at the thought of being offered to Vanyik, but my brain caught on something he had said with a sudden lurch of fear.

"Did you say implant?"

"Of course. It won't hurt much, nor will it scar your lovely, fresh skin," Vanyik stroked my arm with the back of two fingers and licked his lips for a moment. I almost wet myself. His wide eyes shifted back to my face and he made an odd clicking sound that I think was a chuckle.

"I'm far past my years of begetting offspring, lovely Miss Low, but that doesn't mean I don't appreciate beautiful skin when I see it," he made that clicking sound again and I tried to breathe. He motioned to someone else in the room and suddenly the cot I was strapped to started to shift. I was upright and then it started to inch forward, my bedraggled hair falling into my face around the strap on my forehead.

"Make the mark just here," I heard Vanyik say just before I felt his cold touch on the back of my neck at the ridge of my spine. "It will be strongest if we put it close to her brain stem and spine. No no, here."

He tapped again and then kept his finger in place. I swallowed and tried to think of a way out of this. An implant? Since when did the Alliance have implants? What would an implant do?

"What is this implant? Some kind of tracker?"

Vanyik sucked in a breath as though I had physically wounded him.

"A tracker, Miss Low? Oh no no no. The implant is so much more than a simple tracker! This technology is fresh off the line -- better than any nanite technology out there! The chancellor himself has requested that you be the first one to use it because you -- and it -- are so very important to us!"

"Really? How fascinating. Who came up with this amazing new tech?"

As my brain scrolled through the random bits of information I'd heard about his species, I remembered a rumor of ego. Supposedly it wasn't difficult to get a voyag to discuss their creations so much as it was to get them to shut up about it.

"Not to brag…"

But he would…

"It was me. I was tweaking the nanites Professor Talimuck created…good man, that Talimuck. Shame he's an ordinary human…And I noticed that some of the instruction coding in the cells were a little lax. We-ee-ell! When I saw that, I knew what needed to be done!"

"Do tell," I was tugging at my arm constraints, trying to inch my hands closer to the edge of the buckles. No chains, but man I couldn't seem to find a way to slip through. I shifted to moving my ankles to test the restraints there.

"Control the subject, of course. Tracking isn't enough, absolute control is what you need! You should never lose sight of your possession or, Chancellor-forbid, let someone steal the things you hold precious. I couldn't imagine the loss of Adonis, here. He's my most-trusted assistant."

Adonis was a tiny male who stepped forward and nodded at me once. His floppy ears made him look cuter than his diminutive height already did; he was like a baby bunny. He was less cute when he started tightening my restraints and frowning at me. I tried to growl at him, but even annoyed floppy-eared critters are pretty damn adorable.

"Mr. Vanyik, I really think you should start at the beginning, so I can see how this all came about. I am just a pirate after all...I couldn't possibly grasp this amazing breakthrough without more to go on."

"Well...if you must know, I--"

"Chancellor Willett wants to know what's taking so long," a marshal with a bandage across his nose and a black eye came into view. He looked vaguely familiar.

"Of course! She's almost ready," Vanyik went back to tapping the spot on my neck again. The marshal glared at me through one good and one swollen eye and I remembered slamming my head into his face earlier.

"That's a good look on you," I commented with a toothy grin that made him glare harder. "Come closer, though. You really should have a matched set."

The young marshal rolled his eyes, winced at the pain it caused his bruised one, and walked out of sight. Then the screaming began.

For a moment, I wondered what they were doing to some poor woman that she was screaming like that. It was unseemly. Then, the pain brought me back to my body and I realized it was me screaming as Vanyik and Adonis sliced into my neck. Thankfully, the girlish screams likely died off when I passed out, saving my dignity.

Someone was tapping me upside the head, and it caused me to snarl. Or I wanted to snarl. I'm not sure. Though, I did open my eyes to Vanyik smiling down at me and petting the side of my face as though I were a temperamental horse. I tried to say something to get him to stop but couldn't. My mouth felt like it was wired shut.

"Is she ready, Vanyik?"

"She certainly is, Chancellor," Vanyik smiled into my face and I blinked but didn't turn away like I wanted to. Especially when his tongue came out and rolled across his flat lips. I could see ridges and tiny spikes along the appendage, but I couldn't look away no matter how much I wanted to.

"Have the marshals escort her to the podium with you. Do you have the controller?"

"Oh yes, right here. Would you like me to--"?

"Yes. Get on with it, please."

Vanyik motioned to someone, waving them forward. His other hand, with the extended middle two fingers tapping casually against each other, was a round ball-like device. It looked somewhat like an old-style compass, but it didn't have visible nautical directions on it. There was a line that looked like a needle, but that was it.

"Come along, Miss Low." Vanyik nodded and motioned me forward. I saw his long fingers shift and my legs took slow steps without my permission. I couldn't even gasp at the lack of control on my part. There was nothing I could do but be driven around like a passenger in my own body.

Shocked surprise overwhelmed my fear for a moment and all I could think was: *Well, this is new*.

Chancellor Willett waved someone forward and then walked beside me. I moved from an unfamiliar, lushly furnished room to one that was too dark to make out my surroundings. My legs marched me onto a raised podium in what felt like a large room. Air and space surrounded me, and I felt like I was walking blindly through the room without the ability to turn body or head to look. I'd seen little toy soldiers in a market once that you could spin a key and they would lift their legs and march forward with an awkward, ambling gait. I imagined that's what I looked like. It was like I was sleepwalking. I felt so disconnected from my body that I couldn't grasp why everything was suddenly so wrong.

Ahead of me, as I moved forward, was one marshal and I could sense the heat and movement of another at my back. To my right was the chancellor with Vanyik on my left. It was like a twisted parody of an honor guard. The image had a strange giggle rolling up in my throat, but I didn't make a sound.

I *couldn't* make a sound.

The more I thought about the *couldn't* of the scenario, the more my blood started to pump in my body. I *couldn't* stop walking. I *couldn't* turn to look at anyone. I *couldn't* scream.

A rush of energy bubbled up inside me and I felt myself screaming inside, but I couldn't give it voice. I couldn't *do* anything. I couldn't choose to run away, smile, or flip a single motherfucker off. Panic almost made me black out as my insides tried to escape the shell that held me prisoner, but I couldn't. If I could have hyperventilated or vomited, I would have.

I. Just. Couldn't.

When my body and the people around it reached the podium, the marshal to the front peeled off and stepped away. In front of me stood a pedestal holding a tray with a round shell-like disk that I screamed at myself to grab and throw but nothing happened. The chancellor stepped forward and picked up the disk the moment he was behind the podium. He turned to face a dark area that my senses told me was full of people; it was as though I was in the belly of a breathing beast. I could feel the movement of the lungs of the room as though waiting for the moment they could gulp me down.

My heart stuttered as, from the corner of my eye, I saw Sloan step up beside the chancellor. Part of the panic bubble inside me shrunk while new fears grew.

Did he know what had happened? What if Sloan had planned this from the beginning?

I shrunk inside myself as new demons clawed at my brain; some called for me to kill them all, Sloan included, at the first opportunity. Others replayed the vulnerable look the other captain gave me when he was helmless and asking me to go along with his plan to be sold to the Alliance. I didn't know what to believe, but I felt like the helpless girl cowering in the corner as her mother whipped her in a drunken rage; the girl who hid in the forest and watched Alliance soldiers set beasts loose on women and children. I was the girl I swore never to be again.

"This next auction is what so many of you have traveled to see. May I present the former captain of the *MadCap*, Magerious "Maggy" Low?"

Sound rumbled through the darkened room. I couldn't focus on any figures, but I caught hints of movement out in the room beyond the brightly lit podium. Sounds rolled and curled around me: anger, admiration, and laughter. They all stabbed at my senses like needles of rain in a gale. I wanted to glare or snarl or show my dominance in some way, but I was completely impotent.

"The bidding for our next slave will begin at seventy thousand units. Before we begin, I would like to address some of the concerns I've heard from some of you. If you would please voice your questions for the gathering?"

The questioning tone seemed to be pointed very directly at someone specific and I heard a throat clear.

"Chancellor Willett, what proof do we have that this is *the* Maggy Low?"

"Other than my word, Lord Malu?" The chancellor's voice remained uninflected, but the hush in the room showed that everyone perceived the implied threat.

"As you say, Sir. I think we would all feel better if there was...proof? There has been rumors of her capture before."

Were I in any less a panic or rat's trap, I would have smiled at that. I did find myself wondering if the man's testicles crawled back up into his body from the effort of asking that question. Silence was an extended accompaniment until another voice cut in, causing ice to ride up my spine.

"How about my word then, Lord Malu?" The voice was inflected with the slightest hint of a crisp accent resplendent of the proper upbringing that he'd never received. I would have recognized his voice anywhere despite having only heard it once.

Former pirate captain, Edward "Ned" Low's voice held laughter that was almost as much of a threat as the chancellor's lack of emotion. I heard chairs being shifted as they scuffed the invisible floor of the room.

"Of course, Admiral Low," Lord Malu's voice capitulated. "You would be the best to recognize your own flesh and blood."

Under the fear, I could feel the man's hate being spearheaded toward my father. A tingle of heat roiled in my belly to echo the feeling. I would have to remember that I wasn't the only one who wished my father harm and use it to my advantage. *If* I ever had use of my limbs again.

The platform creaked with the addition of new weight being tread on it. In my mind it was echoing the outraged and unavenged voices of the slain Kinship as my father stepped up to the stage. As the man himself stepped into the light to my left, my internal dialogue snorted.

If Sloan was the epitome of a stereotypical pirate, my father was the picture of a romanticized one. His hair was the same blue-black shade as my own but in a mass of long curls streaked with silver. His skin was just a shade darker than my own sun-bronzed skin and it accented the aged color of his mustache and finely trimmed beard as though done mindfully. His eyes were the devil himself; innocent blue with inky black depths to mark the failings of his soul. I knew him to be charm-incarnate despite the clear marks of age and hard living in the lines of his skin. I resembled him so much in swarthiness and innate charm, that denying he was my sire would never be a bluff I could pull off.

"Admiral Low has offered a pre-bid for the slave. As such, it is his choice to request to inspect the slave or a demonstration of skills before we open to all bidders," the chancellor motioned toward me, his arm out, palm up. It was as though he was presenting a show and I was the main act.

"I will see a contest of combat skills to show her worth," Low's voice poured ice into my belly. The tingles of madness that threatened to overcome me were quelled as my muscles seemed to cue in on what was about to happen. My brain charged the cannon holding the adrenaline in my veins; aimed and ready to fire. If will alone could have broken me from the control of the implant, I would have been free then and there as some instinctual aspect of my being came alive.

The chancellor turned to Vanyik with a jerk of his chin. The voyag stepped forward and I saw his eyes widen as he fiddled with the device in his hand for a moment before nodding to the chancellor.

"Who is your chosen combatant, or would you like to face her, Admiral Low?"

Catcalls rose from the audience at the chancellor's question. My father stepped forward enough that the light in the room seemed to be focused on him. His lips curled into a toothy grin.

"I would not damage such valuable merchandise."

For a moment, I wondered if he meant me or himself. Low looked around for a moment in feigned deliberation until his eyes caught on the blue uniform who'd been the last to join us on the stage for this comedy of errors.

"Perhaps your captain…?" My father shifted, his arm out as he indicated Sloan with a slight bow and the chancellor nodded.

"Captain Sloan, if you would please take up arms against the slave? Bring dulled cutlasses for them, marshal."

A cutlass was placed in my hand and my fingers tightened around it immediately. I wanted to but didn't slash out at the marshal who placed it there. My body shifted, and I faced Sloan as though I were a toy being turned by a giant hand.

I still wasn't sure what Sloan knew about the situation, but it occurred to me that he might be blind to the fact that I was not under my own control. I tried to give him a sign, but I couldn't so much as widen my eyes. I felt a single drop of perspiration slide down my face from the effort of trying to regain control, but it was no use.

Vanyik's voice whispered in my ear that I would fight but not kill and I saw the flicker of light hit the odd device in his hand that I realized must be a controller of sorts. My body stepped forward and I bent at the waist in a bow before taking a fighting stance.

"Are you doing that?" Low said in a low tone from where he'd moved near the chancellor. Both men looked to Vanyik, who hurried closer to them.

"It is the instinctual reactions of her muscles, sir. We send a command for her to defend herself and her body does the rest. She must be initially instructed, but as the implant settles, even that won't be necessary," Vanyik's voice rose high with excitement and Low glared him into a hush. Vanyik spoke again at a lower tone. "Her body will follow the will of the implant and knock her out if I hit this part of the control, so we can end the fight whenever we need."

I hoped to Odah that Sloan was close enough to hear that and realize something was off. So much of me wanted to believe that this was not part of a plan he'd neglected to make me aware of.

Sloan lifted his cutlass and moved toward me, the blade cutting through the air in front of him, creating a high-pitched sound as air whistled across the edge. He was determined to show that this was a true battle. My body moved forward, and I spun, slicing up to almost knock the blade from his grip with a strike that caught the pummel.

"Well done, Vanyik."

"The chancellor is too kind."

Yeah, because the voyag was the one with the power behind the swing. Bastard males. The ire for being even more at the whims of the males in society than I already was made me strike out even harder and I kicked Sloan square in the gut as he parried my blade.

Sloan danced to the side and went to kick at my knee, but I shifted away, slicing at his unguarded side. He caught the blade before it struck, but I saw his eyes widen in the metal mask. His claw hand came up and grabbed for my blade, but I parried and struck for his stomach. He barely blocked it in time.

The blade in my hand danced like a graceful wind. My muscles moved on instinct and for a moment I was impressed at how my body reacted once my mind was taken out of the equation. I would have to figure out a way to use that in the future.

If I *had* a future.

Sloan took a chance and chopped at my head with his blade. I curved my upper body to the side, fluid and sure, before spinning to knock his legs out from under him. I finished the spin and jumped; my blade pointed at his exposed neck. My body jerked as though someone had tossed a noose around my neck.

Chapter 17

Despite the fact that it was dulled, the tip of the cutlass in my hand pricked the soft skin of Sloan's neck. My body spasmed once from what I could only assume was a stop command on whatever the device was in Vanyik's hand. A tiny stream of red ran down from just beneath his Adam's apple, where the mask ended, to the floor of the stage beneath him. Sloan swallowed hard, his pupils dilated, and his blue eyes locked on mine. I could imagine the emptiness he saw there, the lack of reaction or emotion in my kill blues. I saw fear sing from his eyes despite the fact he'd fallen partially into the shadows, but I could do nothing but stand as I was. The last command sent to my body locked me in place while Sloan's eyes told me he had no idea that I wasn't acting on my own behalf.

Just because I threatened to kill him the first chance I got to escape didn't mean he had to take it all so seriously. The look in his eyes told me exactly which conversations he was reliving as I stood over him.

I heard the chancellor open the bidding to a frenzy of voices behind me. I told myself to step back, to pull the blade up, but I couldn't. Moisture dripped down my face while the tug continued around my neck, not pulling me back but not letting me move. I could barely breathe. I felt my muscles shaking at the strain of stillness. I stared down at Sloan. My knuckles whitened while my palms grew slick and I worried that the blade would come loose and do the one thing I hadn't been commanded to. I didn't so much as twitch.

Suddenly, like a child's toy, my arms were drawn back, and I bowed. The blade was taken from my hand and I turned sharply on my heel, my back to Sloan as I turned to face down the bidding war in the room.

I could make out some of the faces in the room, the madness in them a hunger. Inside, part of me tried to shrink back while my body remained as steady as the sun. My spine was rigid with artificially induced steel and my blue eyes were blank. I was a toy for the adult children of wealth in the Alliance to purchase and play with at their will.

My father watched me. I felt his eyes and their shrewd assessment of me from where he stood on the stage to my left. He wasn't bidding but was waiting for the weaker hearts to sputter out. I could see the calculation in his frame as he waited; he knew that nothing would stop him from obtaining his prize. Even if there was a *chance* that he might be outbid, it would take no more than a look from him to turn the offending party away. It was all just a power game. One I was set to lose no matter what.

"One million units, Chancellor," my father said, his voice soft. Despite the volume, it cut through the throng like a whip and I imagined several gentry flinching away from the bid or my father or both. I felt the quick movement of the chancellor beside me as he slapped the shell-like gavel on the raised dais.

Aside from just giving a high bid, there was something else, I could sense it. The bid felt more like a signal from my father to the chancellor. A deal had been struck behind closed doors, in dark alleys with knives to pale throats. The deal had been shaken upon on with those words. No one else spoke. No one dared.

"Sold to Admiral Low for the sum of one million units," the chancellor called, and I saw his arm wave out of the corner of my eye, signaling the end of the auction for my soul.

Vanyik walked at my side and I could hear the unusually heavy clunk of Sloan somewhere behind me. My father met us at the edge of the staging area and gave a gentlemanly bow that made me wish I could kick him in the throat.

At least my fantasies were still under my own control.

"Captain Sloan, if you would take the controller from the Voyag?" Daddy-dearest made an elegant motion toward Vanyik, though his eyes caught on the creature with a look of venom.

"Oh now, let's not be rude--"

"*Now*, Voyag. I will have my slave and be done with your presence," Low growled but the accent still made it sound courteous despite the underlying hostility.

Vanyik turned and handed the device to Sloan, who looked at the odd black box for a very long time. Vanyik hastened to give my father whispered instructions for basic control and offered warnings about trying to give too many commands at once. I listened intently when I heard the harried tone of voice, but no indication was given as to what would happen with too many commands.

"Vocal command works well with the controller. It's quite brilliant--"

"Enough. To me, Captain Sloan," Low curled his lip at Vanyik and plucked the controller from Sloan's hands. I wondered if he feared taking something from Vanyik or just didn't want to dirty his hands by dealing with a voyag. Then, Low stepped ahead of us; the people who had gathered to watch me come down from the stage drew back like the tide before Moses.

Sloan didn't dare speak to me, but I saw him focused on the controller in Low's hand so much that I think he almost tripped at one point. His skin, from what I could see at a side angle, was still damp and his shirt collar clung to his neck where it had been dyed red with his blood.

"It's a lucky turn that you're here," Low said as soon as the doors closed behind us. We'd paused as a group of servants entered the hall carrying trays of refreshments and food. Apparently, the gathered gentry was ready to either celebrate their gains or commiserate their losses in the auction. I wondered that Low didn't want to stay and gloat at his assumptive triumph over winning me. As if it would have gone any other way.

"Come. We'll adjourn to my suites to celebrate our victories: yours in bringing the treasure beside us, and mine in acquiring it." Low motioned to someone off to the side who scurried ahead of us, just shy of a run.

I noted his use of it instead of she or calling me by my name. It didn't surprise me that I was an object. I had a strong feeling that as an object I could be labeled a pawn with what he likely had planned for me.

"Oh! But I forget myself. Perhaps you would like to freshen up, Captain?" Low's eyes danced over Sloan's collar as though catching a glimpse of something inappropriate. One of his dark eyebrows arched up and the edge of his mouth curled under the wave of his mustache.

"Of course," Sloan bowed and paused. "Perhaps I'll just escort Mag... your winnings to your rooms, first?"

"Yes, yes of course," he waved a hand in the air around us as though giving the royal blessing for Sloan to continue in his duties. The strut I saw in his gait should have been sickening, but he made even that look elegant. I wondered how often he had to practice to become so adept at his calculated courtliness.

We moved through the halls and instead of a decrease in elegance that marked my descent into the bowels of the Alliance building, the luxury spread like an invasive alga. Precious gems sparkled from ornamentation on the walls or within hardware on tables. Chairs were velvet lined and embroidered with fine thread that likely would have been worth as much as the rest with the jewel tones. Light trickled in from windows in various rich shades at the upper arches with exotic scenes detailed at eye-level. It felt almost like a place of worship and I wondered if I wasn't far off in that comparison. A place not to reach for higher powers like Odah, god of the sea traveler, but to reach for the never-ending ideology of the Alliance: money.

We rounded a corner and found double doors opened and awaiting our arrival. Various servants came forward like flies drawn to a stink. One young man rushed forward to take the coat Low shrugged out of. From the way the servant shifted the coat, with its heavy brocade and ornamentation, it must have weighed several pounds.

I mentally shook my head at the ridiculous marks of power that men in the Alliance wore. Sadly, it wasn't far off from what women did with fine gowns cut high or low meant to mark their marital or societal status.

Peacockery was all it was, no matter who wore it. For Low, it was a tool to intimidate and he used it well. He glared at the older servant that came forward and knelt to take Low's boots off before replacing them with some sort of silk shoe. Apparently, my father was disappointed in the speed with which he was attended to.

As soon as the gray-haired servant was done bowing and scraping, he moved to do the same to my feet. I felt like a shy horse being shod. My body didn't seem to know that it didn't need to keep weight on the lifted foot and I almost fell. The shoes were soft pillows of fabric around my feet and immediately felt too warm against my skin. I wished I could kick them off. Preferably in a way that injured someone if that was even possible.

"Tonight, we shall dine, and you can tell me all about your journey to bring Magerious to me, Captain Sloan," Low waved the servants away. "It will be a casual affair. Please do not come in the ridiculous officer regalia that seems to be the only acceptable dining apparel in this place. I will take it as a personal insult."

Sloan bowed and stepped backward to the still-opened doors. Low turned his back and walked several steps to a sideboard where he picked up a drink that had been waiting. His back was to me, as though I was nothing of consequence. If I'd had my magic, he'd have died on the spot. Instead, I stood, playing statue in slippers as my only hope for escape bowed his way from the room behind me.

I felt Sloan's presence as it lingered behind me and I knew he was taking too long to leave. I didn't know if he was waiting for me to acknowledge him or if he was trying to puzzle things out, but I just hoped that Low didn't look back and catch him. The door clicked behind the captain and echoed the closing of the prison doors I'd grown accustomed to. It was just as ominous despite the sparkle and shine in the room.

"Darling daughter. I had hoped our second meeting would be a bit happier," Low's voice called from my right. He appeared in front of me, the strange controller in his palm. "Let us see if this device is as simple as the Voyag insists."

He pushed a button. "Follow me."

My legs moved, and I kept pace several steps behind him like an obedient, kept woman. I felt my rage rise. I wanted to hiss, spit, and behave like an enraged alley cat but my body would allow no such reaction. *Obey*. I could only follow and obey.

"Be seated," Low ran his thumb across the control and pointed at a luxurious chair of heavy vermillion brocade and pale wood gilded with hand carvings. My body took a stiff posture as it sat in the seat. I could feel the plush cushions beneath me trying to pull me down, but it was as though I sat on a board adjusted a few inches above the seat.

"My servants will see to your dress and grooming for the moment. I am certain I sense your fire, my darling Maggy, and know you will not appreciate their efforts." He gave a broad wave of his hand for a moment before his posture shifted. He clenched his fist and dropped it to his side.

"This situation and having servants handle you like a helpless babe cannot be helped until I get a better grasp on how to control you with this infernal device."

He peered down at the control before leaning forward to stare into my face. I didn't bother trying to look at him or even look away, but my skin crawled when he ran his finger along my face.

"You will allow their ministrations until you are cleaned and presentable. Hopefully, that is enough instruction. Oh, and in case this isn't hardwired into the control: you will not speak, harm anyone, or attempt to escape. I expect to return to see my prized child ready to receive company."

Inside, I spit in his face. Outwardly, I stood as servants entered the room, bowed once, and then I was led to another room.

When I returned to the main sitting room in Low's suite, my hair had been trimmed so that it was evenly shaped around my jawline in a sloping angle that followed the curve of my jaw. I missed the length I'd had, but at least I no longer looked like I'd had my hair cut with a rudder blade. I was dressed in loose harem-type pants that seemed to be a style favored for Low's servants. The only distinction between my clothing and that of most of his servants was a ruffled shirt with extensive tails adorned with a silk and bone corset. The boots that completed the ensemble were almost exactly what I would have picked to wear underway and I could imagine kicking in some skulls with their shining steel-tips.

The servants had been non-reactive in their handling and dressing of me, much to my relief. It was akin to watching someone make the bed: quick, efficient, and without any sort of emotional reaction. The bath would have been mortifying were it not for the concise approach to the entire affair. As it was, I could tell myself that I was not really a participant in any of it since I couldn't react, speak, or assist in any of what was being done. It was like being caught up in some sort of bad dream that wouldn't allow you to participate. Despite the outrageous outfit and helplessness, it was nice to feel well and truly clean.

It didn't stop the urge to rail and scream from where I was locked inside my fleshy cage. I would happily be a grown woman throwing a temper tantrum if I could react.

"My daughter! You look marvelous. I can imagine taking to the seas with you at my side, as I always hoped." Low stepped forward and lifted both of my hands, raising them to his lips. I felt the brush of his whiskers against my fingers and cringed inwardly at the contact. It was too bad that lack of control over my person didn't include a lack of feeling. Perhaps Vanyik would find time to ask for my input about the experience of being a mindless slave so I could give him some recommendations.

Or cut his head off. I was fine with either.

"Let me escort you."

Low spoke as though there was nothing unusual about steering someone around the room. He tucked my hand into the crook of his elbow and walked me into a spacious dining room with a massive table laid out with enough food for a party. I wondered how many guests he was planning to have but recognized the political ploy. He planned to show off his possession to further consolidate his position within the Alliance and grow as a power in his own right. His actions were wholly transparent.

"You will sit here, at my right, as you always should have. May I tell you a secret, my darling?" He leaned in and then laughed. "Not that you will be able to tell anyone, but I digress. I will teach you to become my strongest captain! The implant will keep you under control until I see fit to release you. You will eventually see my way of things, dear heart. You don't know everything I've done for you, but you *will* see."

I felt my jaw twitch and felt the slightest hope that I'd caused it with the desire to kill him rising within me. It was more likely just a spasm from musculature and nerves being restrained by the implant.

"I've done this for you, my sweet Maggy. I've built all that I have to one day put you in the position that I hold," he leaned forward as he spoke, placing his chin on his hand like a lovesick boy. I had a brief fear that I wouldn't be able to fight the urge to vomit and my overly controlled body would make me choke to death on it. A servant filled the doorway of the dining room and Low released me.

"Admiral Low, your guests are arriving."

"Thank you. Captain Magerious...I get ahead of myself...Magerious and I will receive them in the formal sitting room," Low stood and reached for my arm, tucking it again into his own.

Chapter 18

L ow easily steered me from the seat at the table to the next room. It was filled with low chatter and forced-casual movements from players in whatever game my father seemed to be engineering.

My eyes skimmed across the group and took in the stiff postures and tight lips. Apparently, a party with my father was all that I expected it would be. The only smiles I saw were closer to something a giant dragonfish would do before attempting to eat a person alive. It occurred to me that I might be the next meal for Low's guests.

The wealth of the crowd was noticeable in the same subtle way one would acknowledge a steam horn to the ear. Women had gems dripping from ears, necks, fingers, and wrists. Some even had mixes of metal and gemstones attached to various piercings on their faces. One woman had ridges in place of her eyebrows that were tipped with what looked like a very expensive cut of emeralds. The men were equally adorned but with a more understated hint of wealth that was nonetheless enhanced by posture and pose.

In the midst of sparkle and glitter, I felt a distinct lack of something that nagged at my consciousness for a moment as my eyes took in everything around me. When

I realized what it was, I gave a mental shrug at the obviousness: no one laughed or flirted.

The room was filled with calculating humanoid beasts that watched as Low paraded me through the room. When my dead blue gaze caught on the movement of men and women, the looks they gave me were all the same: appraisal. One after another, their eyes gave a quick flick that became a slow draw of the chin as they took me in from head to toe. Freak viewing over, they moved on with the migration of the crowd. It was a dismissal for certain, but also an acknowledgement not to get too close to the admiral's new plaything.

I turned my head just slightly to meet a challenging gaze from a high-ranking officer that didn't immediately step back when we passed. Though I couldn't glare or posture, apparently the lack of emotion in my eyes was enough to make him think better of it and he, too, stepped back after a moment. I wondered if he'd meant to say something to my father or just wanted a better view of the show. Whatever his intent, it was forgotten in his haste.

When a woman dropped a glass on the floor, I followed the path with my eyes before looking back to see her expression. Dead gaze aside, the movement was *my* reaction and it surprised me for a moment. I flicked my eyes to a painting on the wall to see if it was movement or truly my own control making my gaze shift. Though the thoughtful shift was a little sluggish at first, like trying to wake up from a deep sleep or focus over-tired eyes after a long day in the sun, I did it. My eyes landed on a garishly bright painting of a bowl of food but caressed the lines of color and shape as though they were a gorgeous naked man.

I waited until Low was a few steps ahead of me before I tried to turn my face. When I was able to, I started thinking about the small shifts. The only conclusion I came to was that the commands to be tended to by the servants had loosened something in me. Perhaps Low's commands had been too vague or perhaps the implant was like any new technology that would eventually lose some of its strength after the initial start-up. Either way, I kept my movements stiff and forced to keep my father from noticing.

It was a relief to have that small freedom instead of being locked in the stiff posture of the servile that I thought would be part of my torment. I could narrow my eyes or turn my head from side to side, though not with any haste unless something startled me like the dropped glass. Apparently, if it was an instinctual move, I could react. I just couldn't speak out of turn or push for a facial expression no matter how much I wanted to sneer or snarl at anyone. My gaze was dead and emotionless, but it was somewhat of a boon.

Eye contact was good. I could do a lot with clear eye contact. Navigating the crowd would be easier for one. The fish in the room were simply a school for Low to feed from when he felt the need. What they needed to realize that he wasn't the only shark in the water with them. I just needed to keep my head about it so that my father didn't catch on.

Sloan entered without the uniform and dressed to the nines. Sloan had obviously taken my father's thinly veiled threat to heart. His chosen attire, unlike the flair and flouncy ruffles that Low had donned and attired me in, was starched with clean lines and dark colors. He looked like white clouds had met deep blue ocean and then was sliced with the titanium blade that was his head. His clothing was pressed with fine stitching, but little embellishment and I wondered where he'd found it. The sleeves of his dress shirt were long and covered his metal arm to the wrist. His hair too, though short, seemed lighter. It made him look younger around the metal maw that covered his face. The dress trousers he wore completely hid the other metal replacement limb, but I heard the dull thunk of it as he moved.

If he was wearing a weapon other than the ever-present metal claw, it was built into the lines of his clothes. I could see no bulk or bunch of fabric. Even without an additional blade or cannon, if you considered Sloan's leg, claw, and head, he was a weapon sheathed in dress clothing.

The entire look was different and startling in the change it made to him. Everything from his shined shoes to the top of his head were different, though I had to wonder if I wasn't seeing him so changed because of the lack of such a hated uniform.

It was simple and elegant if it was a somewhat unnatural look for him. I watched him work his way through the crowd and wondered if he ever spent any time out of uniform. Not that I'd hoped to see him out of uniform. It had never even crossed my mind prior to that.

I wondered if I could still blush while mind controlled.

Sloan inclined his head here and there as he made his way through the room to where Low held court with me at his side. I watched him come toward us and wished I could tell him pretty much anything. Strange how much I wanted to be chatty now that I couldn't.

I knew from what Low hinted at in the dining room that something larger was at play. Sloan's sources were right about my father having some information, though how valuable it would be or how much of a maniacal plan it was, remained to be seen.

"Admiral Low," Sloan gave a deep bow, and my father inclined his head.

"Captain Sloan, welcome. You will take the seat at my left at dinner and then we will have drinks after to discuss that opportunity I mentioned," Low lifted a hand in the air and the room stilled. I had had similar reactions when I held up a blaster aboard my ship.

"Dinner is waiting. If you would all join me?"

Low steered me back to the dining room with Sloan a step behind us. Low motioned him forward and nodded at Sloan's slight bow. He released my arm and put pressure on my lower back to propel me forward to my assigned seat. Sloan saw the movement and deftly stepped around my father to hold out the seat for me. Low's eyebrows lowered for a moment and then his face lifted in a smile that would have made a fox worry.

"It's the young who remind us of our manners, is it not? Gentlemen, you should take your cue from the young captain and seat *your* ladies," Low seated himself.

There was a scramble around the room as men took positions to seat the lady nearest them, some doubling up or looking confused when they had no one to seat. It caused a spike of uneasiness to think that such a casual command from my father could make such a mass of people react so quickly. I also didn't care for the emphasis in his phrasing.

Sloan stepped away and moved back around the table. I really wanted to kick him for doing something that would draw Low's attention so completely. Instead, when he sat, I gave him a small nod and saw his eyes widen slightly before he looked away. I didn't know how to tell him what was going on, but I wanted him to know that some part of me was still here.

Servants started filling dishes for each guest according to what they said or pointed at from the trays at the center of the table. I could only incline my head.

"Magerious will have the same as me," Low told a servant who nodded and hurried away. My father looked at me and I saw his hand shift to his pocket for a moment, but his eyes never left mine.

"Eat, Maggy," he jutted his chin at me when a plate was placed before me. I wouldn't hazard to guess at half of what was on it, but my hand lifted, and I obeyed my father's command. He watched me eat a bit of everything from the dish and I had the awful feeling that part of my duty as his new slave was food-taster. My stomach roiled at the thought that I might end up giving my life for my bastard father. Low started eating before he turned to Sloan.

"Your quarters are impressive," Sloan said as conversations picked up around the table. "I feel as though I've seen them before...Isn't this the suites the King usually uses when he's here?"

"Charles? Yes. He rarely visits and the chancellor decided that my contributions equated to a suite that was equal to my stature," Low spoke between bites of food. Table manners were obviously one of the things he didn't practice. "The good man offered me his accommodations, to be honest. I, of course, turned him down."

I wondered if the force of my desire to roll my eyes would be enough to short out the implant. Sadly, I still found myself puppeting the commands given.

"That's right. When he visited last, he had all of the officers come by for drinks and smoke," Sloan nodded as he covered his glass with his hand when a servant tried to fill it with wine.

"I don't recall," Low's voice had taken on a sharp edge and I wondered if he'd not been invited to the soiree/meeting. "It is of little significance. Tell me about your voyage. There have been rumors that Magerious got loose from her restraints and a mutiny occurred aboard your vessel. *The Dragon* was it?"

"*Draconis*," Sloan supplied. The plate in front of him remained empty. Low eyed it once or twice. "Maggy didn't get loose at any point, though she did have a few run-ins with other prisoners and crew. It's all normal for an Alliance cargo transport."

"We are all adults here, Captain Sloan. It is an Alliance slave ship, your *Draconis*," Low lifted a glass of deep-red wine to his mouth and I found myself mirroring the movement, much to my displeasure. It wasn't that I didn't like wine, or any alcohol for that matter, but I certainly didn't like that I was in any way inclined toward copying the bastard.

Over the rim of my goblet, I watched the shift in Sloan's eyes at Low referring to the Draconis as a slave vessel. It was the truth, but I don't think the captain liked the implication. When his gaze shifted to me, it lost some of the tension. I cut my eyes to Low's jacket pocket and wondered if I could somehow get Sloan to pick it.

It was a stupid thought. Sloan needed information, even if it meant leaving me under the control of my genocidal father for a while. He'd never learn anything from Low if he took away his new favorite toy.

"I notice that you do not eat, Captain Sloan. Is the meal not to your liking?"

I felt the hush around us as several of the bejeweled guests quieted to hear the response. I probably would have stopped as well. No doubt they had all heard something about Sloan's mask and were hoping for a bit of entertainment if Low decided to press the issue. I felt my blood rise at the thought that anyone else would have to be entertainment for my bastard father.

"The food looks wonderful, Admiral Low. Unfortunately, with this," he gestured at his metal-plated head, "I cannot eat in polite company. I need to reserve that for a time when I wouldn't put others off their meals."

Soft chatter began again when Low nodded and took another sip from his glass, which I again mirrored. *Bastard.* Oh well, maybe he was in the mood to get rip-roaring drunk. That would be something I could fully support.

"I had heard that you were disfigured somehow and that the mask is a precaution against your...illness?... Getting worse," Low tapped at his chin with his index finger. "Can't it be treated with the current level of nanite technology?"

If a metal face could frown, Sloan's would have been.

"Admiral Low, something tells me you know the answer to that," Sloan put his hand up when a well-meaning servant, who hadn't been listening, stepped forward to fill a glass with water.

"I suppose that's true," Low smiled. "Perhaps another time, then."

"As you say," Sloan inclined his head, and I felt his gaze touch on me for a moment. "May I take this opportunity to thank you for your invitation to dinner? It's seldom that a lowly Alliance captain is given the opportunity to dine at your illustrious table."

There went that gag reflex again. Men and their melodramatics.

Low waved the comment away. "Perhaps we can get back to the story? I had heard that there was a mutiny onboard the *Draconis* of some sort? You say that Maggy didn't escape, so what happened?"

Low cut into his food and watched Sloan as the man relayed the *improved* version of the tale. At no point was my part in the tale hinted at, instead the focus was on the escaped prisoners, including the feral humans, and the bloodshed that occurred. Several utensils clunked down on plates near us as Sloan discussed the battle. He left most of the gore out, but I guess the hint of it was too much for some of the guests' sensitive stomachs.

Sloan concluded the embellished story with the bravery of his surviving crew and the loss of his first mate's life to protect me. I didn't care for that part.

Richter having saved my life was a bit too far-fetched, but I wasn't the one telling the story.

"Maggy, I cannot help but think you would like to add something," my father shifted his black gaze to me, and I saw the minute movement of his hand under the table. "Tell me: what do you think of what Captain Sloan has said?"

My jaw released as though it had been sewn shut and someone had cut the strings. I drew in a breath and thought of all the nasty things I wanted to say. I felt what Low wanted in his inquiry but hadn't voiced in his command. Thankfully, I snatched at his loose wording before speaking.

"I think that the captain has done an excellent job of relaying the tale," I picked up my wine glass, again mirroring my father, and took a sip. Low's dark eyes didn't leave my face as we both drank from our glasses.

"Just so," Low said softly as he replaced his glass. A servant rushed forward to refill it before stepping back.

The rest of the meal was filled with idle chit-chat between my father, Captain Sloan, and a few well-dressed guests that inquired about various aspects of Alliance trade and slave running. One of the guests asked me a question about the storm we weathered during the voyage, but I could only stare him down since my father hadn't given me any additional commands to speak. It made the poor man shake for a moment before his eyes dropped and he played with his food. I caught Sloan watching the interaction. Low was distracted as he gave directions to a servant and missed the look.

A mountain of exotic and overly indulgent food later, the meal concluded. Several guests approached my father and commented about me. Two different guests went so far as congratulating him on his winning bid. They probably thought it was what he wanted to hear and seemed to be a good bet from the way his chin lifted a notch and his lips curled. I imagined the cat after eating the mouse that had almost escaped.

Guests left the dining area and sitting room in steady streams. Not that I blamed them, but no one seemed inclined to stay and while away their time with my father. One or two spoke business, which I took note of in my statue-state. Some shared personal information and gossip with Low despite my standing right beside him. Apparently, in the same way they treated servants, I was assumed to be deaf to their dealings.

Low waved them all off with flowery words and grand gestures despite the diminished group. He motioned Sloan forward, summoning him to where he'd been speaking with an older woman and her young, officer escort. I recognized them both from my walk through the hallway at Sloan's side from that morning. Had it really been earlier in the same day?

The woman was again, or still, adorned in her heavy armor of sparkly items and the young man looked me up and down like I was a steak. Keeping my gaze away from him was a struggle when I wanted to stab him with my eyes.

Low continued his conversation with them without acknowledging or introducing Sloan once the captain reached my father's side. I wanted to speak to the metal-mawed man, but my jaw was once again wired shut.

It wouldn't have mattered. Had I spoken to him, it would have drawn Low's attention and I didn't need any more of that right then. I actually preferred being treated like furniture since I couldn't make my presence meaningful enough to kick the old man's ass.

Sloan, however, kept positioning himself to watch me. I caught his gaze more than once. His blue eyes were piercing with intent swirling around in them. I still hadn't decided if he was friend or foe in all of this, but I did my best to play blind.

When Low and the gentry finished their chat, the old woman looked through me while the young man made sure to brush against me as he escorted her away. My gallant father chose to ignore the blatant attempt to feel me up. The visitor was just fluffing the pillows on Low's new furniture when his hand grazed me, I guess.

I had a brief image of checking the working order of his family jewels with a wrench in return.

"Captain Sloan, will you adjourn with me to the terrace? Can I tempt you into joining me for a lovely aged whiskey?"

"Very gracious of you, Admiral." Sloan followed my father who motioned for me as well.

His terrace was around the same size as the main deck of my ship, the *MadCap*. Beyond the ornate balustrade, it boasted an expansive view of the Alliance holding we were housed in. We were probably the same distance from the ground as being in the crow's nest of the ship. Height and direction gave a feeling of isolation but made the breeze cool and the evening peaceful despite proximity to the small town that housed the compound. The ocean was a glittering gemstone in the distance only hinted at with brine on the wind.

One servant waited, almost blending in from his spot on the wall near the doorway, like a potted plant. Drinks were poured and waiting.

"Please, each of you, take a glass and enjoy," Low gestured before he picked his up and strolled to the railing, waiting for us to join him.

Sloan lifted a drink to hand it to me, but my hand was already reaching for the other glass. I wondered how much of my reactions would become intuitive to what my father the slaver wanted. How much of myself would I lose in the process? I tossed back the drink and, in my haste, sloshed some on the frilled shirt and corset. I set down the glass so that the near-invisible servant could step forward and refill it. From the corner of my eye, I saw my father's mouth turn down. The servant handed me a newly replenished glass.

"Sip, Maggy," Low's words were drawn out with his annoyance. He lifted his own glass to his lips, smelled the contents for a moment before taking a small drink as if he were showing me proper drinking etiquette. My body dutifully mirrored him, and I stepped forward to the railing. Sloan was already there, so I was forced to take a position between the two men as though guarding one from the other. Was I given an inherent command or was it something more?

Low's dark gaze snagged on the sloshed amber liquid on my blouse and his lip curled. He motioned for the servant, with a frigid look centered on me.

"Take Magerious to get cleaned up," he snapped his fingers, pulled out the remote for a moment and then looked at me. "Go with the servant and freshen up, my pet."

It was probably one of the most correct endearments he'd ever used with me, I thought as I walked away. Pet or slave worked fine in this...whatever it was we had. Daughter or dearest were earned and/or reciprocated but he hadn't earned shit and I sure as hell didn't reciprocate.

The servant rushed me along, but my feet felt no such compunction and I smiled inwardly at the almost-rebellious response of my body. It wasn't actual rebellion so much as just a lack of clear command, but it gave me a jolt of pleasure just the same.

When we returned, the servant positioned me at the door and hurried back to get something. More whiskey or tobacco or swords so the two men could fight to the death. Maybe a measuring stick? I didn't know and I couldn't ask even if I wanted to. With lack of clear command, I was frozen in place to eavesdrop.

"Captain Sloan, I want you to join my fleet," Low said. "The chancellor has given me leave to make the assignments and I've heard of your outstanding record. Excluding today's tardiness, of course."

I snorted internally at the intended jab. The bastard was really good at knocking someone down a heartbeat after a compliment.

"I'm honored, Admiral Low." I could imagine Sloan inclining his head at my father.

"You have proven to be valuable in keeping my Maggy safe and bringing her to me."

There was that gag reflex again and I contemplated trying to find a way to encourage it just so I could choke to death. My father spoke as though Sloan had brought me from a nearby city on a leisurely carriage ride instead of from an Alliance prison and sold like cattle.

To *him*.

"It was my duty, Admiral," Sloan's voice had that smooth quality that I'd learned hid most of what he was thinking. I still thought he practiced it. Of course, if he was trying to undermine the current Alliance ruling body, that might be a necessary action on his part.

"As I was only doing my job, I'm not sure I'm worthy of such an honor," Sloan hedged. He really should have known that modesty would just make my father demand him more until it became an outright command.

"You did your job commendably. It is time you take a position more reflective of your skills," Low's approving tone made me feel like this was them rehearsing a script. Did they cue each other with gestures or just count out the beats between their lines?

"It's a weighty offer, Admiral. I beg your indulgence in letting me have some time to decide?"

Oh Sloan, you can't play politics with this man, he'll see through it, I raised my eyes and wished I could sigh. The silence stretched on for too long as Low tried to make Sloan squirm for not accepting the offer immediately. I couldn't see them, but I could feel the tension like needle-pricks to my skin.

"You will have time to consider it, yes." Low paused and I imagined him taking a sip from his glass. "Until then, I want you to help me do something about Maggy."

"I'm sorry?"

If Sloan had been drinking whiskey, he would have choked on his surprise. I felt a smile itch at my skin when I heard his smooth tone slip a notch.

"You fight well and have had time to see what she's capable of."

There was a pause and I imagined one or more scrutinizing glares passing between the men.

"But we will need to break Maggy of some of her spirit if she is ever to be useful to me."

"I don't know that I can help with that, Admiral. The combat display during the auction should have shown you that she is a formidable opponent," Sloan's tone leveled out. I imagined him either tapping his fingers on his arm or itching at his cheek over the metal.

"I saw it in the way that she looked at you, Captain Sloan -- both when you brought her in and again at dinner. There is something going on between my daughter and you. I wish to exploit it. Or more correctly, I wish for you to exploit it."

Chapter 19

The servant returned and opened the door in front of me. My father motioned me in.

"My dear, you've returned just in time to escort Captain Sloan out," Low's lips flashed white teeth under his dark whiskers. "Please escort Captain Sloan to the door and you may adjourn to your room for the night."

I saw the remote in his hand and felt my body curve into a graceful bow at the waist that had me shooting mental steam cannons at the bastard. My eyes must have darkened a little because when I came up, Low smiled wider.

So much for keeping my little freedoms to myself.

"Tomorrow we will go see that Voyag as well. I must commend him on his good work, vile creature that he is. Terribly clever, this creation of his," Low's voice dripped with contempt that undermined any true compliment. Would he restrain himself when he saw Vanyik, or would that be too much of a bother? I had good reasons for not wanting to face the creature, but my father's general sense of privilege over others was reprehensible.

"Oh, and Maggy?" My father's address filled me with foreboding. "Please feel free to converse with Captain Sloan as you escort him. I am not, after all, a monster."

I opened my mouth to tell him what I thought of that, feeling my jaw freed and realized he hadn't said anything about speaking to him. I blinked and turned away as Sloan stepped forward. The servant closed the door behind us.

"Don't tell me anything, Maggy," Sloan whispered.

"I was going to give you the same warning," my voice felt strange. The movement of my vocal cords felt like I was gurgling gravel. "That rat bastard has ears everywhere in case we had anything of substance to discuss. Though, I don't mind sharing how I feel about him. Loudly and violently if possible."

Sloan cleared his throat and my muscles held back the grin.

"I didn't know," Sloan's voice dropped to barely above a whisper. All of the smooth confidence I was used to from him was stripped away and I turned to look at him. His eyes were so wide through the eye holes of the mask that they looked like Caribbean water.

I looked away from the raw appeal for forgiveness in his eyes and shook my head.

"Just be glad I didn't kill you," I narrowed my eyes and pictured the red stain on his collar. "Don't apologize to me for anything. I may kill you yet."

"I thought, at first--"

"Stop. Say nothing that can be used against either one of us." I glanced at him and saw him jerk his chin once and turn so that I was looking at his profile. Looking in his eyes made me afraid and uncomfortable in a way that made me want to apologize to him for something that I had no control over. I knew I should be blaming him for my predicament, but I found that I didn't and that annoyed me further.

At least Sloan understood that the freedom to speak, the 'gift' from Low, was to gauge Sloan's loyalties. He probably hoped that either the captain would say something nasty to me and out his opinion of me, or that he'd say something sweet or caring and show a possible weakness in his future employee.

"I can't react, still," I told him in a low tone. "Do you have any idea what it's like to want to smile or growl or snarl and your face stays so still it's as though it were frozen?"

"Yes."

My head snapped to the side when I realized what I'd said, and I cringed inwardly.

"Right. Sorry."

"Did you just apologize to me?" Sloan's tone was light, and it made me want to smile again. Damn. Being without reaction for a day was giving me a hard-on for smiles.

"Don't get used to it. I think I'm just relieved to be speaking at all," I admitted.

"So, you have absolutely no control?" His voice was conversational as though he was discussing the lovely summer breeze, or the delightful smoke of the whiskey Low had given him. Not that he'd drank any of it, I'm sure.

I gave him a bit of side-eye which was the best I could do to let him know that I wouldn't be able to tell him exactly what I'd learned about my implant. I took a deep breath. How to make him understand?

"I must do exactly what Low tells me, exactly the way he tells me to," I met his eyes, willing him to read between the lines. His head nodded once. "If he were to say, go jump out that window, right there, right this moment, I would do exactly that."

"I see. He's right; that it is a terribly clever device."

"Just so," I mimicked my father. "I cannot get a *break*. Not with *you*. Not with anything."

Please, please, please get that reference, I thought, my eyes catching his again. I wanted him to know that I'd heard their conversation and understood what Low intended Sloan to do. I wanted him to understand that I was willing to go along with whatever emotional connection Low thought I'd made with Sloan if it meant we'd have a chance to escape somehow. I would play smitten if it would help us.

Not that I was sure I even knew how to do that much. Vicious, bitchy, angry...I could do those. Love? I'd never tried it and only ever seen stupidity out of those around me who had. I wanted to sigh or snarl, but it would have been an impotent gesture.

Not being able to say exactly what I meant was painful. I'd never been interested in keeping my thoughts to myself prior to that moment. The flip side of it was that sharing everything I could would just cause new problems. I'd never been subtle; I didn't know how to start.

Unfortunately, a servant unfurled himself from where he'd been doing his best to blend into the furnishings and stepped forward to open the door to the hallway.

Sloan faced me and winked before he lifted my right hand, pressing my knuckles to his chin as he bowed. The cold brush of metal touched my knuckles for a moment. He released my hand and quickly stepped from the room, the doors closing behind him. It left the lingering smell of the sea and an odd warmth that remained on my fingertips.

The following morning, servants dressed me in an outfit almost identical to what I'd worn to dinner. We'd gone to Vanyik first thing, where Low left me in the hall with a stay command. He asked something about the controller before shutting me out, so I imagine that's what the discussion revolved around. Locking me out was probably the smartest thing I'd seen him do up to that point. Maybe part of him had come to the realization that I wasn't a bought and paid-for servant that would never discuss what he did or said. Of course, I doubted many of the servants held back much, either.

The command he gave me was simple. So much so that, it hadn't prevented me from shifting around a little or looking around the hallway. It was a strange sensation to have a little freedom but nothing substantial enough to do something about my situation.

I wondered if he even realized that he'd left wiggle room in the command. I wished I could ask Vanyik questions. It wouldn't have been a good idea though as he might see it as an opportunity for improvement of his device. I did not want him to tweak the controller or implant and end up with even less freedom.

When Low came out, he led me to the chancellor's meeting rooms. I saw Sloan once in passing and my jaw unlocked. I knew I could have spoken if I'd wanted to. Something in the initial release command of the night before had given me that freedom. I was in no hurry to let Low know about it and kept my lips locked whenever I saw the captain.

I'd been marched to another area of the villa and positioned behind my father's chair as he attended meetings. I tried to focus on what was being said, but it just seemed like a bunch of made-up words. Capital. Streamlining. Venture.

At one point, I perked up when they said "holding" because I hoped they were going to spill some structural weaknesses or something to the building. Instead they started talking about some deal they had with someone somewhere about some crap.

Instead, I focused on "streamlining." It made me think of the wind running perfectly along a sail. It was a peaceful image that I tried to lock onto as I waited for time to pass.

From what I could tell, my job was to stand behind Low and look like some sort of vicious guard dog. I had free-range of movement for my eyes and head, so it made it easier when he pushed a button on that damned controller and spoke at one of the men or women in the room for me to shift and stare them down. I wondered what they thought when we moved in tandem due to the remote. Did any of them even realize it was simply because of a remote, or was control over me in this way part of the game Low was playing?

"Thank you, Chancellor Willett," Low stood and shook the man's hand. "I have several other things to attend to today. I will have a short list of possible captains to you this evening."

"I look forward to seeing what you've come up with," the chancellor nodded and watched as Low and I walked from the meeting room.

"Ah, Captain Sloan."

Sloan was outside the meeting hall when we exited. I felt that familiar release but ignored it, letting my eyes meet his for less than a heartbeat. I clenched the muscles in my jaw as if fighting against the restraint of the implant. I didn't know if it would fool Low if he decided to check me for a reaction.

"I see you received my message. I hope I'm not keeping you from anything?" He said the words, but Low's gaze made me believe he couldn't care less what he kept the captain from.

"Just time off, Admiral Low," Sloan's reply had the edge of my mouth twitching into a smirk. It was such a shock that it took me a moment to realize I'd reacted. Everything was such a careful play, that, as I struggled to get the reaction from my face, I tried to keep my head faced away. Thankfully neither man seemed to notice.

"We are men of action, Captain Sloan. Time off is best reserved for when we reach our eternal sleep."

Yeah, yeah, sleep when you're fish food. I groaned in my head and locked my eyes on the hallway ahead of us. It was strange how quickly I suddenly seemed to be reacting. Yesterday, I don't think I could have sneezed without Low giving me permission. Just that morning, my face had felt frozen when I tried to speak to a servant. Now, I was suddenly working at maintaining a good poker face.

I caught movement out of the corner of my eye and realized that my father was holding the controller in his right hand. I wouldn't put it past him to loosen the noose a bit on me just to see what happened. Maybe that's something he had learned from Vanyik. Then again, maybe he just had a nervous tic that had him tapping the controller with his thumb. All people have some tells if you know when and how to watch for them. If this was his, maybe I would actually be able to bluff my way through his game.

"I need Maggy run through some combat scenarios and think you would be the best partner to work with her," Low gestured grandly for a moment before tapping his fingers together.

I had a sudden urge to bark like a dog at the way he was planning for Sloan to put me through combat paces. I could imagine the surprise on Low's face, and I had to fight back the grin.

"I have acquired a sparring room for you, but I can't stay to watch you two play. I have another meeting, I must attend, sadly." Low made a small gesture and a marshal came down the hall and stopped in front of him. He gave a deep bow.

"Ah yes, Marshal Ebora will accompany you both to the training rooms," he turned to me. "You will run fighting scenarios with Captain Sloan. Marshal Ebora will take you both to the training hall."

"Maggy, my pet, Captain Sloan will not go easy on you. I expect to hear that you used your skill to best him.

You will not fight to *kill*, but you will fight your hardest. Marshal Ebora will supervise. Follow him."

I gave a deep bow and my father gestured toward the silver-haired marshal who seemed to be pet spy for the day. The man's face was flat-featured which was emphasized by his lack of expression.

If Low thought we were going to let down our guards just because he was out of the room, strategy was not his strong suit. Still, without him there, I could test some of the restraint in little ways without being caught or try to puzzle out a way to pass Sloan information.

I saw Vanyik coming down the hall and fought the urge to groan. Two sets of eyes tightened the leash a bit further, especially when one of them would be looking specifically for failings in the tech that controlled me.

"Ah, Voyag. You will have as you requested. Maggy and the captain will now head to fighting practice. You may observe."

Vanyik's normal expression of creepy joy tilted in a frown, but he reached out for the control in my father's hand. Low hesitated. He didn't like to share any of his toys. Typical.

"If the true control is through commands as you assured me, you do not need the device," Low tucked the controller in his pocket. "I will hold on to this and come to watch as soon as my next meeting comes to a conclusion."

I dropped quickly to a bow which Sloan and Vanyik mirrored. I had dropped first, much to my annoyance. Sloan's was practiced perfection while Vanyik's bow was hesitant and resentful. The creature's face was even more smooth without the child-like parody of a smile.

Ebora led us down the hall to a massive room. The room was an expansive hall that might have been a ballroom. The only humanoid figures in the room were a few sparring dummies that lined the walls. Sloan walked to a rack of weapons behind the dummies lined with blades, staves, whips, and various practice items. He reached up and pulled down two dulled cutlasses. I wondered if he was reliving the combat in the auction room when he looked at them. I know I was.

This time I was sure I could keep from jabbing him or drawing blood. For some reason, the thought of making him bleed again made my palms sweat.

To the left of the doors was a set of couches and chairs. Vanyik took a seat in the comfortable-looking accommodations. Ebora took up a military rest position just beside the seating, probably in case he needed to run at us, run from the room, or jump forward and strangle Vanyik. For the marshal, I'm sure those were all viable scenarios.

As I looked at the luxurious seats and ornamental tables, I wondered how often lords or ladies took their entertainment in watching others train to protect them. I wondered if they pitted good sailors against each other, betting at the outcome. Blood sport was probably the epitome of high entertainment for bored gentry if their treatment of those they considered beneath them was anything to go by. The bruised and scarred servants in the building whispered the silent evils in the walls to me. They say pirates are cruel, but we don't go for endless abuse. We fight: if you lose, you're either captured and dropped off somewhere, dead, or you become part of the crew.

Sloan brought the training weapons to the middle of the floor where I stood almost at attention as I waited. I was trying to forget that there were others watching us, waiting for one of us to get beaten bloody or do something otherwise noteworthy.

I focused on the metallic head framing pale blue eyes and tried to think of it as a simple bit of training. I liked training. My muscles were feeling lax from having been walked around like a puppet for a day. It would feel good to unroll my body and let the rage inside me stretch beyond my limbs. I no longer had an immediate urge to kill Sloan, but that didn't mean I wouldn't always be up for giving him a good ass kicking.

"Try to follow the rules of training combat if you would, Maggy?" Sloan's voice was low as he reached forward to hand me one of the weapons. I felt my mouth twitch as his comment made me think of the last time he and I had "trained."

I took the practice blade from his grasp and gave a courtly bow. I was able to add an extra bit of flourish to it. I'm sure Low would be pleased at the peacocking.

"Taking you down with a nut shot doesn't work with you, remember?" I whispered. Shock widened his eyes before they crinkled. I wanted to grin, and my face wanted to grin when I saw a smile in Sloan's eyes, but I bit down on my lip to keep my face bland. I shifted so that my back was to the two audience members and let my control slip a little.

"Ready to have your ass handed to you, Sloan?" I raised my voice and let one edge of my mouth curl up, being careful to position my body so that our watchers couldn't see my face. I saw Sloan's eyes crinkle again.

"I can't tell you how happy I am at the possibility, Maggy," he struck toward me, a feint that I slapped aside with a snort. The clang of the weapons was deafening in the cavernous, windowless room. I quickly realized the real reason Sloan had gone for metal practice swords over wooden ones.

"I can react and respond to you, now," I swiped back and forth in rapid blows, letting my voice dip under the sound of the strikes. "When Low gave me the command to speak to you last night, it freed something in me, I think."

Sloan whirled in front of me, spinning the blade toward me and I arched backward, dropping far enough that I almost touched the floor behind me. As I rose, he spun forward and got his metal arm around my waist, his practice blade coming toward my neck. I found myself in a dance-like dip with his blade coming toward me. I wedged my blade up before he could strike. I could feel my muscles bunching as the strength of my father's command to fight this man pushed at me, killing any hesitation. I pushed up, but Sloan spun me to get behind me, his blade sliding free of mine. His metal arm was a vice around my waist that I was struggling to break free from.

"I will figure out a way to free you from this," Sloan squeezed with his claw, causing pain and distraction. He whispered into my ear, his body locked against my back as he fought to free his weapon and strike. I elbowed him in the stomach and dropped, kicking backwards at him, going for his inner thigh. He shifted to the side and struck down.

"Be careful what you say to me. I cannot guarantee that my idiot father won't figure out the right questions to ask." I caught the blow at the high end of my cutlass, near the hilt. I windmilled my legs and spun one leg up at him, intending to catch his neck with my foot.

"I trust you."

The words were like a throat punch, but it didn't affect the outward me and my body kept moving in combat. Sloan curved backwards and avoided my leg, aiming a new blow at my temporarily exposed back. He didn't realize it was what I had intended. I'm not even sure I realized it through the blur of instinctual attack and defend. My blade came around and I caught the edge of his weapon and spun it away from him.

"That's the worst thing you could possibly do," I panted and stood with two swords. I swung both at my sides before advancing. At least I could still play at showmanship during battle. It was possible that I could use that to my advantage and keep from truly injuring the man in front of me.

Sloan ducked the first swing and caught the second with his claw, yanking the cutlass from my grasp.

"I know," he frowned and put the sword back in his hand before charging me.

Chapter 20

Between swings and kicks, Sloan managed to tell me that he'd uncovered some of what Low was planning in his desire to create his own fleet. The admiral was using his fleet to transport nanite tech to out-lying Alliance holdings. Sloan believed that my father was probably skimming off some of the tech and making side deals with some of the less-than-Alliance-friendly humanoid races that didn't enjoy being under their thumb.

It seemed like something dear old dad would do; very self-serving and back-stabby of him. I would have admired it if somehow I forget that it was this same approach he'd used to get his cushy seat with the Alliance. I also wasn't sure it felt like it was large enough game to keep Low's interest. I hinted as much to Sloan.

Even with small ventures that worked against his Alliance compatriots, it would never make up for what he'd done. Low completely turned away from the other pirates; men and women who'd been his friends and support for most of his life. He'd offered them up as a sacrifice to the Alliance gods. He might have been part of the same group of seafaring population that I counted as my kin, but he'd gone far beyond simple traitorous actions.

When Low set forth with Alliance airships to kill the coordinated command of the pirates, the Kinship, he'd become the worst sort of mass murderer. To kill them as though they were nothing? Destroy every person who'd supported him? Who does that shit?

I crossed paths with the bastard for the first time about a month prior to the bloodbath. It had been in Cartagena during Las Hogueras. The festival was loud, wild, and perfect for my crew to celebrate. I was selling some spoils we'd gotten from a few Alliance skimmers and drinking myself oblivious from the need to be underway. We'd been in port for almost a week waiting on supplies we desperately needed before heading out again and I was getting anxious. Shore life brought too many bad memories.

I heard the whispering about el Capitan, and looked over to see a too-precise, too put-together man geared up and armed to the hilt. That alone had been a surprise since most of the bars in the area wouldn't let anyone in without taking at least the visible weapons. They were hesitant to pat-down some of the less-friendly members of my crew, but it hadn't stopped them. They had made my own weapon check fast when I smiled at them and let my newly tattoo-lengthened teeth show. It hadn't been hard to call on the rage power of the tattoo because I was itching for a fight.

I'd given the man a nod over my glass; normal polite greeting between pirates. It wasn't so much a sign of respect or a fuck-off, but it was generally enough to maintain distance without offense. It was also good manners to acknowledge another predator. His eyes lingered, made me uncomfortable, and I showed him my teeth. The shark-smile made him smile and annoyed the shit out of me.

It was the next moments that will be forever burned into my brain. He walked over, set a bottle of incredibly good rum next to me and spoke. The sound of his voice, it's rich timbre and smooth confidence, haunted my dreams like a boogieman.

"Fair winds, Captain Low," he tilted his hat and walked away. He left before I could tell him to fuck off for calling me "Low."

I was a little unnerved and decided to pay my tab and leave. When I called the barmaid, she explained that my tab had been covered by Captain Ned Low. I'd wanted to bring all that fine alcohol back up to color the bar when I realized I'd just had a run-in with dear old dad.

I found my suppliers, put the fear of Odah in them if they didn't cough up my supplies and yanked my ship and crew the hell out of port. There was no way I wanted any dealings with him, no matter the friendly gesture. I'd grown up hating his existence without ever having laid eyes on him and I was loath to give that up. That was before I'd had anything other than my birthright, or lack thereof, to hate him for.

Later, while we stopped in Lisbon, we heard about his mass destruction in the ruse of a meet-up with the other Kinship. The crewmen-for-hire in that area were spooked, thinking that my father would come for them. More than a few looked at me as though I'd been sent to do his dirty work.

Rumor got back to me that there'd been a messenger looking for me in Cartagena to give me the details for the meeting. He'd been found cut to pieces in some back alley, the missive still in his pouch with my name on it. Luck sometimes found even the unlucky, or at least I'd assumed.

The double-doors clicked open as if I'd summoned the devil with my memories. Low walked in with a woman that was dressed in the gentry uniform of a dress with a low-cut neckline and a smattering of gems. Her painted lady make-up made me question her actual station or how she'd gotten to be gentry. Women in the higher echelon wore their wealth as armor, not the bold color this woman wore. Behind her was a rainbow of foppishly dressed men and women but none moved with the air about them that she had. The room suddenly smelled of jasmine and posturing.

"He said he saved you in Cartagena," Sloan had whispered just before we parted ways after training. His eyes cut to my father before he stepped away and slapped the cutlass to his side. He bowed to my father and my body followed suit. Sloan's words knocked any flourish I'd been tempted to show right out of my spine.

It was as if he'd been privy to my thoughts, but also that he'd killed my thoughts of luck and thrown Low's motivations toward me further into dispute.

"I take it we've come just as you're finishing, Captain Sloan?" Low stood in front of the comfortable seating. "Pity."

"Would you like us to begin again, Admiral?"

"No." Low's fingers formed a steeple in front of his mouth and declined with a single shake of his head. "I did promise my guests a demonstration, though. Perhaps it will just have to be something else?"

He gave his guests a wide smile that I recognized from my own musings in a mirror; without the facial hair, of course, but no less ball-shriveling. Low turned back to us and motioned us forward. He leaned down and pulled a knife from his boot. It was an expensive-looking blade and wickedly sharp from what I could tell. Sloan and I stopped directly in front of him, good little minions awaiting further instruction.

"Maggy, you will cut your arm."

My hand grasped the hilt, and I sliced a quick gash across my bare forearm before I could even think or react. The pain ran through my body and mixed with the shock of what I'd just done, but I fought my face to remain impassive and unreactive. My brain screamed at the pain and about how pissed off I was.

"Good." Low reached forward and took the blade, but I held it tight in my hand for a moment, using the commands he hadn't given against him. My every muscle fought to shift forward and stab him with the blade that was already dyed red with Low blood. He motioned, with a finger snap for good measure, and I shifted the blade in my grip to offer it hilt-first. The action played as though it was what I'd intended from the first.

"As you can see, she is unflinching in her loyalty to me," Low pulled a cloth from his pocket and proceeded to clean the blade. "Her life is mine to use as I see fit, just as I've told you."

"The chancellor said that the technology you're using is new. Could it not be faulty?" The woman stepped forward and pursed cherry-painted lips. Her words held the light roll of a French accent. I wondered if it was mindfully done or an actual mark of birth. She looked like the type that would pretend to be French even if she wasn't. No doubt she was considered attractive with a cascade of dark hair that fell just short of her exposed cleavage. She leaned forward and looked me over. "How do we know that this is something we can use and not just...a fluke."

Her eyes took me in, distrust heavy in the narrowing of her eyes. Her gaze indicated she thought that I might be the sort of person who would consider hurting myself simply to curry favor with my father. I felt my nostrils flare but just eyed her back. I reminded myself that I was an empty shell that would someday have the good fortune of cleaving my father's head from his neck.

"Captain Magerious Low is one of the most ferocious captains to have ever sailed," Low sheathed the blade. "As much as I would enjoy the idea that she does something like this for my honor alone, she is not that sort of person. Any more than you would give up something important to you just to prove a point, Baroness."

"I cannot say that I'm convinced enough to put my vote behind you, Admiral Low," the baroness tapped a long-nailed finger to her lips. Her lips curled up at the side as she narrowed her eyes at me. "Have her strip."

My teeth dragged against each other and sent a screeching through my head. It was painful and loud, but no one reacted to the sound as all eyes shifted to my father. His lips pursed for a moment as he kept eye contact with the baroness. She dropped her gaze after a few heartbeats but then Low's gaze shifted to me, his lips turned down and I knew he was going to grant her request.

"I don't think playing into the baroness' sexual taste is what you intend for this display, Admiral," Sloan's voice cut through the air and sliced at the baroness like a throwing dagger. "She is a fighter, after all, not something for one of the pleasure houses the baroness so enjoys."

I saw the woman's face purple and she turned furious eyes to my savior. The baroness was not happy to have been caught with her skirts around her ankles by Sloan. Low saw that and laughed loudly. Everyone but the baroness joined in.

"He is not wrong, if memory serves, Baroness Critue," Low nodded. "It would be a good display of her loyalty to make her vulnerable, but I will not cater to your tastes. Despite everything, she *is* my daughter."

Low looked from Sloan to me and I saw something in his eyes darken. Fear clenched my stomach for a second as I considered that the last time he'd looked at me this way was just before I ended up with my blade swinging for Sloan's neck.

"Maggy, you will try to kill me."

The words barely left my father's lips before my body reacted. Bloodlust roared through me like a living thing as every restrained part of me released all at once. I leapt at him like a starved beast intent on a meal. My hands were like claws that latched onto his throat and I rode the momentum of his fall to the floor. His arm came up and broke my hold, sending me to the floor beside him.

Low, spry for someone easily twenty years my senior, jumped to his feet. He swung a fist that grazed my cheek. I might be lying to myself, but I think surprise at his quick recovery allowed him to make the connection. It didn't last long, though.

I caught the arm before he could withdraw and pulled his weight into an arc over me. I used the momentum to send him over my head and rolled with him. My knees slammed into him as I landed on his chest before I hauled back cold cocked him. My other arm was swinging to second the blow when that damned tech leash snapped tight.

"Stop."

My hand skidded to a stop almost touching the side of his face with my knuckles. I panted, and my muscles shivered under my skin, but the command was absolute; I couldn't resist it.

"Stand up and step back," Low's voice directed my movements and I fought with every bit of energy to ignore him; to stay and finish what he'd allowed me to start. My body obeyed and I shook as I stood before him and watched him climb to his feet.

"Kneel before me and your betters. Show your obedience, Maggy."

I dropped to my knees and bowed my head, the perfect slave. A single drop of salty moisture from my eye mixed with sweat that rolled down my flushed cheek. It dripped onto the collar of my shirt, unwanted and unheeded.

I would make the bastard pay. I would paint my ship with his blood for this and every other abasement.

"That was quite a right hook, my pet," Low was shifting his jaw from side to side as we entered his suites. He turned his dark eyes on me, and a cold smile rose over his features. "The passion in you; the fire, rage, and fury. It was truly a sight to behold. I doubt the baroness will ever forget watching you. I wouldn't be surprised if she begs me to get her the tech currently in your body on the assumption she can somehow recreate it in one of her pets."

He picked up a cup and poured himself a water from a nearby pitcher, drinking deeply before he continued.

"When she does, others will follow. They will want me to get them this implant for all their enemies, hell their lovers! Can you imagine?"

I could and it sickened me to the core.

A servant brought out ice wrapped in a cloth and handed it to my father, who put it to his jaw. I felt my eyebrow twitch and he nodded at me.

"You wonder why they would come to me if they can go to the chancellor? It's a good question, my daughter. It isn't one I'm ready to answer yet, but just know that I have my ways," Low laughed and then winced. "That *really* was a good punch! I'm impressed.

"Davide, please go to the medic and get some healing nanites for myself and for Maggy," he set the cloth bundle down on the table beside him and walked toward me, his eyes on the gash on my arm. I hadn't pressed hard with the knife, but it had been sharp, and the cut stung.

Low stepped over to me and lifted my arm, inspecting the cut. He met my eyes and dug his thumb into the cut, his lips curling and nostrils flaring.

"You enjoyed attacking me a little too much, daughter. You would do well to remember who holds your leash. I would hate to order you to walk your own plank," he sneered, and his eyes glowed with hellish fury. I thought I was the master of crazy eyes, but apparently, I'd inherited that from the bastard as well. Still, it was nice to see the real Low for a moment.

I couldn't make a noise, not that I wanted to give him the satisfaction of crying out in pain. The fury in my blood just then would have fired up my tattoos for a good, long battle. I could picture my teeth sharpening just before I leaned forward to rip out my father's throat. My nostrils flared as though I could already smell his spilt blood and his eyes narrowed.

Low stepped away when the servant re-entered the sitting area.

"Davide will take you to get cleaned up, and have you dressed for dinner. Davide, we will be dining with the chancellor, so make sure to find something appropriate for my darling girl. Go with Davide, Maggy."

Low took a vial from the servant and walked away. Davide turned away and walked toward my room without a word.

I walked behind the young man and thought about everything that had happened. I knew there had to be some way out of the predicament I was in. I knew if Sloan could find a way to get me away from Low, he would. The damned controller meant that I was collared, though. I would never be able to act on my own without having the implant removed, if that could be done, or having possession of the controller -- if I could even control it. I was pretty certain Vanyik would have thought of what would happen if the controller fell into the hands of the controlled.

"The maid will be in shortly, Miss Magerious," Davide opened the door for me and bowed. "If you would please have a seat, I will see to your wound."

I didn't sit. His words did not compel or repel me without the command behind them. I had no urge to sit and my father wasn't in the room to make me, so I stood and watched the servant who sighed.

He went to the washroom and I was left looking at the ridiculously large room that had replaced my prison cell. It was furnished in feminine fabrics and decor. The room was done in shades of purple; none of which looked like something from nature. It was garish and ornate with heavy velvet curtains at the window and around the massive bed. I could put an entire hold's prisoners in that bed, and they'd have more room than they would on the ship.

The carpet under my boots was like walking in wet sand, it was so thick. The furniture was dark and plentiful with two desks set with jewelry boxes and various writing implements. Each desk or table had a mirror nearby in case the occupant fancied admiring him or herself. The wardrobe nearest the washroom was open and looked as though it had eaten so many silk and velvet gowns that it had indigestion.

Davide returned and used a damp cloth to clean my arm. I stared at the wall and waited for him to finish and leave me.

"The nanites for healing that the medic has are the best available. Your skin will probably close in a moment and the pain should go away quickly," Davide prattled on as he filled a syringe from the vial and injected me just below the cut, close to the vein in my wrist. I looked down as it pinched me and then felt the pressure of the tiny bot-like technology as it followed my vein to the wound.

He was right though: the skin closed as I watched. The blood dried quickly as though it had been on my skin for hours instead of moments after Davide finished cleaning the wound. He wiped at my arm again and all that was left was a thin red line that faded almost immediately.

The door opened behind me and two young women came in, chatting. They stopped when they spotted Davide and me. I turned my head to look at them and watched their eyes lock on the floor.

"Admiral Low wants Miss Magerious cleaned up and dressed to dine with the chancellor," Davide gathered the bloody cloth and remaining nanites. He exited the room, and the maids came forward.

I put my hands out when they went to take my clothes, realizing that I had enough freedom to do so myself. They wrung their hands for a moment and watched me as though they didn't know what to do.

I needed to tell them that I needed a...

"Bath," I managed to say. I blinked at them, and myself, in surprise. I hadn't expected to be able to direct them in any way. I guess reminding them of my father's directions wasn't against his orders. He also hadn't commanded my silence.

The women jumped at the word and hurried away to the washing room.

I left the filthy training clothes, spattered with my blood, on the floor of the room once I had everything removed. The maids came out and I walked past them to clean myself up. It was a tiny freedom, but it was welcome. I settled into the tub and sunk deep into the hot water, submerging and just enjoying the heat across my skin, soft and caressing. I emerged like the love goddesses of old, smelling like night blooms and citrus.

The gown that was waiting for me made me want to crawl back in the tub and attempt drowning. It, unlike the bath, was not welcoming with its various buttons, ties, and heavy material. Nor were the ridiculous underpinnings needed to wear it. I'd always had a trim figure, mostly due to regular bouts of near starvation. Even without that, I'd never seen the need to wear a corset under my clothes. I'm not sure how male pirates felt about it but wearing clothing that had a cage to hold you in seemed like a new form of tortured imprisonment.

Over clothes, on the other hand, with thick plates instead of narrow strips of bone or metal, was somewhat useful. The right type of corset was armor that could keep a blade from catching you between the ribs. It wouldn't stop a cannon blast that I knew of, but remade female garments with titanium fittings could save a life and look damn good while doing so.

The accoutrements that were sitting on the garish purple coverlet, however, were painfully useless unless I wanted to look skeletally thin and shove my breasts up under my ears. My bosom would make a nice shelf for my dinner plate, but I doubted anyone would appreciate that trick if I tried it.

The maids unfolded the bone-lined and lace-covered corset for me. I tried to put some will into stepping back but felt the pull of "dress for dinner" working against me. There was no way I could maneuver away as the cage closed around my body. The daft maids pulled it tight enough to almost end my lungs' ability to expand. I was sure that I wouldn't be able to sit at dinner, but that didn't seem to be what was important to my two helpers.

Laced in, they pulled a forest green gown over me. At first, I thought it was just a skirt and then realized that the top consisted of mostly something to drape over my shoulders and button behind me. My cleavage would rival that of the upright-standing Baroness Critue. I wondered, briefly, if they were locked in tight enough that I could spin right and cause some damage to a foe. Not that my father would likely command such an action, but it would be nice to think my breasts could be a weapon, too.

The shoes, much like the rest of the garments, were useless pieces of fabric. They were dyed to match the flouncy satin gown and shone like a gaudy gem. Unfortunately, they had soft bottoms and no heel with which to kick someone in the head. What if I needed to throw them? These were just bits of cloth. I could imagine the laughter I'd get if I tried to defend myself by throwing the flimsy shoes.

There was one spot of useful attire on the bed. I hadn't noticed it at first, blocked as it was with all the flouffery. Two daggers decorated with a gem that, disgustingly, matched my dress waited. The sheaths were made of dark leather and had enough strap that I knew they wrapped around my thighs. The maids had to hike up the dress to outfit me with them. The leather belt strapped around me at the same level my boots normally would have, giving me comfort in the familiarity of the feel.

After I was outfitted, the two women then went to work on my hair and makeup. Again, I was forced to sit still and take it since I couldn't go against the command I'd been given. They powdered and painted me before putting some stuff in my hair and flattened it out. Then came enough jewelry to tempt a good person into thievery. My neck and fingers felt like they were covered in armor but looked clunky and shrunken by the sparkly ornamentation. The scars across my knuckles and calluses on my skin stuck out more than usual with the adornments. I wondered how much some of it would sell for in town if I tried to hock it.

The maids walked me out to the sitting area where my father was dressed much as he had the night before, but with a jeweled scabbard at his hip.

"*No*. Remove the make-up. I will not have her looking like one of those gentry whores," Low flicked his hand at the maid who hurried away. It was the first time I ever considered thanking him for something. It would probably be the only time.

I was somewhat surprised he complained. I'd assumed he thought women were useful for physical needs and little more. Granted, he wanted to make me a captain, but it seemed out of character for him to otherwise care.

"Take the necklaces and rings, too," he picked up a necklace where it hung on my neck and released it with an eye roll. "Bring me the case on the table over there."

At the center of the main table in the sitting room sat a wooden box with no decoration whatsoever. It looked like it could be anything from a box for cigars or dice. One of the maids handed it to Low who waited until they'd divested me of the various sparkly raiment before he opened it.

Inside was a metal band. It wasn't overly shiny and had no decoration or engraving. As I looked at what looked like a metal bracelet, I realized that the odd white-yellow tone of the metal identified it as titanium. Brushed, unpolished titanium similar to Sloan's arm and leg.

He lifted it and pulled. It popped apart into two half circles. He placed one at either side of my neck and then rejoined them. The metal felt like ice against my soul and rage against my skin. I'd seen slaves wear bands at wrist or ankle, but never on their necks.

Until now.

I had no doubt it was a slave collar. My father wished to mark me as a possession as clearly as he could.

"Beautiful," he leaned in and brushed a kiss at my cheek. A keening scream rent through my body, starting at the core of who I was. Somehow, it never erupted from my lips.

He turned, tucked my arm in his and said, "Come."

It was sad that such a simple command could send me into the bowels of hell, and I would never utter a single complaint.

MadCap

Chapter 21

If I'd thought my father's rooms were overabundant in space, they were nothing when viewed through the scope of the chancellor's rooms. I wasn't really surprised so much as disgusted.

Men and women chatted and laughed as they wandered back and forth in the immense sitting room. Low walked me forward to greet the chancellor and then steered me around the room like the feminine decoration I was. I spotted Sloan talking to a few Alliance captains near a window, but Low never went near them.

Not speaking or reacting to those around you is apparently almost as intimidating as snarling and baring your teeth. Of course, that might just be for high society, but I found myself wishing I could try it on sailors.

It was somewhat satisfying to see people look at me and then walk away as though I were a potted plant. The ones that spoke to my father, tried to shoot intimidating glances in my direction and I just looked back until they left. Despite the joy of them hurrying away, I felt defeat wrapped in cold metal at my neck. Fear coiled in my stomach in place of the anger and rage that usually waited, and I felt like the slave that I was. The collar had done more damage to my spirit than anything Low had done up to that point.

"I see that you've collared your pet," Baroness Critue reached over to run a long fingernail across the band at my neck and I found myself wishing for the ability to bite. Guard dogs didn't have to take that crap, why should I?

"Be careful in how you speak of my daughter, Baroness," Low pulled her hand away and then kissed her fingers. I saw the woman's skin go sallow under the powder that coated her face. I couldn't blame her since I felt the same way any time he touched me.

"Our deal, Admiral?" The baroness looked at me, her eyes narrowed as my father watched.

"Of course! I hadn't forgotten, Baroness," his teeth gleamed in the white light of the room. "Magerious, about two years ago, you stole a necklace from a ship. The rubies formed a starburst around a diamond the size of my thumbnail. What did you do with it? Answer."

"I traded it for several cases of Barbados rum, food stores, and munitions in Tortuga," I told them without hesitation.

The baroness swore and Low started laughing.

"Next time, don't bother with that idiot Spinner, just come to me for answers, dear Baroness," Low's voice was heavy with laughter and the baroness shot fury at me from her eyes. It tempered and a different sort of heat rested there as she looked me up and down.

"I would love to see another demonstration," the baroness's voice went breathy as though she were exhaling the words. "I mentioned it to a few...friends, who wish to discuss it with you."

"Who are these friends? Perhaps I should discuss it with them?"

That was code for, tell me who you told so I can kill them if I think they're a risk to my plans. I could see it all over his smooth, smiling face.

"I would be happy to make introductions, Admiral."

Low offered her his other arm and I could see the shudder slide up her spine at the thought of touching him. She recovered quickly.

"It's a bit chilly tonight," she smiled and took his arm. She looked back at me and gave me a slow wink. My father finally remembered I was there. He released my arm and dropped his hand into his coat pocket.

"Maggy, go wait with Captain Sloan. I'll be over to escort you when dinner is announced," Low's dark eyes were as full of command as his hand was of controller. It was tucked away in his jacket pocket, but I knew what he'd reached for the moment he released me. "Feel free to partake of refreshments while you wait."

I followed the order of his commands, finding Sloan first. I pulled the drink he was holding right out of his hand, knowing he wouldn't drink anything anyway, and downed it. When a servant came past, I grabbed two more glasses, placing one in Sloan's hand so he could continue the charade and simultaneously act as my spare drink holder.

"Captain Maggy Low, may I introduce Captains Taloo and Schael of the Alliance Navy," Sloan gestured to the two men dressed in formal attire and looking incredibly uncomfortable with my arrival.

"I wasn't instructed to speak to anyone but you, Sloan," I said before downing my drink and swapping glasses with him. "Honestly, I was only told to wait with you, but earlier commands still apply, it seems."

"Kip, Hans, if you would excuse us?" Sloan took my arm and walked me away from the two captains quickly, handing his/my empty glass to a passing servant and snagging another drink.

"Did you notice my lovely jewelry?" I asked, sipping at the new drink and watching him over the rim. "My father gave it to me this evening."

"Yes, I noticed," Sloan's Adam's apple bobbed. "Is it charged?"

"Beg your pardon?" I paused, the glass at my lips as my brain struggled to understand what he'd just said as panic fogged my vision. My brain was too successful for my own good and I choked. "Did you say charged?"

"It was something Low had created for some of his more hesitant crewmen," Sloan cut his eyes to me. His grip on my arm got tighter. "It's an electric collar, if I'm not mistaken."

"The fuck you say," I hissed, and a few people turned to look but I ignored them. "Tell me this is an awful joke meant to get me back for being such a bitch to you."

"I wish I could, Maggy," Sloan's eyes dropped, and I watched him tapping at his arm. I downed the rest of my drink and quickly followed with his.

Several drinks later, my mood did not improve with the reappearance of my father.

"Maggy, my pet, let me escort you to dinner," he held out his arm. "Captain Sloan, if you would follow? I would like you to sit at Maggy's side."

He bowed, "It would be my honor."

I missed the rough verbal abuse of pirates, dammit. The political, overly polite shit, which was sometimes just as rude, really got on my last nerve.

We walked into a dining room that seemed to stretch the length of the estate. I didn't bother to count the place settings or try to figure out how many guests, servants, and miscellaneous bodies moved throughout the room. It was too big. I felt like I was being walked through a crowded market during a slow-moving riot.

My father took the seat to the chancellor's right. Sloan seated me beside Low and settled in to my right. Across from us were a young man with an annoyed expression and probably the oldest man I'd ever seen in my life. If the lines on his face were year markers, he was older than the ball of dirt we resided on.

Dishes were placed in front of us by silent servants. The chatter continued with shrill laughter punctuating the sounds at random intervals. At least things were more upbeat than Low's soiree had been. Despite that, I settled in to die of boredom.

Low didn't need to command me to eat or drink anymore, thankfully. I did manage to keep the servant pouring wine very busy as I set about pickling my insides as quickly as possible.

"The South Atlantic component of the Alliance has sent word that they will begin mining for the ore, Admiral," the chancellor lifted his fork to his mouth. Every piece of food on his plate was cut into precise bites. He chewed slowly as he watched my father.

"That's wonderful, Chancellor. I'm pleased to hear that they followed through with your plan," Low scooped a few choice pieces of food from his plate with his fingers and dropped them in his mouth. My father's less-delicate eating tendencies were one of few mannerisms he had that reminded me of his roots. Knives were generally the only utensil that most sailors bothered with. Either food was taken in like a drink or stabbed and chewed. In the absence of either, or as a supplement, fingers worked just fine.

The chancellor motioned the plate away with at least half of the food still present. I wondered if it would find its way to one of the starved residents of the town. If not directly, it likely would via squabble in a waste heap.

"Would you like me to see to the southern territories once we mobilize the fleet?" Low asked and the chancellor took a drink from his glass before cocking his head at my father.

"As you say, Admiral. Your help would be greatly welcomed as always," the chancellor put the glass down and a new plate of food was placed before him. I watched as he cut the food again into tiny, perfect portions. It was like watching a colony of ants moving in straight, thought-out lines. Either that or the alcohol was hitting my bloodstream hard enough that stupid things were becoming interesting.

"This lass is your daughter?" The ancient man suddenly half-yelled the question across the table. The chancellor didn't look up from his activities. My father blinked slowly before responding.

"Yes, Master Malaki, this is my daughter, Maggy," Low raised his voice a little to address the old man who nodded with a mindless smile.

"She looks like her mother," Malaki yelled back, and I saw the storm clouds gather in my father's eyes out of the corner of my eye. I half wanted to let my face slide into a smirk at the reaction. Low didn't respond.

I wanted to ask how the old codger knew anything about my mother, but I didn't have permission. He leaned into the young man beside him and yelled into his ear.

"She's a pretty thing. You should ask her to dance."

The young man looked at me with flared nostrils and peeled the old man's hands off his sleeve. He then continued ignoring everyone except the chancellor whose movements he focused on with intensity.

"I hear that you'll begin the academy in a few weeks. Is that correct, Frederique?" Sloan asked from beside me, snagging the attention of the young man and answering my unasked questions about the arrogant youth.

"That's correct, Captain Sloan. I expect I'll graduate early, and we'll see each other on the seas by next summer," the youth lifted his chin and looked at Sloan. It was a challenging look and I felt amusement coming from Sloan. His posture was relaxed with his hands resting on the table in front of him.

"I look forward to it," Sloan said. I could practically hear the quirk of a grin on his mouth under the helm. Young Frederique, however, looked at Sloan with narrowed eyes as though insulted by his mirth.

"I must say that sitting at dinners whilst not eating just strikes me as rude, Captain Sloan," my father said from the other side of me, drawing the attention back to him. His dark gaze was pointed at the empty place setting in front of Sloan. "I don't see why you don't just join us."

"I'm certain that the view would be off-putting to many of the guests. Parties are a time of frivolity and pleasure, Admiral. They should enjoy their meals, not regret them after viewing my countenance," Sloan's voice had picked up that rolling surety that covered most of the underlying tension. His fingers twitched where they rested on his metal arm.

"Ridiculous. Most of those near you shouldn't have such weak stomachs. I have no doubt that Maggy would enjoy having an active dining companion."

I downed my glass and held it out for the servant. I had a bad feeling that I knew where this was going as Low waved a servant forward. I had felt the emphasis on my name in his statement as though hinting at some level of intimacy between Sloan and myself. I managed to keep my wine-coated lips from flapping, somehow. I knew, with Sloan beside me, I could speak, so it was a near thing in preventing it with the level of alcohol in my veins.

A young servant shook as he placed a plate of food in front of Sloan at my father's behest. Sloan looked down to find the fish course. I couldn't imagine him having any way of pulling a fast one with what he had to eat. Soup, he could shift somehow to only remove the mask a little and sip it...maybe? Some sort of salad or crudités, he could push around if there weren't so many eyes suddenly on him. But fish in this setting required filleting and the use of both fork and knife to consume.

Sloan picked up the required utensils and began slicing food in almost the same manner that the chancellor, who still hadn't looked up. It was a stall tactic, I knew. I couldn't think of a thing to do to help him, though.

Thankfully, my next drink came. I decided that if I couldn't help, maybe I could just enjoy the spectacle within the safety of further intoxication. Sadly, or fortunately, my reflexes were already feeling the expensive booze humming happily through my body.

I reached to grab the slow-moving bottle from the startled servant instead of my refilled glass. I ended up giving the wine glass a good shove and sent it flying at my father, the chancellor, his son, and the doddering old fool across from me. It crested in this beautiful burgundy wave of grape innards that was a truly spectacular mess. It was also a roaring waste of good booze. I let out a disappointed grunt that they were wearing my drink.

The chancellor and I were the only ones who didn't jump to our feet at the mess. I wanted to as I watched the wine making its way back across the tablecloth to me. It was one of those delicate lace tablecloths; expensive and non-absorbent.

"Chancellor! I must apologize!" Low exclaimed and the Alliance leader looked from his food to the wine, to my father without concern. His cold eyes took in the scene around him.

"Crackers!" the old coot suddenly yelled, and heads snapped in his direction. "She'll need some crackers after all that wine!"

A choking snort came from Sloan at my right, but it cut off when my father cut a sharp look at him. I surveyed the color change on my father's shirt impassively. I kind of liked it better with the purplish red splatter over the fluffy white; it looked closer to blood and therefore was much more suitable for him than anything white.

"Captain Sloan, escort Maggy to the training room," Low's voice had the low tone of a dog giving a warning growl. I knew his choice of location did not bode well for me and I recalled the whips that had hung alongside the blades on the weapons rack. "Maggy, you will go with Captain Sloan."

We stood and did as he ordered. The dining room was almost hushed for our departure, but some of the people at the far side of the table hadn't yet been told what happened on the chancellor's end, so they continued murmured conversations.

Sloan hurried me out of the suites.

Did you ever notice that suites sounds like sweets? I thought on that with my addled mind, deciding that it was almost sweet of Sloan to escort me away. I didn't like sweet and took a swing at him to express my displeasure.

"Maggy!" Sloan grabbed my fist and walked me into a nearby room.

"Tis not the training room," I slurred, trying to pull my fist out of his grasp. "You were ordered to take me to the training room. Why are you not following orders?"

That choked noise came again, and I frowned up at him as I tugged at my fist again. Sloan shook his head, and his body shook. For a moment, I was worried he was having some sort of seizure or attack. I stopped trying to tug my hand away and lifted my hand to press his bowed head up by cupping his cheek.

"S'all right. Breathe. Do we need to go to a medic? Or maybe get some wine?" I patted his metal face and tried to frown and look serious, but my face wouldn't let me. "Don't have an attack. I'm not a doctor. We'll get you some wine."

His blue eyes widened, and the familiar rasping noise came out to mix with the strange choked sound. He tucked one hand into his stomach and leaned back against the door.

"Stop...just stop...talking...I can't..." he huffed, and the rasp became a rattle that was truly alarming to hear. He fought for breath and I went to pull my hand back, but he caught it and kept it on his metal cheek. Taking a few slow breaths, he nodded.

"You're absolutely hilarious when you're drunk, Maggy," he shook his head. "I don't know how you broke free from Low to spill that wine but thank you."

"Pah. I didn't do it on purpose," I shook my head sadly. "That was good wine that got poured on them. I was planning to drink that wine. Do you think they still have some? We should go back!"

"No," Sloan's voice was warmer than I ever remembered hearing. "We have to get you out of here while we can, Maggy. He only ordered you to go with me, so that's what you'll do. It won't be to a training room where he can whip you for what happened, though."

My eyes widened, and the information rattled around in my brain enough to have a sobering effect on me. I nodded and shook my head frantically.

"The controller!" I had serious doubts at my ability to escape. I knew freedom was impossible with that device still in Low's hands.

"We'll get it. Low won't go to the training room until he goes back to his rooms to change," Sloan's voice dropped to a low hum that gave me goosebumps. "Davide can get the controller and meet us at the ship. We'll have to take him with -- he can't remain after this."

"Davide? My father's favorite servant?"

"He's been playing Low's favor for years and feeding us information about him," Sloan opened the door and peeked out before motioning me forward. "He's the spy I actually came to meet."

Chapter 22

Sloan started off escorting me through the Alliance base openly, like the good lackey he was supposed to be. It wasn't until we reached a descent toward one of the exits from the massive villa, that he started looking nervous and ducking around corners. He paused only once to whisper in the ear of a young maid who looked remarkably like Bree and then hurried me on.

"Our best bet is going to be the *MadCap*," Sloan cocked his head at me. "A lot of her munitions have been stripped, but she's been re-outfitted with a faster steam engine. They also haven't figured out how to engage the bladders you installed for flight so they can replace them with something newer.

"Impressive craftsmanship from what I hear," Sloan's voice was casual. "I hope you'll train me on the ins and outs of the ship?"

"That sounded dirty, the way you said it," I cut my eyes to him, cocking my head. "I kind of like this side of you, Captain Sloan."

"First Mate Sloan, maybe?" his eyes were lost in the sudden dark as we made it outside. I gave him a slow nod, wishing I could smile or give him a wink. Sad that an implant could kill my playful side.

"Just get me to my ship, Sloan. We'll work out who gets to order who around later," I whispered.

"Now who sounds like they're talking dirty?" Sloan said and rasped beside me.

We kept to the walls of the villa, trying to find our way through the shadows in the massive courtyard that wrapped around it. It was much bigger than a normal Spanish villa, almost like a tiny city. It was surrounded by massive stone walls that loomed darkly on the edge of open space that would leave us exposed when we tried to cross it. I wondered if there was a moat, too.

When it seemed clear, Sloan tugged at my arm and we raced for the wall. No one called out or came running toward us to the sound of a drawn cutlass or blaster; we seemed to be in the clear. Sloan felt his way along the wall, looking for a gate. He seemed to have a good idea of where he was going, thankfully. My eyes were quick to adjust to the darkness, but I had no clue which direction would mean out.

A loud click sounded, and I froze. Sloan's arm came around my waist and he jerked me into motion. He'd found and opened the gate to our freedom.

"You wouldn't be planning to escape now, would you Maggy?"

That voice, more than my fathers, more than anyone I'd ever gotten a beating from, haunted my dreams. Whispers of metal on leather sounded as well as a few clicks of hand cannons being readied. Flashes of memory passed through my mind as I turned to face the man who had us surrounded on the edge of liberty.

Images flashed through my brain in rapid succession. Taking my first Alliance vessel with a smiling Jim at my side. Fighting my way through a whorehouse because Jim pissed off the madam. Pulling Jim from the brink of death with an infusion of nanites. Jim jumping at me and trying to take a chunk of flesh from my arm. Jim, clear eyed and looking at me as he did now.

"What, no 'hello Jim you old salty bastard'? Or maybe even 'No Jim, don't return me to the Alliance who pulls your chain'?"

He stepped closer and I wanted to swing, kick, shake him, anything but being frozen like a saddled kelpie. I couldn't do it though. The damned implant wouldn't let me do anything but follow Sloan and we weren't moving

"'Tis just as well, Maggy m'dear," Jim stepped forward and lifted my chin to meet his eyes. "Admiral Low will be pleased as a sailor on furlough when I bring you to him and whoever your...wait, Captain Sloan?"

Jim's eyes got wide as he looked Sloan up and down as though he hadn't noticed him before that moment.

"Too bad, but I'm sure there'll be a reward in it for me for bringing in a traitor," Jim still held my chin and I wanted to jerk away but couldn't. For good measure, he punched me hard in the stomach, doubling me over.

He'd always been a bit of an ass, but this was more. In his prison visits, I'd seen hints of aggression when he carried out Spinner's orders; even taking a whip to me once. This was worse. The previous bouts of rage, I'd always thought to blame on his upbringing, but he'd always been exceptionally close-lipped about where he'd come from.

Jim reached down and tugged at my hair until I was again facing him. Unfortunately for him, his ire and the fact that his breath smelled like rotten meat kicked my gag reflex into high gear. I didn't try to stop it. I'm not sure if it was one of the few willful acts I was able to do or if some unknown god was smiling on me.

"Fuck!" Jim let go and jumped back a few feet as the wine, whiskey, and bourbon I'd consumed painted his front.

"Maggy, I'm escaping," Sloan leaned in and hissed suddenly. "And you need to follow me, which means you're going to have to do whatever you can to escape, too."

I caught his eye and felt the edge of my mouth twitch as I caught his meaning and gave him a sharp nod. We both dove forward into a couple of guards who were busy looking at Jim with disgust. We knocked them down and made our escape to the accompaniment of shooting and lots of cussing.

We cut around buildings and through patches of weeds and greenery that were most likely someone's attempt at a garden. The sound of footfalls and shouting egged us on to keep moving as fast as we could. Sloan reached back and grabbed my arm, yanking me sideways where I fell against him and almost knocked us both into the darkened entry of someone's home. His hand flew up to cover my mouth as if I *could* have called out to our pursuers, much less would have. I shoved his hand down to make it easier to slow my breathing and stood as still as I was able.

Someone passed very near us; I could hear the quick step of movement and heavy breathing. Part of me wanted to step forward from the shadows and slit a few throats to even the odds, but I was stuck following Sloan. Not that I was in the mind to complain just then.

After both of us had calmed and night birds began soft calls beyond our hiding place, Sloan removed the arm he'd wrapped around me. I hadn't noticed it was there, but I noticed the moist air dancing on my skin at its absence.

"We'll need to run to the docks," Sloan whispered. "If even one of them goes back, it will be only too easy to guess where we're going."

"I aim to follow," I grunted, he snorted. I bent forward and pulled at the useless and heavy gown, lifting the skirts to get at one of the leather sheaths. "Grab a handful of this damned fabric."

"I'm flattered Maggy, but now isn't the time," Sloan's voice roiled in a low tone just above a whisper. I shook my head.

"I figure that I need to be able to keep up with you in order to keep to the command to follow," I pulled the knife out and cut at the fabric. "If I'm to do that, I need less to weigh me down or trip me as I run."

I cut a swath of fabric from the front and ran the blade up the back, tossing the excess material to the side before I unbuckled both sheaths from my thighs. Using some of the fabric and the belts that held the knives in place, I fastened the fabric around my legs, shifting from foot to foot.

"At least the frilly underthings they made me wear cover up my lady parts somewhat," I grumbled.

"Frilly what now?" Sloan's voice was strangled and heavy all at once, but I fought to ignore him. Moonlight reflected off of my shiny slippers. I leaned down and tugged off the useless slippers, flinging them at Sloan where they bounced off his metal face. He flinched, but I think it was more from surprise.

"Um?"

"I just wanted to see if those shoes were even slightly useful," I gave him a sharp nod. "Let's go then. Time's a-wasting."

"What was that you said about frilly underthings?" He asked just before he grabbed my hand and set off at a sprint.

Davide was waiting for us when we reached the *MadCap*. I wanted to drop down and kiss the deck when I saw her. She was scuffed, and her deck needed a good cleaning, but she was still the most beautiful ship in the world.

I'm *not* biased.

"Are the others aboard?" Sloan asked Davide who flashed him a salute before handing him the controller. *My* controller.

"They are sir. They've been making ready to depart. The Walrusoid went below decks to gather night sails?"

"Tell them Captain Maggy and I are aboard and that they need to make haste," he nodded, and Davide saluted again before running off.

"What are your orders, Captain?"

He looked at me and I could practically feel a grin coming from him.

"My first order is that you lose my chain, Sloan," I said slowly. "At the moment, I can't seem to do anything other than stand here and wait for you to lead me somewhere."

"Oh, right!" Sloan lifted the controller and pressed down in the center of the pad. "Maggy, you can do or say what you want. You will captain this ship and its crew and get us all out of here. You are free to react as you feel. You are free."

The world fell out from under my feet and I fell to the deck, hard. My body started spasming and little whimpers came out of me as my body warred with the last series of commands. Sloan dropped the controller and dropped to the deck beside me. I felt his arms under me as I shook and choked on air and saliva. Agonized sounds came out of me as pain raged along my every nerve.

"I'm afraid that won't do at all, Captain Sloan," the voice of my captor was too clear despite my agony. I shook and shuddered on the deck as a lantern floated nearer to me and I looked upon the countenance of my father as he stood over me. "She's my daughter and my possession. She'll only obey my commands. Didn't you listen to the Voyag's warnings about too many commands at once?"

Tears were streaming freely down the sides of my face as it felt like every blood vessel in my body was being burst in rapid succession. I felt my heart trying to flee from my chest and my lungs burning without breath that I couldn't seem to draw in. Low crouched down on the other side of me as two men stepped up to stand next to Sloan, taking his arms.

"I had hoped that if I ever had to kill you, that it would be years from now, Maggy," Low brushed a strand of hair from my sweat-covered face. "How disappointing this is, but I knew someday it would come to this. That's why I gave you the collar."

Low tapped my neck just above the hated titanium ring and pressed something in his hand. Piercing pain jabbed through the back of my neck and I felt as though I was lit on fire. My spine arched up off of the deck and I screamed a garbled sound as I continued to choke on my own spit. My whole body felt like it was being drawn like a mast in gale winds. Pain sung through every nerve while the spasms made my teeth rattle.

"I noticed more and more of you coming to the surface despite the nanites that kept you following commands, my pet. This was my failsafe in case you learned to fight back. It injects you with an exquisite poison I got from a witch woman," Low stood. "Your whole body will go against you until your muscles melt, your organs turn to goo, and your heart will stutter and die in your chest. I tested it on one of the chancellor's lieutenants. It was truly a sight to see."

"Search the ship and bring me any others," Low ordered. I could no longer see him. My eyes had become a wash of red and gray and my spine felt as though it were trying to dig its way out of my back. The only noise I could make was a gurgling sound as I continued to shake and spasm.

"Take Sloan to Vanyik. He's got another implant. He's not the captain I originally planned to use it on, but..."

I heard a snap and then the shuffling and scuffing of feet. I felt liquid rise from my throat and gurgle past my lips, running down my face and across skin that screamed in contact. I felt Low's presence standing over me as my life drained onto the deck of my beloved

MadCap. The spasms slowed and stopped. I felt my heart slow and stutter and blackness took me.

Chapter 23

You'd think death would finish off anyone, even a violent, crazed pirate such as myself. I'd heard some of my crew say I was too tough a bitch to die, but I'd never really taken the idea to heart. We all die at some point, don't we? Strange how things don't always work out the way you expect.

Sometime after things went black, my heart started again. I lay there, on the deck of my ship, feeling a buzzing return to my limbs as though every nerve ending was suddenly charged with electricity. My lungs pulled air in slowly and I felt them expand as though I were using bellows to do so. My heart chugged, and I heard it in my ears like the low throb of a steam engine. My skin puckered at the feel of the cold night air that brushed across me in a Northern wind that smelled of rain and hinted at colder seasons coming.

Silence surrounded me other than the gentle creak of the *MadCap* where she rested in the water, waiting at the dock for someone to throw off her lines and set her free. I think it was that thought that lifted me: my girl called me to the freedom that we both sought.

I felt my body roll up into a sitting position. My eyesight was still blurry, but it was starting to clear enough that I could see the shape of the ship around me.

I was alone on deck. Low had taken Sloan and the others. I didn't know if I'd been dead for a minute, an hour, or a day, but I didn't think it was long.

My vision grew stronger and I could feel that the night was still in its honeymoon period. The moon had not yet risen, the night birds were singing softly in the distance, and the stars shone like pinpoints of familiarity to my ravaged soul.

When I stood up, I felt strength roll through my limbs. My entire body felt...new. *Strong*.

I won't lie. I considered setting sail right then. I thought about how I could just drop the lines and take the *MadCap* out onto the dark, welcoming embrace of the ocean. I would be free, I *knew* it. I knew that no one would be able to touch, leash, or hurt me again. I knew that no one would ever raise a hand to me again. The world would be a calm, welcoming place and I could sail until I found a secluded spot to make anchor near an island to live out my days in relative peace.

What was the fun in that?

I had some bastards that needed to face me for what they'd done. I turned my body, faced the plank, and felt madness born of pure, undiluted apoplectic anger. The rise of it, mercurial, rolled up inside me like pure energy. I reveled in the feel of it and knew that I would put it to good use in hunting down my enemies and saving my crew. Low had taken everything from me and tried to kill me. That shit just was *not* going to fly.

The power riding my blood had my legs pumping with speed as I ran from the *MadCap* and down to the pier. As I moved, a new yet familiar feeling flooded me, and I smiled. At a hanging lantern on the pier, I slowed a tiny bit, lifting my left hand to the glow and saw lava-like markings growing to spread across my hand like tiny vines. The lines stretched and grew, wrapping around my fingers and taking root under my nails as though my veins had decided to grow above my skin instead of beneath it. I knew the familiar, beautifully intricate tattoo, but it had changed. It was just like my power tattoo, but it moved and glowed in an odd way in the dim light.

I felt the same warmth spreading on my lips and the back of my calves. I knew that if I had a mirror, I would see similar lines blooming across my skin. My lips would be stained like they'd been brushed with pomegranate juice. Under my shredded skirt, long spiking vines would be climbing onto the back of my knees and wrapping around my thighs. Whatever had happened to me, some version of my witch-cursed tattoos was back.

Odah'd decided it was time for me to tear some people apart.

I saw a lantern bobbing not far from the end of the pier and realized that my quarry had not made it back to the villa. I slowed long enough to pull the daggers from the holsters at my thighs and ran after the beacon. I knew, if the magic I felt was any indication, my leg tattoos would be charged by the time I hit dry land.

A few paces onto shore, I slowed and crouched down, feeling my core pull down like the drop of a ship over a high swell. I launched myself into the night air.

The drop from using my leg tattoos is always like feeling as though the ground has been lifted to meet you in a jolting, uncomfortable sort of way. This was the first time I'd ever used them without boots on and it was more comfortable when I landed. It was as though it was almost natural for my feet to kiss the ground and curve with the hard-packed earth. That doesn't mean it made the rush of my landing any less gentle for those around me.

Sadly, as prey and prisoners were within the midst of the town, my landing did more than knock over the bodies of those near me. The wave from my gods-granted tattoo magic was strong enough to rip open the side of a tiny house. As the occupants were practicing their privileges as husband and wife, it was a little embarrassing for them to be suddenly exposed to our party. It became more so when one of the lanterns landed on the street in some trash that promptly ignited, turning their bedroom into a well-lit stage.

As I was surveying the fallen bodies around me, I spotted the husband and wife by firelight and giggled. It might have been hysteria, but it was also damn funny.

"You folks may want to grab your clothes and run to the neighbor's house," I told them with a nod. "This is about to get violent."

They scurried away, and I turned back in time to find that one of Low's crew had gained his feet and was coming at me with a cutlass. I dipped back from his swing and swung forward, bringing my daggers together. I crossed them in a quick movement that slit his throat before he could take a second swing.

"What do we call that, Smitters? An eternal smile?" I called as I saw the Walrusoid rolling his girth over to crush a guard before standing to kick him in the head.

"That we do, Captain," he called back as he pulled a cutlass from the fallen foe.

"Do you really think this is the time for jokes?" Sloan's voice called from somewhere ahead where I heard him, or someone, grunt in a flurry of movement. "As a side note: didn't you *die*, Maggy? Not that I'm complaining, but I'm pretty sure I watched it happen."

"You can't kill something as evil as Captain Maggy Low, Mister Sloan," Smitters retorted.

I smiled as another guard came at me, pulling a steam hand cannon a little too slowly. I kicked out and caught his hand, the residual energy in my legs snapped his wrist and he screamed in pain.

"Funny thing about that: Never leave a pirate for dead without making damn sure. They tend to wake up pissed off and kill everyone," I danced forward and sliced up into the man's gut where my blade snagged as he dropped. "It's just common sense to make sure your enemy is dead."

"Duly noted," Low said as he popped out of the shadows beside me. I saw his blade arc toward my neck, but my nearest dagger had just been taken by his guard's death and I didn't have time to bring up the dagger in my other hand to block. I rolled back on instinct, but I was too slow, and the blade connected.

The metal ring that was still around my neck connected with the blade and something cracked. At first, I thought it was my spine from the pain that wrenched through me, but I realized I was only feeling reverb from the connection of Low's sword to the metal. It fell apart and clattered to the ground in two half-crescents, whatever was holding it together on my neck was fully spent.

Low pulled back, but there was no way I was going to give him another swing. I leaned back and kicked out, sending him flying back a few feet where he landed and gasped for air.

I turned back to the recently fallen and borrowed a cutlass. I faced back toward where I'd last seen Low, but he was gone. I didn't have a chance to look for him as another body came flying at me from the darkness between buildings.

A cutlass swung down, and I caught it with an upstroke of my own. My arms were caught at the same time as I caught my opponent's, both of us intending to give a body blow to get the advantage.

"Seems we're as well matched as ever, Maggy, my love," Jim leered down at me. My lip curled, and anger rose inside me, recharging the blood fury tattoos across my body.

"We were never well matched, Jimmy-boy," I pushed and went low as I spun, knocking his legs out from under him. "I just let you win a lot."

Jim rolled before I could bring a fist down into his face. Despite the dagger in one hand and the cutlass in the other, I didn't immediately go for the killing blow. Part of me was always remembering those damned nanites in his system. Jim grinned when he gained his feet.

"That was a mistake, Maggy. You'll never get the chance to kill me again," Jim's face broke into a parody of the boyish grin I knew so well.

"It might have been a mistake, but I have no doubt you're stupid enough to let me try again, Jim," I jumped at him, swinging my blade in slicing arcs, my dagger held against my forearm in guard. "It's just a pity that I spent so much time and effort getting nanites to put you back together just to be the one to slice you apart."

"Stop, Maggy," Low's voice called from behind me and I felt a tugging sensation in my neck. I jerked but stopped swinging the blade.

"That's right, now *turn*," Low said softly. I kept the blades up but turned to face him.

"Go contain the prisoners, Jim. I have Maggy," my father lifted his chin and I heard Jim comply. "I don't know why the collar didn't work on you, Maggy, but we'll figure that out together at the holding. Now, come closer and drop your weapons."

I took slow steps toward him, my arms at my side, knife and sword clattering on the stones at my feet.

"Much better. Let's go back up to the holding and see what we can do to fix this," Low motioned toward the villa and turned his body, his fingers pressing at the controller in his hand.

I reached out, grabbed the device with my magically powered left and crushed it, the tattoos twisting and glowing gently in the dark night.

"Fixed. Anything else, Father?" I let my mouth curve into the terrifying grin that I had so missed giving. I reached forward and picked him up by the throat, lifting him until his feet dangled in the air despite our height differences.

Most children probably dream of the moment that a parent will look down at them, pride swimming in their eyes at something their offspring has done. They dream about that approval and embrace as the best moment of their lives.

I had a similar perception as my father looked down at me, eyes wide, mouth gaping, and pants wet. The difference was that this best moment was never about approval and absolutely about comeuppance. It really was the little things that made life worth living.

Noise and pain shattered through my left shoulder and my fingers released, dropping Low to the ground. I curled, and another shot rang out, this one missing me. A body came at me, knocking me sideways and pinning me to the ground as more shots rang out around us.

"Captain, might I suggest that we head back to the ship and set sail before the guards, who had apparently already been summoned by Jim after we escaped him, can come to claim us?" Sloan's voice was music to my ears, but his arm was pressing into the wound on my shoulder. I punched him with my good arm, making him grunt.

"Where the fuck's Low?" I growled, my voice the death call of a wolf.

"Gone, but we'll get him," Sloan panted in my ear. "Don't you think it will be better to run now and return when they don't expect us?"

"Yes, but first get the fuck off me," I growled to hide the pain in my voice.

"Of course," Sloan shifted beside me and helped me rise to a crouch.

"The others?"

"Here, Captain," a voice hissed from nearby and I recognized the odd slurring speech of Smitters. "Stuart's dead, but the rest of us are here."

"Then shut your yap and run for the *MadCap*! I expect to set sail the moment I step aboard!"

"Aye Captain!"

Shots peppered the walls around us, and we ran for all we were worth.

We reached the *MadCap* with several more holes than most of us started off with. Blood of different colors dripped on the deck of my glorious ship. It pissed me off to see her stained by friendly blood. The only blood that should ever spill on her deck was that of our enemies. I must have complained out loud because Sloan gave me a gentle shove toward the wheel.

"Later, Captain," Sloan grunted. "For now, let's get her out to sea before we have any further casualties."

"Smitters! Cast off!" I yelled. I moved around the deck with the tiny crew we'd gathered, pulling in lines and readying the sails. The gangplank had been pulled the moment my crew was aboard.

As soon as we were ready, I ran to the helm and we pushed off. Hand cannons blasted at us from the pier and I saw lines cast at us as Low, Jim, and the surviving Alliance party that had taken my crew tried to get a foothold on my ship. More were running down the pier behind them. Malcolm and Davide stayed on their bellies near the balustrades to throw off any grapples that caught. I heard the old sailor swear and call out insults to our would-be captors. I'd always known Malcolm would be an excellent addition to my crew.

It took longer than I would have liked, but we finally got the *MadCap* free from the piers. It was just in time, too. I saw a small militia of Alliance join Low and Jim.

"They've likely got a few low-air skiffs at one of the nearby piers and this ship does not have her cannons," Sloan stepped up to the helm bringing nothing but happy news. "It might be best if we take to the skies instead. Those skiffs might not be able to get altitude, but they'll be on us quick."

"That's where you're wrong, Sloan." My eyes went wide as I gave him a full-tooth grin of madness. "You forget what ship you're on. This is a pirate ship, mate. We don't always go for the throat, sometimes we go for the nut-shot."

"I don't think I could ever forget that if I tried, *Captain*." Humor warmed his voice. "Though if you'll recall, a 'nut-shot' was how…"

"Okay, we aren't being literal here, Sloan," I snapped. "Go tell Smitters that we need to go dark."

"There's only one lantern lit--"

"Please just do as I say," I was not used to repeating my orders. Sloan as a crewman was not going to work out if this was our future. I realized I might just need to throw him overboard. It might be a fun game; we could take bets on how quickly he'd sink out of sight.

"Aye Captain," Sloan hurried off to find the walrusoid and relay my message.

Moments later, Sloan returned and handed me a black cloth bag which I pushed back at him.

"Strip," I eyed his dirty white shirt and ridiculous blue jacket with the bright shiny buttons and pins.

"Maggy, this is so sudden. I figured you'd at least get me drunk first."

"Hardee har har," I shook my head. "You need to disappear, and you won't be able to do it in that ridiculous uniform with your metal shining a beacon to anyone looking, so strip!"

I watched. Sloan turned his back to me, but that didn't mean I turned away. It was my damn ship; I could watch if I wanted to. If he wanted privacy, he wouldn't have stayed on the helm.

When he finished, he turned to face me.

"Why are you grinning, Maggy?"

"*Captain* Maggy," I cleared my throat and then looked at the shining beacon that was Sloan's head. "You're going to have to do something about your face, Sloan."

"And here I thought you liked how I looked," He quipped but didn't hesitate to take off the metallic dome that had kept him from prying eyes for who knows how long at my request. I had a great deal of respect for him right at that moment that had nothing to do with seeing his naked ass a few minutes prior.

"Tuck it in the bag and take the wheel."

We switched positions and I pulled out a black suit from the bag. After wearing the itchy green dress and various useless feminine apparel, I was looking forward to wearing one of the 'night suits.'

I unstrapped the belts and untied the fabric from around my legs, but when I went to tug the rest of the dress off, I couldn't reach the odd fasteners at the back and tearing it just shredded the skirt further. I finally huffed a sigh and turned to Sloan, who quickly turned his head to face away from where I stood.

"Were you watching?" I tried to keep the laugh from my voice.

"A gentleman never watches," Sloan responded with a non-answer.

"You're a pirate, Sloan," I grunted. "Can you get this gown off of me, please?"

"Oh Maggy--"

"Shut it!" I growled and handed him the knife. "Just cut the damn thing away -- as much as you can without filleting me, if you would?"

He cleared his throat and used his claw to pull fabric away from me before sliding the knife between corset and fabric and slicing up quickly. Good thing the blade was sharp, or I would have had to stand there with him sawing at it, making it more awkward. As it was, it felt ridiculously intimate.

"Thanks," I grunted.

"Thank *you*." One of his ruined eyebrows wagged and there was warm laughter in his voice. I momentarily wondered if it would be in bad form to throw one of my knives at him. I found I kind of liked the humor though and gave him a smile before turning away.

I was stuck with the corset and frilly underthings until I could have some light to cut away the various cords and pins that held them in place. I hadn't noticed how much went into the damned things when the maids were forcing my body into them, but now they were just a time sink I couldn't afford.

I pulled the black silk up over my body, fastening the buttons at the side and tightening the laces to make it fit snug against my body. When I was done, I turned and chucked the bag at Sloan and took my place at the helm.

"Go help Smitters. He'll need all hands if he's going to swap the mast," I shooed him away. The main mast had already been dropped, which had probably helped make us invisible to any incoming Alliance vessels. Once the black, oiled canvas was raised, though, we would be damned near impossible to spot. As long as everyone had night suits on and kept movement to a minimum, that is.

I was the best pirate on the seas thanks to my battle skills, strategic ability, outstanding leadership, and modesty. Though, it helped that I knew how to truly go dark with a few tricks and some dark fabric. My ship, the *MadCap*, could truly become invisible.

Chapter 24

Blame it on my early life as a thief in a world of vicious cutthroats and murderous whores, but I learned the values of invisibility at an early age. Being invisible meant you were less likely to get knocked around when your ma was short on money and high on something unnatural. It meant that you could cut someone's purse strings and blend into the shadows before they even realized you were there.

When I took to the seas, I went from thinking about making myself invisible to making my world invisible. Oiled black canvas used as sails, dark stain on the decks, and tarred rigging could make a ship practically disappear during the day and especially at night. The moon and sun could be a spotlight if you let them; I preferred the shadows. All of the other ships spent coin and effort on getting the best flying gear and steam engines, but you couldn't disappear in the sky. Not like you could on the ocean.

Smitters showed the crew how to open the pockets in the hull and decking that held our night-rigging. It didn't take long for everything we had to fade to black. I turned the ship so that her bow was cutting into the waves at a direct angle, allowing them to part around my ship like a curtain. The sound of the water against the hull was almost negligible. It would take a miracle for one of the skiffs to find us like this.

"There's a skiff heading right for us, Maggy."

Fuck.

I turned to where Sloan indicated and, sure enough, there was a boat hovering just above the water headed straight for our starboard side. It was as if they were being pulled in by a rope, the route was so direct.

I let out a low growl, grabbed Sloan's hand and put it on the wheel. I was too angry for words as I rushed down to the main deck, watching the boat and gauging the point of intersection for the skiff. They were ridiculously close and obviously planning to just set down right on our main deck.

I tapped a couple of shadows as I hurried along, pulling my oiled cutlass from my belt and motioning they do the same. A massive shadow met me at the line of sight for the skiff and I dropped the entirety of my weight toward the smallest point. I felt tusk and bone grind together before I shifted and slid my cutlass just underneath.

"Make a sound and it's your last, Smitters," I pressed my lips to his ear holes and spoke in a low tone. I leaned back just a little and let my teeth go pointy as I looked down at him.

The skiff buzzed over the balustrade and skidded across the deck. The shadows around me came alive and jumped the three men that came barreling off before they could shout or get a shot off. Someone killed the engine and another set about deflating the air bladders.

I heard the scuffle and half wanted to join, but I was too busy making sure that Smitters knew that the devil was on his chest and it was time to pay his dues.

"Do you want us to kill them, Captain?"

"No. Gag them and take them below decks. Knock them out if you have to, but don't kill them just yet," I returned, never taking my eyes from the fat man beneath me. "Send over Malcolm with some oiled rope for this fat fuck."

"Aye, Captain."

Malcolm came around and tied up Smitters, running the line from his bound wrists to his ankles, forcing my former crewmate into a kneeling position on the deck. I hazarded a look behind me and saw that my new crew had covered the skiff with black tarp and the Alliance men had been dealt with.

"Are we going to kill him, Captain?"

I looked at Malcolm and saw his arched eyebrow and clear expectation of me.

"Killing Smitters and chopping him to bits, as I would so like to do right now, would then require tossing his remains overboard -- lest we want to draw carrion birds and therefore attention," I kept my blade tight enough against the walrusoid's neck that any movement on his part would separate his head from his shoulders as I faced the old sailor. "Any captain worth his salt would follow the line of predators in the water and be able to map out our movements from it, making our getaway even more difficult than it currently is."

I paused, looking back down at the sniveling mass who looked ready to plead for his forfeit life.

"How'd you escape when the *MadCap* was taken?"

"They tortured me for information on the ship and then threw me in the swell, bloodied and beaten with most of the crew," Smitters said. "Spinner'd decided that taking pirate hostages, yourself excluded, wasn't worth the hassle."

"He didn't realize you'd heal up and be able to take to the surface," I shook my head and he nodded. "So, why help them now?"

"The *MadCap*," Smitters shrugged and looked half-smug for a Deadman. "When they brought me to the holding, they heard I was part of your original crew and took me to meet with Admiral Low. He promised that if you ever escaped and I helped retrieve you that he'd give me the *MadCap* as a reward."

"You're dumber than I thought," I tsked. "Low wants to control my ship as much as he wants to control me. He dangled a treat and you rolled over."

I looked at him for a moment and thought about what we needed to do. Riding off into the sunrise wasn't going to make this end or even slow down. It was time to take a stand. Well, time to sneak in and kill people as a way of taking a stand but a stand, nonetheless.

"Clean him up and check his wounds. I don't want him to bleed," I nodded to Malcolm and Davide. I walked up to where Sloan was maintaining our heading, his ruined face drawn tight against the salty air.

"You said they took the munitions off of the *MadCap*, correct?"

"Everything but an old, rusted cannon. I think it's stuck. I looked at it when we were prepping to leave, and the wheels look jammed." Sloan narrowed his eyes at me, trying to see what I was thinking. I don't know why he bothered when he should have figured I'd just tell him.

"They left Betsy, how nice. Damn. I'm gonna miss her," I sighed. I took the wheel and adjusted our course, so we were going in a northwesterly direction before tying off the wheel. "Come with me. Betsy's a lady. You have to know how to touch her to get her where you want her."

"Are you offering pointers, Captain?"

I kept my face forward so he couldn't see the smile that curved my lips.

Somehow, we got Smitters down to the weapons deck. I found a good length of chain and locked it around Betsy's legs. I hated what I was about to do but explained to Sloan that it was necessary.

I ran the chain to the line restraining Smitters and wound it through. We only found one lock on board, but we only really needed one.

"Did you know that a walrusoid, like Smitters here, can hold his breath for about fifteen minutes? Twenty if they're in good shape," I looked down at the glowering and gagged mass of the man currently attached to my beloved cannon, Betsy. "So, we'll assume closer to ten for Smitters."

"Betsy's a heavy girl, so even with his exceptional ability to swim, Smitters is only going to have a few minutes of her sinking before he has to get himself free if he wants to make it back to the surface without dying. His natural buoyancy thanks to the many, many layers of lard will slow her descent, of course, but not by a lot."

I leaned down to investigate the face of my former crewman.

"This is my mercy to you, not that you deserve it, you fat, stupid piece of shit," I snarled. "If you get yourself free, you can face the Alliance roaming the waters and possibly survive another day. We, however, will be long beyond San Miguel by the time that happens."

I saw Malcolm's eyes widen on me and felt Sloan shift behind me, either to give the man a look or gesture to keep his mouth shut.

"If not, say hello to the deep feeders for me, would you? I hear they're particularly ravenous during their mating cycle which happens...oh, right around now," I leaned forward and tweaked his nose before standing upright beside Sloan. I motioned for the crew to open the cannon doors, so I could slide Betsy and her new best friend forward. We'd already taken away the break and blocks to stop her from rolling off, so it just took a good shove.

Sloan and I shoved Betsy and she dropped off the side of the ship making a loud thunk as she submerged. The chain rattled on the deck before going taut and jerking Smitters away from our little gathering. I waved as he went over before lifting a finger to wipe away a tiny bit of moisture running from the corner of my eye.

"I'm sorry Maggy," Sloan's hand rested on my shoulder.

I nodded. "She was a damn fine cannon."

I turned and headed back to the wheel to re-adjust our course.

"The Alliance will find Smitters..."

"Are you sure he'll survive?" Sloan asked, his metal face in place so I couldn't see the frown I was sure was there. He'd put it on the moment we'd gone into the officer mess to go over my plans. He told me it did slow the decay rate of his wounds because of something in how it was made or some coating on the metal. It didn't sound like something that would ever be useful to me, so I tuned him out a few words into his explanation.

"He'll survive and find his way to the surface, so he can float there like a piece of driftwood until he gets picked up. Then, he'll re-sell his soul and ours to get back to safety," I tapped my finger on San Miguel. "He'll point them in this direction, assuming, as he always has, that I'm a pretty face who's always succeeded through luck or circumstance. Possibly because of Jim. I don't know."

"Okay, so the Alliance heads in that direction but we're going back, aren't we?"

I smiled at the brightest student in the room. The only student, but good enough.

"We are. Say, are you a fan of mythology?"

"Some, why?"

"Because I think we face the Alliance hydra and chop off its head."

Night was ending as we shifted into a tiny bay on the other side of Santa Maria. We covered everything we could and brought down the masts, tying them to the deck so the *Madcap* would look like a disheveled wreck of a ship to anyone who caught sight of her. We brought her in, catching her on a sandbar and found seaweed and flotsam to drape across her deck. We left a ghost crew, led by Davide, and took the Alliance skiff to shore.

By the time we made it back to the Alliance holding in the village Sloan told me was called Vila do Porto, the sun was burning down on us. The town was quiet as most of the residents hid from the heat with afternoon naps. The holding, crouched like a giant spider on a web, was quiet as well.

I was certain Low had sent most of the available ships and militia to try to capture us. Some might have stayed coastal, but we weren't on the water, so it didn't matter. Any ships circling the island either at sea or above, if they spotted the *MadCap*, would not recognize her and would keep looking. I hoped.

Sloan led us through a side gate after knocking out a sleepy guard and into the servant's quarters of the villa. After skirting through a few occupied rooms where the residents took one look at us and rolled over on their mats, we made our way through quiet hallways. The villa was practically deserted as we made our way up.

Sloan knew how to get us to the chancellor's offices, but we still had to blend in. Malcolm found a guard who was close enough to his size that when we knocked him out and took his uniform, it mostly fit. Hopefully, no one would think much about the puckered buttons on the jacket or would at least be polite enough not to point it out.

I dressed as a servant. It was either that or a whore. I had no desire to do the latter and Sloan pointed out that my face would be too recognizable even with tawdry make-up and my breasts to distract them. He did suggest we take the clothing with us 'just in case' we needed it for something in the future. Bastard.

I kept my eyes down and did my best to look cowed as I walked with the two men. Sloan had removed his helmet and tucked it in a bag, donning the disguise of a servant as well. I was pretty sure, without the helmet and his metal limbs covered with loose clothing, no one would recognize him.

We entered the chancellor's rooms unaccosted. In fact, it went so well that the chancellor himself was sitting in his parlor with only a couple of guards that didn't stand a chance.

I walked forward and grabbed the Alliance head by the neck, forcing him to his feet as I choked him. Chancellor Willett didn't fight back. He just gasped.

"You have to stop," a voice called from behind a couch and I saw a familiar face peek up.

Though it was a surprise to see Professor Talimuck, I itched to repay him for what he'd started when my crew took the *Interrogator*. In my mind, he was the scientist responsible for everything that had happened. He was the man responsible for putting me in prison and taking away the only friend I'd ever had to become part of the one thing I hated more than my father: the Alliance.

Talimuck stood slowly, shaking as I strode toward him with death in my eyes. He put both hands up to beg or entreaty, I didn't know, and I didn't care.

"Talimuck," I snarled.

"Captain Maggy, please," he danced out of my way, running to the other side of the room where Sloan reached out a metal arm and knocked him to the ground.

"Clumsy," Sloan tsked.

"You don't understand, you're being set up," Talimuck gasped as Sloan lifted him by the neck with his metal claw.

I didn't want to listen to him. I just wanted to watch Sloan's claw tick closed and crush the man's windpipe, but the last few hours tugged at me. We'd gotten in so easily. The chancellor hadn't even fought back when I went to choke him to death. Something wasn't right.

"Keep your grip on him, Sloan, but I want to hear what he has to say."

I cut my eyes from where the chancellor still sat to where Talimuck was caught in Sloan's grip. I glared and he took the cue.

"Low pulled the militia away, leaving almost no one behind. He knew you would come for the chancellor. He knew you would think that killing him would take down the Alliance. Hell, he put me in here to make you rage blind until we were dead and Low could step up and take charge of the entire organization."

I was really beginning to hate that people understood me. It did not bode well for my days as a thief and a pirate. How could I defeat my enemies if they saw me coming? Would a kick in the nuts turn into, 'Good old Maggy, going for the nut shot again?'

"Why the hell would he want the chancellor dead? They seem to be on the exact same page. It seems like the perfect set-up for him." My father was the type to seek power, but never positions of responsibility. I couldn't see that ever being on his holiday wish list.

"The chancellor is controlled by Low," Talimuck lowered his eyes, his mouth clenched. "Low put some kind of experimental implant in the chancellor and it took away Willett's ability to do anything without direction."

I reached up and rubbed my neck and Talimuck bobbed in Sloan's grip, the closest thing he could do to nodding. Sloan loosened his grip, cocking his head at me before stepping back. Talimuck dropped to the floor and didn't try to stand back up.

"You weren't the first he tried that technology on. Unfortunately, the first implant was too powerful. I don't even know if Willett is still in there," Talimuck eyed where the chancellor still sat on the couch where I'd dropped him like a statue. He was about as lively as one of the cushions. We all watched him for a few moments until he blinked.

"If you killed him, Low wouldn't have to work so hard at controlling him anymore -- feeding him commands, reminding him to eat, sleep, breath…" Talimuck closed his eyes and sighed. "I've been trying to figure out a way to break the hold of the implant on him."

His eyes narrowed on me.

"Then, you broke free. I think something about you is the key to freeing the chancellor," Talimuck said.

"It was too many commands…" I started and Talimuck shook his head.

"That would have just sent you into shock. The poison in the collar should have killed you though," he tapped his finger on his leg. I arched an eyebrow.

"Low came back and raged about it before he locked us in and set the handful of guards in place." He tilted his head and looked up at me. I saw so many questions there and realized that Talimuck had been trying to puzzle something about me out for quite a while.

"Would you be willing to give me a sample of your blood?"

I narrowed my eyes at him and curled my lips back to show my teeth. Sloan took a step toward the downed man who lifted his hands and shook his head.

"I'll take that as a no," Talimuck shrunk back. "I have a theory, several actually, but one that I want to test. It has to do with my original nanites."

I gave him a slow blink to continue but said nothing.

"They're still active in Jim's blood, though the virus that lives in him seems to have changed them somehow. They, and he, have become more aggressive than I could have ever imagined. I think even if I wanted to release him from the control we have over him, I'm not sure it would be possible. They must have altered his brain too much."

The idea was a kick in the gut, though I'd already seen the changes wrought in Jim. He'd always been a bit on the aggressive side when fighting but was otherwise prone to...idiocy. Jim was a good guy but, in the time I'd known him, rarely thought through the possible recourse of his actions. He dove in first and then complained about it later. Example A: Siren civil war.

"That brings me to you," Talimuck slowly stood, his hands out, palms forward to show that he wasn't planning anything immediately stupid. "I would like a sample of your blood to see if the nanites are still alive in your blood as well. If the virus in Jim's blood changed them, who's to say something in yours didn't change them as well?"

"You think your nanites might be what helped me overcome the implant," I leapt to the conclusion I think he was hoping to make, and he nodded his head. "Have you tried your nanites on the chancellor?"

"Yes. They swam around for a while, healing minor injuries and then went dormant," he looked over at the man in question on the couch. "There must be something else that makes the nanites change. For you, my assumption would be that the loss of your tattoos and whatever magic was in them, somehow changed the nanites."

"I have my tattoos," I grinned. I lifted my hand to show him, but the tattoo was gone. I frowned. "Okay, I had them last night…"

"Before or after you died?"

When in the world did this become a normal question?

"After. I assumed that they regenerated or something," I shrugged. "Honestly, I didn't question it too much, I was just happy to have them back."

"I'm sure you were in a rage-state?" Talimuck nodded slowly and I shrugged. "I can't be certain, but they're probably in your blood now, possibly with the nanites or the nanites have become them...I won't know until I test your blood."

"Captain, there's someone coming," Malcolm stepped inside, and closed the doors quietly before locking them behind him.

"A lot of someones?"

"A few, possibly roving guards. I didn't wait for them to see me and find out."

I couldn't fault him for that prudent decision.

"So, I don't get to kill the chancellor today? Damn. I was really looking forward to adding that to my list of accomplishments," I sighed. "I think we need to get out of here."

"But what about the chancellor?" Talimuck gave me an outraged look.

"What about him? He's a shell. We'll leave him here," I shrugged.

"Maggy, be reasonable. Do you think that if you don't kill him that Low won't just come back and kill him to blame you and get what he wants anyways?" Sloan asked, and I wanted to punch him for being logical. Apparently, everyone was on their logic game. I just didn't really want to be saddled with whatever the hell this mess was.

"I was hoping no one would consider that," I sighed. "Fine. I assume you know a way out, Talimuck?"

"Yes, we just have to head to my lab, first. I need to take the samples I've collected and some of the nanites," he nodded and walked over to the chancellor. "He'll come; we just have to kind of tug him along. He'll also work well to get us through the compound if anyone tries to stop us."

"As much as I hate to say this...Lead on, Professor Talimuck," I sighed and opened the door.

Chapter 25

The chancellor did very well as a puppet. Some of his previous programming must have included nodding when someone called out or returning salutes when they were given. It was almost like he was the chancellor instead of a chancellor-shell

When we got down to the professor's lab, we had a new surprise waiting for us: Vanyik.

He turned, saw us, and his eyes went wide. Sloan was the first to react and the claw hand closed around Vanyik's neck before he could do more than utter, "What?"

Sloan tapped his hand, and the claw locked its grip around the voyag's neck. Vanyik made odd gurgling noises, and that disgusting tongue made an appearance as he fought to breath.

"How do we break the chancellor's implant?" I asked as I leaned forward and peeked over Sloan's shoulder at the dangling Voyag. He had a strange metallic smell like oiled weapons that I suddenly found appealing and very distracting.

Sloan, not the Voyag. The Voyag was starting to smell like swamp juice and his pants were wet.

Vanyik gurgled at me and I remembered my first interaction with him. I tapped Sloan, who turned his face to me for a moment longer than was required before tapping his arm once to loosen the grip slightly.

"I don't know why we bother. He doesn't know how to fix it, or he would have," I turned my face to Sloan and tapped lightly on his metallic faceplate. "Hell, he probably doesn't even know how to fix the mess of your face, Sloan."

I felt him still beside me, his back stiffened, and his breathing stopped. I felt the insult slide through him and wanted to apologize, but it would look less like posturing if I did. It was a risk just to ask but one that I figured might work.

"Ridiculous human, I know a great deal more than you think. Though, the implant is not meant to be stopped, it does have safeguards as I told you. Were you listening?" Vanyik's voice was haughty and higher than I remembered it being. He was obviously highly offended at my assumptions of his lack of skill.

"As for Captain Sloan's degenerative virus, a simple dose of the reworked Talimuck nanites would easily start the healing process and kill the bacteria in his skin. The nanites should even help with the magical properties in his blood."

Sloan's eyes went wide, and I fought not to react to this new information. He turned his head away and straightened the sleeve of his tunic over his arm. I had to control facial expressions, he just had to hide his eyes. I inspected my nails and shook my head, forcing disbelief and boredom to pull the edges of anxiety away.

"I don't believe you," I sighed and stepped away. "There's no way you've figured that out when no one else seemed to be able to. Your kind is so arrogant, you think you know everything, but you can't fix a simple flesh-eating virus."

"Oh Miss Magerious, it isn't something so...mundane as a flesh-eating virus that afflicts Captain Sloan," Vanyik tsked at my ignorance. "I've already adjusted the nanites for his illness, per Admiral Low's request. He planned to give it to the captain prior to the implant to see if it was enough to buy his control without having to take over his mind. I told him it would certainly be enough as you humans are so vain about your appearance."

I knew, though Sloan had never said so, that it was so much more to him than how he looked. When his skin was exposed, I saw the way parts of it twitched and he flinched as though being bitten by tiny insects over and over. His affliction caused him daily pain that was exacerbated any time he removed the helmet.

"How do I know you aren't just trying to trick us into believing you're brilliant?" I waved my hands around. "I'm certain that you couldn't have overcome the controlling aspect of the nanites in Talimuck's creation to simply heal his wounds. Obviously if you couldn't do that with the implant, there is no way you could have done it with the nanites."

"Miss Magerious!" Vanyik was truly outraged now. "Not only is there zero chance of the newest version of Talimuck's nanites taking over Captain Sloan -- that was a glitch due to Jim's weakened brain matter, by the way and would have never worked like that on any other human -- but the new nanites have a self-destruct that can be activated to turn them into normal cellular waste in the host's body."

"Prove it," I lifted my chin and stared down my nose at him. My mind was ticking through what he'd said, and I saw Talimuck's eyes widened as we both drew similar conclusions about how the new nanites might help with our current predicament outside of healing Sloan.

"Get the cream from the storage box behind my desk labeled Xybb9," Vanyik had his face turned away from us as though trying to express his disgust at my insults. "You will find nanite-proof gloves, another of my inventions by the way, in my second desk drawer. Just apply them to Captain Sloan's face and be prepared to marvel at my brilliance."

I kept my face locked in a look of boredom as I did what he said, donning the gloves after carefully removing Sloan's metal head. I pointed at Vanyik with a nod of my head and Sloan dropped him. Malcolm came forward to push the Voyag to the floor, his knee in the creature's back.

Other than the initial grunt, Vanyik's gaze was locked on us. His eyes were greedy as he waited, and I hesitated for just a moment. The last time I'd smeared nanites on someone, they'd been taken from me forever. I kind of liked having Sloan around.

Okay, I really liked having Sloan around for reasons I wasn't willing to admit to myself. I didn't want to admit that I was scared to lose him like I'd lost Jim. I peered into his eyes and watched the skin bunch on his cheek for a moment and the pain flutter through his eyes but still I hesitated.

"Sloan, I don't know what this will do," I whispered. I reached over as though I would place my gloved hand on his cheek but stopped before I could touch him.

"I trust you," his voice was barely a whisper of breath, but I felt the words like a shock of ice water on my back. I felt what he said hit me as hard the second time as they had the first time.

Vanyik hissed from the floor.

"Miss Magerious, I have been waiting weeks to watch the miracle of healing from my newest creation work. Watching the skin sample knit itself back together had been amazing, but it will be insignificant to what Captain Sloan's skin will do! Please! I must see my creation in action!"

I looked down to Vanyik and saw that he was begging me. His wide eyes were dilated as though he was high on something as he begged me. It was the strangest thing I think I'd ever witnessed in a lifetime of weird and unusual. It was also earnest, and I realized that, despite the ego and gross procreative activities of his species, they were child-like. He was like a kid being offered the last cookie if he'd just behave for a moment more. Hesitation that had been nagging in the back of my mind that it might be a trap fell away.

I looked back at Sloan whose cheek lifted slightly, and he gave me a slow nod.

Trust. *Dammit.*

I held my breath and smeared the cream-like solution on his cheek and across his face. It was thin like an oil as I spread it, coating every inch of exposed skin on his face, head, and neck. I dabbed at especially red spots on his skin, not sure how much I needed to do or how evenly the coverage had to be. Vanyik was on the floor practically panting from excitement. I took a step back and waited.

I think I expected rainbows of color to flicker from iridescent skin that was newly formed and as fresh as new snow and soft as silk to grow before my eyes. The reality was less fantastical. The first thing that happened was his skin stopped twitching and I saw relief in Sloan's face as he closed his eyes and sighed. The redness slowly faded to a pale olive tone that was less upper Atlantic like his accent and more Mediterranean in coloring.

The biggest difference was the gaping, sponge-like wounds across his cheeks, ears, and jaw closed. It was so sudden that I think I blinked, and his skin was just whole. His ears took a normal shape and the dome of his forehead smoothed out. No hair grew at his eyebrows or lip, and some redness remained to his tone, but it was a very clear healing.

"Remarkable," Vanyik sighed. "Your skin is truly marvelous, Captain Sloan. Might I request that, if you are to lose an ear or something...well, I would love to taste the newly healed--"

"Gross! Vanyik, no," I turned a disgusted look to the creature on the floor who looked surprisingly abashed.

"It will continue to heal through normal skin cell regeneration," Vanyik said softly, peeking up now and then to look at Sloan in a disgustingly adoring sort of way. "The years of damage his skin has taken will take a few weeks to fully regenerate, but this is still truly marvelous. The magic in his blood may cause some changes, so you will need to monitor it."

"I thought you said there was a kill switch for the nanites?" I asked, my mind shifted back to the other matter at hand.

"You would kill the nanites before they complete their work, Miss Magerious?" Vanyik gasped. "But his skin will be beautiful if you let them finish!"

"I just don't believe it can be done," I shrugged, lifting my eyes for a moment to Sloan who kept watching me. The side of his mouth quirked into a smile and his eyes widened as he caught on to what I was at.

"Can so!" Vanyik practically banged his fist on the floor in frustration of my disbelief. "I made a tonic for just such a scenario and it is in the same cabinet as the rest of the samples, labeled Xybb9A. I just cannot believe you would be so cruel as to not let me see...let Captain Sloan have his face fully healed."

There it was again, that need to see his creations be successful. I jerked my head at Talimuck, who grabbed another sample of the nanites as he grabbed the tonic. He nodded at me once and I smiled.

We made it out of the villa with limited resistance, the chancellor still in tow, and nanites that had a chance of deactivating what was in Jim, in hand. Talimuck had made a case for staying to run tests, but I could feel the invisible sands of time trickling through my fingers the longer we stayed in the Alliance holding.

Leaving Vanyik behind was too big of a risk, so we brought him along for the ride. He was so busy salivating over Sloan's new skin that it wasn't hard to do.

"If you can get us to Bunce Island, I can get the chancellor and Talimuck to people who will help," Sloan whispered to me as we were making our hike back across the island. Neither of us were overly inclined to trust our new friends even if they did seem to have the same end goal as we did.

"Without the chancellor in his pocket, Low will be hunted by the rest of the Alliance if we can get the word out about what he tried to do. I know an Alliance admiral in the southern region who will be very happy to spearhead that operation."

"Once an Alliance Captain, always an Alliance--"

Sloan grabbed my arm and spun me, leaning in to lock his faded blue eyes on mine.

"The Alliance you know is not the Alliance I thought I was joining," he told me. "I think I've served my time after this, though. I'm thinking of going privateer once the chancellor and Talimuck have been dropped off."

"You mean pirate?" I grinned up at him and he smiled back.

"Privateer," he shook his head and stepped slowly away with a shake of his head. He held onto my arm for a moment longer before releasing me.

"You know that's just the polite term for pirate," I rolled my eyes and tried to drop the ridiculous grin from my face.

"Maybe," he paused, looking around a tree before we stepped out on the path that led down to the bay that currently held the *MadCap*. "Do you know anyone who's hiring?"

"I'll ask around," I nodded and stepped out beside him. "Have any references?"

I heard a sound come from him that was part rasp and part warm chuckle. Hooray for nanites.

We returned to the *Madcap* and cleared away the sea rubbish. At least if we headed in the direction that Sloan was suggesting, it was unlikely that Low would head the same way or think to look for us. For now.

"What will you need to help the chancellor, Professor?

Talimuck cocked his head to one side and I could practically see a list of supplies drifting through his mind. He shook his head and turned to answer Sloan with a tight smile.

"Get us all out of here and away from Low. We'll worry about lab space after that!"

"For a spineless tool, you say some smart things now and again, Professor," I quipped, and Sloan let out another rasping laugh.

"As if you could fix my implant, human," Vanyik lifted his nose and straightened his spine. I think that if his species had a chin, it would be pointed like a knife at the professor. "I shall think over what I'll need when we get wherever it is you're taking me."

He paused.

"Where are you taking me?"

"Tell you when we get there." I jerked my chin in the direction of the ship and watched the creature roll his eyes before walking on.

"Do you think the nanites with the kill switch can really help Jim," Sloan asked after a few minutes more of making our way to the ship. It came into view and we both waved our cutlasses at the remaining crew so they could start prepping us for departure.

"I don't know, but I'm willing to give it a shot," I nodded. "Of course, that means we'll have to catch the smarmy bastard and take him somewhere so we can watch him."

"Just get us to Bunce Island and we'll go from there," Sloan stepped down into the dingy we'd parked at shore before turning to offer a hand down. I looked at it and laughed before deciding to take it.

"I don't think Bunce Island is going to welcome us," I said through a smile full of teeth.

"I know it's an Alliance port, but I'll signal that we're friendly," Sloan's forehead puckered, and I have to admit that confusion was a good look when it can be gauged by more than just blue eyes.

"Signal or no, the *MadCap* is a pretty well-known ship…" I hedged and he saw it.

"What did you do?" His eyes narrowed and his mouth drew into a tight line that I think had a bit of laughter behind the disapproval.

"Nothing big...We set fire to their piers…"

Sloan's eyes went wide, and I looked over the side of the boat and swirled my fingers in the clear blue water.

"Twice."

It was lucky that we were on the far side of the island because I have no doubt Sloan's laughter could have been heard for a mile. I grinned as the boat shoved forward and we headed for the *MadCap*.

The End

If the world was fair, all biographies would read like the introduction to a Star Wars movie and coffee would flow endlessly. Thus would begin the biopic of Charity Ayres.

Charity writes stories that allow the sarcastic voices in her head to have free reign. Her published works include *Loki Bound, Ice Burns, Secret in the Wings*, and a plethora of upcoming releases. Though she considers herself a fantasy author, her books are a mix of various genres, interlaced with humor, sarcasm, and whatever words are produced by over-consumption of coffee or wine. Charity has also written and published short pieces in Science Fiction, mystery, romance, and non-fiction because she believes that life is too small to stick with one story type.

Charity grew up in South Dakota but left to join the Navy when she graduated high school and has resided in Virginia since the end of her enlistment. She lives with her daughter, two dogs, and a cat which she tries to reassure her daughter is enough pets for one family to have. She teaches high school English, creative writing, and journalism. She has a Bachelor's of English and a Master's in Creative Writing but is committed to life-long learning like the drug that it is. In her free time, whatever that is, Charity can be found on panels at various conventions, teaching writing workshops, or online researching history or interesting ways to kill people for her next novel.

Her current published works are available on Amazon.
www.amazon.com/Charity-Ayres/e/B00J7QW06K

Charity can be reached through her Facebook author's page at:
https://www.facebook.com/CharityAyresAuthor/